THE YEAR *of* DAN PALACE

by

KRISTEN TSETSI

PENXERE PRESS
Connecticut

FOREWORD

I originally published this novel under the pen name Chris Jane, even though I'd never been the kind of writer who'd be likely to adopt a pen name. I'd always believed in taking blame—or credit—for my fiction, but after the release of my debut wartime novel *Pretty Much True* failed to get more than a few men to flip to the first page even out of passing curiosity, I wondered whether it might have been because it was written by a woman.

"Your novel will obviously appeal to other military spouses," said a man by way of an incidental answer. He was interviewing me at the time for his literary blog. "Have you been focusing your marketing efforts on the military community?"

I almost asked whether he thought the target market for *The Things They Carried* had been veterans and active service members. (Silly question. It's assumed the general public will be interested in the masculine war experience.)

I started imagining a parallel universe in which *Pretty Much True* had been published under a male name, and the temptation to approach future projects with a less gendered name grew. By the time I was ready to publish *The Year of Dan Palace* for the first time in 2014, I had chosen the pseudonym Chris Jane.

But ten years of someone else's name being on my book was long enough. It's mine, and it's time I take the blame. If you've bought this copy or checked it out from the library, thank you for reading *The Year of Dan Palace* by Kristen Tsetsi.

For my dad, Steve Tsetsi.

ONE

Dan tore at the skin around his thumb nail, his attention tight on his watch. It had been ten minutes since he'd last looked directly at Nina, ten minutes since he'd told her he was leaving. She stood in the space behind the sofa with her back against the wall and her head turned toward the dark window, gin and tonic in hand. Weeks ago, before this, they'd made a date to stand together at the window and watch whatever they could see of the city's New Year's Eve fireworks, shot off every year from a park about a mile away. They had thirty-three minutes and eighteen seconds until midnight.

"You can't come over here and comfort me?" she said. "Why won't you even look at me?"

He stared at his hands and stayed seated on the fireplace hearth. The cold stone bit through his pants. He stopped picking at his skin when a narrow line of blood traced a path along the nail bed.

She said, "I know people sometimes say things they think they can't take back, but—"

"I said it, Nina. Not 'they.'" He looked at her, finally. Strain and tears had reddened and shined her nose and stamped pink blots on her cheeks. Her hazel eyes, usually a dull olive, had brightened to a distracting green. "I won't be taking it back."

"—but I'm giving you the chance. Please take it. Before everything changes. Sometimes people s—"

"Not 'people.' Me. I. And you."

"But you're saying there is no 'I and you.' Right? That's what you're saying. You have to go. To her."

"Yes."

She nodded. "Yes. *Yes.*" She slid down along the wall, her rough sweater catching behind her and exposing her sides as it collected under her armpits. When she'd fallen all the way to the floor and was seated beside their change jar, she leaned forward and pulled at the knit until she was covered.

Dan wanted another drink, but he would have to pass by her to get to the kitchen and he didn't want to seem dismissive. "I don't want you to think I'm not taking your—this—everything that's happening, here, seriously," he said, standing, "but I need a refill. That okay? You want one?"

Without looking at him, she held up her own glass.

He crossed the room, the backs of his thighs numb with cold, and took it from her. She reached out and wrapped her arms around his knees. It was the first time they'd touched since he'd told her, and the first of what he imagined would be a series of goodbye embraces. "I'm sorry, Neen," he said. She was warm, her arms and chest a snug cocoon encircling him, but her curled fingers dug deep, painfully, into his calves. When he moved his legs to signal to her that it was time to let go, she clutched tighter. She slid her body close and trapped his ankles—the whole bottom half of his legs—in her web of limbs. "Nina."

"This is why you love me, because I'm crazy, remember?" She pressed her face against his knees and whispered into his pants, "Don't leave me, Dan. Please don't leave me. If she loved you she never would have left."

He moved to touch her, but his hands were full. He used the bottom edge of his pinkie to stroke the top of her head. She looked up at him. Fine strands of hair clung to her cheeks where the tears had slid down. She said, "Let's—Let's listen to music and get silly drunk. Let's have sex we won't even remember in the morning."

He wanted to say yes. He didn't dislike her (he was sure he still loved her, if maybe not enough), and the sex they had was a small, but not insignificant, part of what had kept him with her the last two times he'd considered breaking away. He wanted to say yes. But if he did, she would make him feel silly for wanting to leave, crazy for believing in crazy things. Not because she would say so, but because her body and the quiet moments afterward would bring him to complacency, pull him back when he was finally halfway gone. For years he had known that as good as it was, as treasured as she made him feel, *something wasn't right.* Even so, had it not been for the story he'd heard on NPR's "Science Friday," he might have stayed forever.

"Never mind," she said, but without loosening her grip. "I forgot. What morning?"

"I can't get either of us drinks with you holding on like that."

"I don't want one, anymore."

"Well, I do."

"No," she said in a pouty baby voice he'd never heard before and didn't like.

"Nina, come on. I have glasses in all my hands, and—"

"Just one more minute." She re-squeezed, pressed her face deeper into his legs.

But it had already been a minute, possibly one and a half. The additional seconds she was stealing started to tug at him. He thought he might work her loose by jerking one of his legs up and down and side to side, the unpredictable movements confusing her muscles and making them give. He went left, then right, then raised his knee. It smacked something hard and he was free. Nina scooted away, back to her spot against the wall, her fingers to her nose and mouth.

Dan crouched in front of her. "Nina, I'm—It was an accident. Are you okay? Are you bleeding?"

She pulled her hand away from her face, looked at it, and nodded. "A little."

She cleaned her mouth at the kitchen sink with an arm held out to keep him away. She had taken another three minutes, according to the microwave clock. He tried to avoid looking at his watch and being obvious about checking the time. When she finished, she turned to face him but stayed wedged in the corner, the washcloth held in both hands. "Did you ever really love me?"

Of course he did, he said.

"When did you know?"

"What?"

"When did you know you loved me?" She sniffed, then grimaced. With the washcloth held to her nostrils, she said, "It should be easy enough to answer. I can tell you when I knew I loved you. We were meeting at the matinee. You saw me on the sidewalk and opened your arms, and you smiled at me the way you do. Did."

He smiled, not in that special way he supposed he used to but in a way he hoped said "I remember," even if he didn't. There had been no such moment for him. His love for her had crept up on him the way language does with children: naturally, and without much notice. "Mine was the same moment," he said.

Laughter erupted from behind the washcloth she still held to her face.

"What's funny?"

"Nothing." She bent forward with more laughter and started gasping. Whether she was laughing or crying now was hard for him to tell. She wiped her eyes and blew her nose into the terrycloth. "Ow." She looked at it when she pulled it away from her face and pressed it into a ball before setting it on the counter. "You never really did, did you? Love me, I mean."

"Yes," he said. "Nina, yes."

The tears that had settled in her eyes during the burst of laughter now spilled over.

He checked the microwave: six minutes until midnight, by that clock, with a thirty-second allowance between that time and actual time. Farling's prediction was that an uncharted asteroid would collide with the planet sometime between midnight on January first and midnight on June first. If it was going to happen at midnight, he had six minutes to do something. He pulled out the gas station receipt he'd been carrying in his pocket for a week and unfolded it.

He would have to reach past Nina to get the phone. She stared dead ahead into nothing.

"I don't want to hurt you, Neen," he said, "but I have to call."

"Right now? You have to call her right now when we're in the middle of this?"

"I'm s—Yes."

"'Sorry?' Is that what you were going to say?"

He looked at his watch. Four minutes and forty-eight seconds. "I am sorry." He crossed the kitchen one short, cautious step at a time, wishing not for the first time that he had a cell phone. Nina had read too many articles about cell phones and smart phones testing relationships, and he'd agreed at the time that a landline was all they needed. Nina had never owned a cell phone, but Dan had liked his flip phone. He'd meant to keep it for long car trips or a future change of heart, but Nina had reminded him that he never went anywhere and convinced him to donate it to an organization that passed them along to people who needed them for emergencies.

When the only thing preventing him from reaching the phone was Nina standing in the way, he looked down at her until she moved aside, her back sliding against the counter's edge. He grabbed it from the base and pressed the first button of April's number. The tone was loud in the still room.

"Go ahead," she said. "—Well? Keep going."

He punched in the rest and waited for the connection. The rings buzzed through the earpiece.

"What if she doesn't want to talk to you?"

Dan tried again, but again, unanswered rings. He let them go on and on, waiting for an opportunity to leave a message. It never came.

"Doesn't she have voicemail?" she sniffed.

He hung up and dialed again.

"God, Dan."

Unanswered rings.

Two minutes until midnight. He stood at the living room window. Nina, who'd told him she wasn't done loving him, yet, stood beside him. They were waiting for fireworks. Just fireworks. Just like the others on their street who probably stood in their own windows waiting for the same thing. He looked past the glass, avoiding making eye contact with Nina in the reflection. He refused to see her pain or confusion or anger or whatever else she was feeling that he couldn't make his own, anymore, and that he couldn't make go away. The moment he'd accepted it was possible that Farling's prediction could come true—a convincing segment he'd heard on the way to work that had discussed asteroids in general more than Farling in particular—he'd told himself he would have the courage to live honestly. To comfort her would be to mislead her.

Lights were on in all of the houses he could see. At a time like this, it would seem everyone would brave the cold and come together. He supposed, though, that if it really was the end, it was just too damn cold to stand around outside staring at the sky waiting for it.

Or maybe it was too much for anyone to think about at any length. He couldn't comprehend the end of his own existence, never mind the end of all existence. As much as he wanted to believe the fairy tales of angels and demons, a place for good and a place for bad, or the cross-over psychics who claimed to speak to the dead, he'd had to acknowledge three years ago, when the lilies he'd brought home for Nina had killed their cat, Paulie, that he believed in none of that. Back when they'd buried him they were still living in the second-floor apartment and didn't have a yard of their own to put him in. Late that night they'd brought Paulie to the park in a refrigerated box given to them by the vet. Dan had dug a hole near an old oak they thought they would remember while Nina kicked at leaves, hoping to uncover a rock they could use as a marker. As he dug, and as he gently lowered the box into the hole, and as Nina jammed a stick (no rocks to be found) into the ground, and as he drove home blurry-eyed with Nina crying into the cheetah toy Dan had rescued before Nina could pack it away, and in the living room that night with the empty spot next to the TV where his bed used to be, and every day after that, Dan felt nothing of the cat's presence. He had always been sure that when someone—or something—he loved died, he would have a sense of its lingering energy. But Paulie was nowhere. Just dead.

"Are you okay?" Nina's fingers grazed his, her touch so light he almost didn't feel it. He closed them in his fist and said, "I can't breathe."

"Nothing's going to happen, Dan. Don't worry."

One minute and five seconds until midnight at the first sound of fireworks. White and pink and green spots burned in the sky and dropped colored light on the lawn and on the neighborhood cat balanced on the fence. At the next flash and sparkle of light, the cat was gone.

"I forgot to feed him today," Nina said.

"He'll be fine."

"What if he's not? I'm probably the only one feeding him."

"He'll find mice. And we have all these squirrels."

She smiled up at him. "You're right." She circled his waist with her arm. "You always make me feel better."

"Neen." He peeled her fingers away and lowered her hand to her side.

"Not even that?" she said.

"You know it's—"

"Never mind." She took a long, slow breath that she exhaled silently.

The fireworks, popping faster, pulsed purple and gold. When he was younger, they'd seemed to take up more of the sky. His parents would drive to a viewing field and let him watch from the back of the station wagon. Because they didn't think the shows were safe, because "anything could go wrong," he was never allowed to get out.

"How did you get her number?" she said.

"Her name came up."

"When?"

"A few weeks ago." Their agency bought unpaid debts from other agencies. April's had been in collections for some time, the history showing a series of small, unpredictable payments agents referred to as a borrower's blow-off. The lazy effort was little more than a passive-aggressive "Fuck you."

"And you never called her before tonight?"

"No."

"I don't believe you."

He felt her watching his reflection in the window. He caught her stare in the glass and held it. "It's the truth."

"Why did you wait until now?"

As much end-of-the-world speculation as there had been in the months leading up to New Year's Eve, Dan had known it would still sound ridiculous coming out of his mouth. He wouldn't have (and he hadn't) been able to explain with confidence why Farling's prediction, which the media and experts treated with heavy skepticism (and some eye rolls), should be given any more credence than the earlier predictions of the Mesoamerican calendar, Nostradamus, Hagee and Bitz, or even Camping. He had wanted to put off for as long as possible the way Nina, who knew him well, would look at him when he told her and her justifiable accusation that he was latching onto this year's manufactured panic to give himself an excuse to go.

He had also been afraid of what April would say, or that she might say nothing at all, when she heard his voice on the other end of the line.

"I guess I didn't believe until tonight that it could really happen," he said. "Or maybe I had to build the courage."

"To call her?"

"Yes." Everything he said now would be the truth.

"Why did her name come up? Who does she owe?"

"A hospital."

"Which one?"

"I don't know."

"What happened?"

He said "I don't know" again, and re-resolved that everything he said would be the truth. There were things Nina didn't need to know.

"Where does she live?"

"Not far." The address was a post office box, two towns over. The only street address on file was her place of employment, a university admissions office.

"You're not going to tell me?"

"Nina."

She ran a section of her hair through and through and through her fingers. "I'm already out? You don't even know if she'll talk to you, but it's you and her. And I'm out."

The fireworks crackled and blasted, one on top of the other. *Pop! Poppop! Pop!* Midnight. Dan watched for a bright light or streaks unrelated to the fireworks and felt himself pulling Nina close and tight. He had only some awareness of the liquid limpness of her body.

Twenty-three minutes after midnight and time was still moving along. Nina sat on the couch and watched the dissipating Times Square chaos on TV. She'd told Dan he could stay until he managed to get in touch with April, that she was "committed to loving even when it's hard, and not because we're married, but because I love you the way someone is supposed to when they truly love someone."

He didn't want her to be loving, to be understanding. To be weak. Not kind, but weak, he would often tell himself. She had always been weak when it came to him, unwittingly encouraging him to exploit that weakness. When he fell into one of his regular phases of discontent—which were as much about their not-quite-rightness together as they were standard middle-aged angst and feelings of wanting…*something*—she would give him space. It was, she would say, the way her parents, still happily married after forty years, handled their rough spots.

When he got bored with his self-pity, was ready to be present with her and recognized that he had probably even missed her, she would infuriate him with an "I'm glad you're back" or an equally sincere "I hope you're feeling better." His guilt would lash out at her. Where had he gone? he would ask. Who'd said he felt anything but normal? He would blame the distance on her, gently and rationally accusing her of imagining his withdrawal or of having done something to cause his coolness, because he didn't want (couldn't stand) to be the source of her pain. He was so relentless in his deflection that she would ultimately, inevitably, apologize. He hated himself for feeling better when she did.

They'd finally remembered about pouring new drinks after the fireworks. Nina had a sip or two left in her glass on the coffee table. Dan had finished his and was halfway into another, watching TV and Nina from the kitchen where he had easy access to the dining room and a private place to hit the REDIAL button. He knew he should pack his things and leave, but he was afraid to get too far away from Nina until he knew April would be there to accept him, if only to talk. If he was on the way out with nowhere to go, he would be alone, untethered to anyone who cared about him in what could be his final moments. The thought of that kind of drifting isolation filled him with unmanageable panic.

"Another?" he said.

When she twisted to look at him, he displayed his glass. She shook her head and turned back to the TV. Dan took the cordless into the dining room and tried April again, listening to the rings as he walked over to the window that faced the Belowskis' house. A light, steady snow fell on Belowski himself, who stood beside his red sports car in open-laced boots, flannel pajama pants, and an unzipped coat. After seven rings, Dan pushed the OFF button and watched Belowski light a cigarette. "Hey, Neen," he called. "I'm going outside for a minute, okay?"

"Where are you going?"

"Outside, I said." He took the phone with him to the coat closet. He opened the door and looked down the hallway and through the kitchen to the living room, where Nina still sat on the couch facing the TV. He pulled his coat off the hanger and stuffed the phone in an inside pocket.

"Hey, Dan?"

He stopped messing around with his coat and waited for her to say more, but nothing came. "Yes?"

"Can you please come here? What are you doing?"

"I'm putting—" He sighed and walked down the hall to the kitchen. "What's up?" He sneaked a swallow from the glass he'd left on the counter.

She kept her back to him. "This is hard for me, so please … um," Her voice thinned and wavered. "Just a second." She inflated with a breath and started again, her voice this time sharp, strong, and with an authority that was unusual for her. "I want you to know that I want you to do whatever you need to do. When you're finished, when you see the way things really are, you'll come back. And I'll let you. But only once."

Belowski—Carl, with a wife named Kristie and two kids, Cameron and Karen—tipped back a beer can Dan hadn't seen from the window. He wasn't holding the cigarette, anymore, that had prompted Dan to come outside to ask for one. Dan waved, stepping toward him through the snow.

Carl said, "Hey, neighbor," with his eyes on the lit window of the small white house across the street. "Happy New Year. Nina, too. Tell her for me, okay, when you … Hey, you drinking, man? Want a beer?"

"I'll take a beer."

Carl dragged tracks across his driveway and stumbled inside, letting the screen door slam behind him. Dan pulled the phone out of his pocket and pressed REDIAL. While the rings played through the line, he studied the houses on his street (making occasional checks of the sky for anything heavier than a snowflake). Next door, on the side opposite the Belowskis, lived a neighbor he and Nina had never seen and whose curtains never opened. A Hispanic family of six—two teenage boys, a teenage girl, their parents, and an older woman he assumed was the grandmother—lived in the gray ranch directly across the street. Blinking blue Christmas lights lit up their walkway hedges. To their right, in the pale yellow house, lived the old white couple with the short, shaggy dog Dan saw leashed now and then to the front porch. To the left of the Hispanic family, in the small, white box of a house with green and white striped awnings shading the windows, lived a blond woman and her husband. Dan, filling the mower with gas one day last summer, had been startled by the woman's roaring "Fucking roses!" and had looked over to see her trying to escape a tangle of thorny branches clinging to her shirt. Her husband was a daily jogger, a smart phone strapped to his arm and wires snaking up to his ears. Weekday mornings at eight sharp he pulled out of the garage in a throaty yellow Charger. His wife drove a silver Audi two-seater. Curious, Dan had once checked the system for their names. They had no outstanding debts with his company.

The phone continued to ring. He hung up and returned it to his pocket.

He knew none of his street mates' names but Carl's and had exchanged little more than a friendly "Morning" or "Hot today!" with any of them in the three years he and Nina had lived in the house. His neighborly conversations with Carl had begun the previous summer when Carl, drunk, had wandered over in a suit and an Uncle Sam top hat to invite Dan and Nina to a Fourth of July party he and Kristie were hosting. Until that evening, they'd known him only as Belowski, the man whose license plate displayed his last name. Belowski, who slicked back his hair. Belowski, the late-night drinker who sometimes stood in his driveway in a bathrobe and muttered and smoked while gesturing at the white house across the street. If they were awake for it, Dan and Nina would crawl out of bed and watch him through the window, knees on the cold floor and their fingers pressed flat to the window sill.

Dan wondered what his neighbors had observed about him, if anything.

Carl's screen door squeaked and slammed.

Dan brushed the snow off his hair and took the cold can. "Thanks." He popped the top and licked the spray from his fingers.

Carl tapped Dan's can with his own. "New Year."

"New Year." Dan slurped the watery beer and thought it would be the perfect time for the world to end, were life a movie. Quiet snowfall, a few yellow windows, two men drinking beer on the lawn. And then: Carl's house and wife and two kids flaming hot in the fire of Farling's asteroid. The gray house kids and their grandmother, the old couple and their dog, the rose wrestler and the runner, all ash, along with April, Nina, himself. He said, "What are you going to do with it?"

Carl lit a cigarette. "What's that?"

"This year. Doing anything different?" He allowed a short pause before asking for a cigarette. He'd quit a year after he started seeing Nina. A choice he'd never regretted for health reasons, but that he'd been sad to make. There was nothing about smoking he hadn't loved.

"I told Kristie I'd quit smoking," Carl said, cigarette pressed between his lips while he pulled the pack from his coat pocket and opened it for Dan. "She's big on resolutions. Always keeps them for at least six months. You make any?"

Dan lit his first cigarette in seven years and sucked on the filter. He turned away and coughed to hide the gag. "Something like a resolution." He wiped his eyes. "You can't take chances."

"What do you mean? Chances on what?"

"Oh, you know. The talk on the blogs. End of the world. That kind of thing."

"What, that jackass Farling?" Carl made a dismissive sound with his lips, then looked up into the falling snow. "I don't know.

Sometimes I wish, though, man. Maybe not total world destruction, or anything, but something—Fuck, just *something*. You know? Something."

"It could happen."

"What could happen?"

"Something."

"You one of those end-of-the-world nuts, or what?"

"Me? No." Dan was still holding his cigarette, not much of it burned down. He'd have tossed it after the first drag but didn't want Carl to think he was wasting it, so he'd held it at his side. He turned to hide his hand and let it fall, then stomped as if to warm his feet and covered it with snow. "But I guess it doesn't matter what anyone believes. Things happen or they don't."

Carl flicked his own fully smoked cigarette in the direction of his driveway and used the now-free hand swoop back his hair. "Everything'll go on just the way it always h—"

The creak of a tight spring on a screen door carried across the street. Carl folded his arms over his stomach and watched as the blond in the white house walked down her front stairs with a sagging bag of trash. After dropping it in a barrel parked against the garage, she saw Dan and Carl and waved. Dan waved back and called "Happy New Year" as she bounced through her tracks to the stairs and went inside.

"She's teasing me," Carl said. "Tormenting. Taunting. Tempting."

"She was just taking out the trash."

"Who takes out the trash at—What time is it? One?"

"Someone who's cleaning up after New Year's, maybe."

"Maybe. Or maybe she knew I was here."

"We're standing in the middle of my yard."

"You don't know her, all right?"

"All right."

Carl jutted his chin at her window. "She's pregnant. Told Kristie a few days ago. Everyone's pregnant. Babies, babies, babies." He twisted to look at his house and lit another cigarette. "You two having kids?"

Dan said no. Nina couldn't have them, but he didn't tell Carl that. He'd become more selective about who received that information after too many people had "tsked" and looked at him with pity. He'd stopped talking about it entirely after Nina had overheard him telling someone at a dinner. Shaking, she'd dragged him into a closet to tell him *It's nobody's business, it's personal.* He'd apologized and held her, the two of them tucked between a red door and coat sleeves. "I can't give you what you want," she'd whispered, crying, not believing his own whisper that it didn't matter. He'd never consciously wanted kids as much as he'd thought it would be okay if one happened to come along. In the dark closet with Nina that night he'd thought about April's pregnancy for the first time in years and had taken almost visceral pleasure in the privacy of the past, in not feeling compelled to share. As ambivalent as he'd always been about being a father, even with April, Nina so intensely wanted her own baby that she would never have forgiven a past that included him impregnating another woman. So, he'd kept April's pregnancy, and her abortion three weeks in, to himself.

Carl didn't ask why Dan and Nina had no plans for kids. Instead he said, "I guess nothing's holding you back from doing ... shit, whatever the hell you want, really." He raised his beer in a salute. "Kids are great. Don't get me wrong." He poured the can into his mouth until it was empty. "We make our choices." He held out his hand and Dan shook it. "Good to see you, neighbor. Don't let the world end while I'm asleep."

When Carl's front door thudded shut, Dan pulled out the phone and hit REDIAL. It rang once. Twi—

"Hello?"

It was a curious "hello." She had no idea who was on the other end, but right now she wanted to know. Dan could have been anybody. Someone she actually liked.

He heard her hand moving on the phone.

Time was passing. And then time passed. Seconds, maybe a minute. April breathed into the phone. He hadn't been this close to her in nine years.

"I can sit here as long as you can," she said.

He started to laugh. He pressed the OFF button. He hadn't planned what to say, had no idea what his first words to her should be.

Nina said, "Was it just as good for her?" She stood in the open front door, a skinny silhouette dwarfed by their 1930s, mint-green Dutch Colonial. They hadn't liked the green and had meant to paint it gray. Dan supposed they wouldn't be doing that, now. "What are you looking at?" she said.

"Our house."

"You must mean *the* house." She packed a snowball and tossed it to Dan. He caught it and crumbled it in his fingers. They turned hot from the cold. "Our house, then," he said. "I mean, *the*. The."

"Have you seen the cat?"

"No."

Nina patted snow from her mittens and stomped her shoes on the porch before going inside. Dan turned back toward the street and pressed REDIAL again, and again it rang, this time only once before she said hello.

Dan said, "April," and waited for her to respond, but she didn't. He heard music and voices in the background. "Hi," he said.

"Hello."

"It's me."

"I know who it is."

He had missed the smooth strength of her voice. She spoke like a blues singer.

She did not sing like one.

He'd asked her, once, why singing hadn't been one of her talents when she was a girl on the pageant circuit, and in answer she'd tortured Streisand's "The Way We Were" from "Mem'ries" to "Smiles we gave to one another." He'd stopped her by throwing one of his socks at her.

"How did you get this number?"

A rumble sounded overhead and a bright white light glowed through thin spots in the clouds. It sounded like one of the many airplanes that routinely passed by on the way to the airport a few miles away, but louder.

"How did you get this number, I said."

That it sounded like an airplane didn't mean it was an airplane. What did an asteroid sound like? Dan's head turned heavy and cold. His body stiffened, tightened, and he couldn't move, didn't feel real. He didn't want to enter the same nothingness that had taken Paulie. He felt the phone in his hand and the pain of having it pressed too hard to his ear. "I love you! April!" The rumble became a deafening whine. "Can you hear me? I love y—!"

Her disconnect was a click he heard over the fading noise above. The light glowing through the holes in the clouds followed the approach path and disappeared quietly behind a line of aged maples.

TWO

"Your 'I love you' was very convincing," Nina said. "I could hear it all the way in here. I'm sure everyone else on the street heard it, too." She was removing him—his books, odd knickknacks she'd given him as gifts, photographs of the two of them she'd peeled from their frames, all in a pile on the living room floor—when he went inside. He didn't take off his coat. "One nice thing about not getting to know most of our neighbors, at least, is that they probably don't know my name is Nina and that you were just screaming 'I love you' at your ex-wife in the middle of a snowstorm."

Dan could see that she'd taken obvious care to not break or bend anything while placing it all in a neat heap between the coffee table and the fireplace. Her hand shook when she pushed her hair away from her eyes. "You can pack your own clothes. You left some of them in the washing machine, so I put them in the dryer."

A steady, clicking rhythm sounded from behind the accordion closet doors in the living room. Nina's parents, retired and living in Texas just two years after buying the Connecticut house for themselves, had intended it to be a coat closet when they'd built the addition, a "bonus" room Dan and Nina had turned into a regular living room after taking over the mortgage. But Nina had hated basements since her childhood confrontation in her grandmother's cellar with what she insisted were ghosts ("Not unfriendly, and more like shadows on the wall, but I was six and they scared me to death," she'd told him their first week in the house). She refused to do

25

laundry, or anything else, in a dark, downstairs room. Dan was the only one who had been down there since the day they moved in.

He said, "You want me to go right now?"

"I said you could stay until you talked to her. You talked to her."

Her attention wasn't on him, but on something over his head. He looked up. It was the crack in the molding they'd tried to hide with caulk the previous spring. It had rained heavy the next day, and water coming through a roof leak had squeezed through the caulk, leaving it split and ragged.

He said, "She hung up on me."

"Oh."

"I don't want sympathy. That's not why I told you. But I—What I mean is that our agreement, I thought, was that I would leave when I had somewhere … . None of this is coming out right."

"There are hotels."

Another rumble built over the house. He stiffened and his sinuses cleared, a sudden and almost painful thing, and a cold whirling erupted under his ribs. An airplane, his rational self knew, but he ignored logic and conjured vivid flashes of everything he would never have the chance to do and see if he died this instant.

Not much came to him. There was little he wanted to see and less he wanted to do. He had never been an ambitious person, which had made not advancing at the collection agency for so long tolerable, and as much as he wanted one he'd never really had a passion, which had made simply working at the collection agency for so long tolerable. When he'd started, he was a twenty-year-old college freshman trying to make rent money, and he'd stayed after graduating with a major in journalism because the money was better in collections. The job was more challenging for the collectors who felt every day spent at the agency was a day stolen from a more fulfilling pursuit. Shana, who was six thousand hours into her ten thousand hours of mastery, wanted to be in her basement workshop with her wood carving tool set. Blake was trying to develop his own beer for retail sale but had little time to himself after work and on weekends because he had a wife and son. Molly had an idea for a graphic design magazine, but not enough time to put it together.

The images that did come to him were April's. Places he remembered April wanting to go, landmarks April had wanted to see. And then there was April herself, sitting at the kitchen table in their old apartment with her hair in a ball on top of her head while she drank coffee and watched the news in a long, red bathrobe.

"Dan?" Nina said.

He rubbed his hands together and felt the deep grooves where the joints bent, the firm softness of his finger pads, the unevenness of his nails. He laced his fingers together, and it felt strange, holding his own hand. It was something he'd never noticed before, the way his hand felt inside another hand. It was oddly intimate, like talking to himself in the mirror, looking himself in the eye. This was the hand Nina felt when he would put it on her narrow waist. April had had more of a curve, there. More flesh. Dan remembered her wearing faded jeans that rested at that curve. He used to like running his fingers just above the waistline.

"My name is Nina. It's always been Nina," she said.

He opened his eyes. She was sitting on the counter with her bent knees tucked in her arms.

"You said 'April,'" she said.

The sound in the sky was gone. A draft from the heating vent played with the thin hairs on her big toe. She caught him looking and used one foot to cover the other.

"It's cute," he said.

She rested her chin on a knee. "I think you have to go, now."

THREE

A large duffel bag stuffed with clothes and a rigid suitcase filled with the pile Nina had made on the floor fit nicely in the trunk. Dan started the car and something *thwapped* the passenger window and slid down, leaving a streak. Dan lowered the window. Nina crossed the lawn wiping a hand on her pants, the bottoms loosely tucked into boots. "I forgot to get the key," she said.

"My key?"

"Do you have everything you need?"

"I think so."

She crossed her arms. "Please give me your key. And I need the phone back, too."

He'd forgotten he still had it in his coat. He pulled the key off the ring and gave her the phone from his pocket. She took them without touching him and followed her tracks back to the front door.

He drove to the nearest hotel, less than a quarter mile from their house near the interstate on-ramp, and sat in the empty lot with the engine off. It didn't take long for snow to cover the windshield.

Two hours and thirty-five minutes since midnight.

It would be easy enough to go home. He would tell Nina he'd had a panic attack that had manifested as a fixation on April, and he would apologize. He would put away his clothes, return his books to the living room shelves, and go to sleep.

And then what?

And then what.

The *ding!* of the brass bell elicited no movement in the empty lobby. An accompanying note read, "Please do not ring more than twice." Dan tapped it twice more. On the other side of the counter, where the business of a hotel was maintained on a lower shelf, the clerk had left a tabloid magazine and an open box of caramel corn. One of the lights on the hotel phone blinked red with ringing and went dark when the ringing stopped. Dan walked around the counter and picked up the receiver, pressed a line, pulled April's number from his pocket, and dialed. She answered in five rings, her voice low. Alcohol-scratched. He cupped the phone with both hands.

"Helloooo," she said again.

"It's me."

After a moment, she said, "I'm sleeping."

He flipped magazine pages. "Can I see you?"

"No."

"Are you sure?"

"What do you want, Dan?"

"I have to see you."

"I'm not at home."

"Where are you? I'll meet you."

"Call me tomorrow, okay? Or …"

Her voice trailed off in a mutter he didn't understand. He looked at his watch. "What time tomorrow?" he said. "—April?"

Silence and no red light on the phone. He hung up. A toilet flushed and Dan returned to his side of the counter. The wind had picked up outside and blew snow at the doors, made wild, glowing swirls of it around the parking lot's yellow lamp heads. A woman, young, hurried past without looking at him. Once behind her computer, she busied herself closing the magazine while asking "May I help you?" before looking up at him. Her eyes were unusually large, and her skin had the faux tan tint so many young women seemed to like. "I'm— I'm so sorry." She clasped her hands together and then let them fall at her sides. "I hope you weren't waiting long, or anything. I was—I had to—Um … ." She brought her hands up to the counter and pressed them flat, palms down, on either side of the keyboard. "What can I do for you, sir?"

"I'd like a room," he said.

"Right."

Dan smiled at the pink spreading under her spray tan. "You okay?"

"Oh, yeah, I'm just … ." She tapped at the keyboard with her attention on the monitor. "Do you want anything in particular? We have Jacuzzi suites. Not that I think … that you—It's just, people seem to like them, and they're all available, and … ."

Dan thought he heard her whisper *Fuck*, but he ignored it and said okay to a suite. Not because he was particularly fond of Jacuzzis, but because the suites sounded more like apartments and less like hotel rooms. He asked if the hotel charged by the week at a reduced rate, and she told him while handing him his key cards that the manager handled extended stays and to come back after five in the morning.

The room was at the far end of a long hallway. No noise, television or other, came from behind the neighboring rooms. He opened his door and turned on the light to a bedroom with a sitting room in the entry and a Jacuzzi in the far corner. The wall art was generic landscape: a red-barn farm, a garden of purple flowers. He pulled the remote control from the base screwed to the dresser and listened to the TV for company, then turned on the Jacuzzi. It spit tan, black-flecked water. He turned it off. The heating unit under the window vibrated against the wall.

Dan reached for Nina before opening his eyes to the television, still on and dropping a blue glow on the patterned polyester comforter. Bright red alarm clock numbers told him it was twenty after five. He called the manager about long-term prices and was quoted a figure that was more than he could imagine paying. If the world didn't end appropriately soon—if impact were closer to June than to January— he would also need to have enough money for food and gas, and because he planned to quit his job, all he had was all he had.

Plows had started work on the main roads but hadn't yet made it to residential areas. He steered into the tire tracks of the only car on his street that seemed to have ventured out and followed them until he reached his house, still dark. Looking at it from outside, he could smell the kitchen, hear the hallway echo, feel the fluff of the living room rug under his toes.

He could ring the doorbell and tell her that they still couldn't be together, but that he was legally entitled to stay in the house.

He parked one block over and swung his duffel bag over his shoulder. The fresh snow reached just higher than his ankles, high enough to get into his shoes with every step he took until he reached the tire tracks on his own street. His and Carl's prints had been covered, and the lawn and driveway were pristine, sparkling white. He continued past his driveway and used their reclusive neighbor's yard to get close to the basement window least likely to be noticed by Nina. He heaved his bag over the shared waist-high fence onto the stiff branches of their overgrown hydrangea and climbed after it, kicking snow into his footprints before stooping to push at the small basement window. It was rough at the hinges, but unlocked. Snow from the seam in the frame dropped into darkness. The window was big enough to accommodate him, but just. First the coat went in, and then his legs and butt and back scraping against the sharp metal frame as he scooted through. With nothing to use as a brace between the window and the floor, he landed hard and allowed a few seconds of silence to pass before tugging in his bag and taking off his soaked shoes.

A plush carpet remnant left over from when they'd remodeled the spare bedroom made a diagonal path across concrete flooring to the shelves. It was the basement's only comfort. On the shelves sat the various sizes of empty boxes Nina would allow to collect by the door until Dan brought them down, along with plastic tubs filled with objects from Dan's past (the World War II kalis sword handed down on his father's side, high school yearbooks, pictures of old girlfriends) and Nina's boxes, labeled with black marker on masking tape: "Grandma," "Toby," "Paulie," the latter two filled, sealed, and named before the bodies were even buried.

They also saved boxes of things they didn't need but couldn't part with because they might use them someday. In one corner sat a wardrobe box stuffed with paper-wrapped china Nina's grandmother had given her when she turned eighteen, and which had proved useful when she and Dan had needed, and Dan had found tucked deep in the packing paper, a gravy boat for their first living-together Thanksgiving dinner. Others stored old appliances they'd replaced with new versions: microwave, toaster oven, blender. They kept them in case one of the new ones, bought primarily for aesthetic reasons, broke. Dan searched the boxes with no labels and some weight to them, hoping to find extra pillows or blankets, but there was nothing like that. Just an old lamp with its bulb, some books, and a deflated basketball of unknown origin.

He took off his wet socks, dried his feet with a t-shirt from the duffel bag, and put on a dry pair. The rest of his clothes served as a bed: thicker items down for cushioning, a rolled wool sweater wrapped in a t-shirt for his head, and the rest—minus the coat, which he wore again—piled on top of him.

Twenty-four minutes later he wasn't sleeping and his feet were cold. He listened for movement upstairs, not expecting to hear anything. Nina never woke up before seven o'clock, her standard time on workdays and some weekends. Today, though a holiday, was a workday for Nina. In her ten years of dedicated, uncomplaining service, she had been and continued to be the only employee her boss, an excitable Albanian named Valbon Bogdani, could count on when everyone else wanted a day off.

Dan took off his coat and climbed the stairs to the main floor. At the landing, he turned the knob a fraction of a rotation at a time, wincing at the clicking sound made by the pull of the latch. He pushed the door open a crack and listened again, then looked at the microwave clock. Her alarm would go off in twenty minutes.

A square of light coming through the back door illuminated the fireplace wall on the other side of the breakfast bar. Nina had already replaced the empty spots on the shelves with things she'd taken from different parts of the house. He went to the back door and looked outside at the snow that had started up again and fell thick around the Belowskis' bright deck light. April would probably not like Carl if she met him and would immediately, and maybe accurately, label him an aged frat boy. He wondered if—awarded the benefit of time—she would live in the house with him. It was easy to imagine her clothes sharing closet space with his, coffee with her in the morning. On a morning like this she would drag him outside to play. She would throw ice balls at him and shove snow in his face, because she was rough like that, but she would take the same roughness from him, and afterward, as soft as she was hard, she would get warm with him by the fire and kiss the spot she'd always kissed, the one behind his earlobe.

The neighborhood cat jarred Dan out of his daydream with a sudden appearance on their fence, white flakes clinging to his whiskers. He leapt off after something, dropping into the deep snow in the Belowskis' yard and popping out with each spring across the property and down their brightly lit driveway. The Belowskis' lights were Dan and Nina's winter morning sun, always shining in their windows when they woke up to the same alarm. He and Nina left at the same time for much of the work week. Collections started early to catch East Coast debtors at the earliest legal hour, and Nina had to be at the jewelry store an hour and a half before they opened. Dan thought the owner's son liked to have her there early so he could watch her pushing the vacuum cleaner around the display cases. Nina said he would talk to her as he arranged bracelets and rings on their velvet platforms under the glass, but that Dan was wrong about why he wanted her there early—after all, he was a married man. She'd added, in case being married wasn't enough, that he also believed in a literal interpretation of the Bible. Dan had told her she didn't know shit about men.

He checked his watch. Ten minutes until he would have to return to the basement, where his feet would be cold again until his shoes dried. He remembered, then, a pair of slippers tucked under his bedside table that he'd forgotten to pack when he was throwing things together. He treaded quietly down the hall and listened at the bottom of the stairs for movement from the bedroom above. Nothing. Bypassing the creaky first, third, and fifth steps, he made his way to the second floor and tiptoed into the bedroom.

Nina's nose squeaked in her sleep. She lay on his side of the bed with a book open and face down on hers. The sheets were different. Dark. He recognized them as the extra set they kept on the shelf over the washer and dryer. Nina's sister, on an overnight after too much wine that first Thanksgiving in their apartment, had called them "scratchy" and said she would bring by some of the sheets she sold in her store, "One hundred percent certified organic cotton, handmade, and priced better than anything you'd ever get at Pottery Barn." They never came. Nina was wrapped up tight in their substandard bedding, the comforter pulled to her neck, her pale face on the pillow like a half moon in a black sky.

She moved.

He dropped to the floor, knees cracking. He held his breath and listened, but her nose continued its even song. He exhaled slowly through his mouth, the walls of this throat expanded for silence. He crept to his side of the bed and reached around for his slippers, stuffed so far under the nightstand that Nina wouldn't notice their absence. He'd just hooked a finger into each of the heels when he heard the repeating, high-pitched beeping that had always made Dan want to hurl her clock at the wall. He lowered himself to his stomach. As Nina dragged herself across the mattress to turn off the alarm, he squeezed under the bed, using her noises to mask his. She yawned— a vocal activity for her—and her feet dropped to the floor. Dan watched them slap around the bed and out of the room. When the bathroom door closed and the shower turned on, he slithered out from under the bed and hurried to the basement.

Dan watched the news in the living room with his slippered feet on the coffee table. Nine hours into the first day of the year and they'd made no mention in the two hours since he'd turned on the TV of Farling's asteroid. He wasn't too surprised. Prior to New Year's, most of the media hadn't given Farling serious coverage beyond time-filler conjecture about what people would do, and how many would die, if a mile-wide asteroid were to gouge a hole in the planet. The channels that did treat him with respect (whether that respect was genuine or dictated by audience preference was hard to say) were the same channels whose experts gravely discussed the psychological impact of alien abductions.

He'd called April twice. No answer. Without knowing where she lived there was little he could do to find her. He'd called the university's admissions office, but they said she'd left months before. Dan assumed she had a new job. April liked to feel useful even if she didn't need to work. When her parents died—the last text the man had sent on that narrow road before steering directly into them had read "socks and a dragon!"—she'd been the sole beneficiary of an interesting amount of money left by her father, who'd founded an investment firm. It would have gone to her mother, who'd made a profession of being a beautiful and supportive wife, had she lived. Dan had wanted April to use some of the inheritance to get her mind off things, buy the perfect "April" house and a new car, but she had promptly donated half to charity, hired a financial planner, and assigned herself a strict annual salary of sixty thousand dollars.

She made that much every year in interest alone and had more than enough to pay off the bill sitting in collections.

He turned down the TV and called work.

Pictures. That was another difference in the living room, on the walls. She'd moved them, exchanged big with small.

Howie answered, sounding distracted and busy. Howie was rarely distracted or busy, but Dan appreciated the solid effort he made to sound that way. He told Howie he would be out sick, that it was bad, and that he didn't know how long he'd be gone. Howie said he didn't sound sick and asked if he was quitting. Dan hung up before he'd have to turn down any of Howie's persuasive pleas to make him stay. The next call, to April, rewarded him with her voice asking him to leave a message if he wanted her to call him back.

"April. Hi," he said. "It's me. I'm—I'm just here at …" He looked around. She couldn't call him at the house. He said, "I'll call you back," and hung up.

He needed a cell phone.

He turned off the TV and ran down to the basement, packed his clothes back into the duffel bag, and hid the bag in the water heater closet (just in case) before going back upstairs to the kitchen for the extra key they kept in the junk drawer. He left through the front door, sticking his toes in Nina's footprints from the porch to the garage. She'd left without shoveling, leaving deep tire tracks in the snow. Across the street, each of the three children worked to clear the final section of their driveway. Dan waved, hoping to appear normal, but they were focused on something else. A massive yellow truck led by a rolling wall of heavy, collecting snow lumbered toward them and then passed, leaving a fresh mound of heavy, dirty slush at the end of the family's driveway. "Asshole!" the oldest boy screamed before tossing his shovel into the road.

Dan opened the garage for his own shovel and spent the next hour and a half clearing his driveway and the snowplow mound. He also got rid of the fresh mound in front of the Belowskis' driveway, which he'd seen Carl shoveling earlier that morning for Kristie and the kids to go somewhere in the Belowski-mobile.

When he finished, he put away his shovel and walked over to the Belowskis' house and knocked until Carl came to the door.

Dan brought the borrowed shovel to his driveway and speared it into a snow pile. He yelled to Carl, watching from his doorway, "Let her find it. Say you forgot it when she brings it over, will you?"

"Sure thing."

FOUR

Dan bought a phone from a sick-looking kid who smelled like morning-after tequila. He wanted a flip phone like his old one, but no one sold it, anymore, so he bought a two-year contract he reasoned he would never have to fulfill and a smart phone that would have made Nina "Oh, Dan, come on" him. His service began right away, he was told. Outside in the parking lot, he tested it with a call to April.

She said, "I'm busy," and hung up.

Following the teenager's instructions about how to use the texting application, Dan sent April his new number in a text message and put the phone in his pocket. His phone chimed almost immediately and he took it out to read her reply: *Don't text me.*

The sun, a white blur in the clouds, had begun to drop and would soon disappear behind the mall. Nina would be there about now, cleaning the bank closed for the holiday. When she finished, she would drive five miles to the small financial services building downtown to dust the desks, empty cubicle trash cans, and clean toilets, a three-person job in larger buildings. She wouldn't be home until late, ten or eleven, her hair in a ponytail and smelling like urinal cakes, hands clammy and soft from sweating in latex gloves. Dan would make it home long before she did.

He read store signs as he waited for the light to change. Many of the smaller businesses had their CLOSED signs facing out, but the rest, the chains—electronics stores, computer stores—were open New

Year's Day, a logical consequence of the Black Friday creep. A healthy percentage of the season's shoppers determined to have the smartest TV, the latest tablet, or the trendiest phone would end up in his calling queue within six months, each giving him some variation of the argument that blood couldn't be extracted from an object that didn't have blood to give.

The light turned green and Dan pressed the gas, slowing when he saw, blocks ahead, a billboard over *Wexler's Rent and Buy* advertising low, low prices on used RVs.

There was something he'd always wanted to do, after all. He'd just forgotten.

As a child, he would watch TV commercials advertising the joys of seeing the big, wide world from behind the wheel of a mobile home. The clouds were fluffy and high in the distance where the road came to a point on the horizon, even the looming rain promising a journey of beauty and freedom. He hadn't cared about any of that, but had thought an RV was *the coolest* fort *on Earth*. It was an entire house *in one car!* He had pleaded with his parents to buy one for the back yard (never including among his reasons for wanting one the longing to escape their forced politeness with one another, their pasted smiles), but they had said it was "wholly impractical."

As impractical as it may have been at the time, it made good sense, now. He was homeless, it was cold, and if he could get the right deal, it would be less expensive than staying in hotels.

Wexler and Dan toed through puddled slush to seven RVs, beginning at the top of the previously-owned line with a gently used Monaco Dynasty—porcelain tile floor, two bathrooms (each bigger than either of his and Nina's two bathrooms at home), marble countertops, leather sofas—and ending with a collapsing 1977 Dodge Jamboree. He had just over thirty thousand dollars in his personal checking account, kept separate from Nina's personal checking and from the joint account they shared for bills. Dan's Honda and two thousand in cash bought a 1987, thirty-four-foot

Fleetwood Pace Arrow with plush carpeting, stove, microwave, refrigerator, double sink, full bath, tan velour sofa and barrel chairs, a dining booth, and what Wexler said was a brand new queen bed.

"Most people will buy anything used, but not a bed," he said.

It was dark by the time Wexler finished his thorough tutorial on the key basics of RV ownership. Dan found the lights, then pushed and pulled at the shift lever to lock it into DRIVE and turned onto the road. The seat, soft and springy, bounced him over potholes.

He needed to pick up his clothes and get some supplies from home—dishes, glasses, utensils. Nina wouldn't be there, yet, but he parked around the block to be less conspicuous to any curious neighbors. A full moon reflected off the snow, lighting the neighborhood and making Dan feel too visible as a lone figure on the road. It was dark enough for curtains to be drawn, but only a few houses had pulled them closed. On his street, in the small white house with the green and white awnings, running husband and rose-mangling wife sat in their living room in strobing TV glow, her legs tossed over his lap. Carl's house was dark but for the driveway lamp. That meant Kristie might not happen to see him and then happen to talk to Nina and then happen to mention she'd seen him around. That any of it was unlikely—Kristie and Nina talked even less than Dan and Carl—didn't mean he wanted to take the risk.

He passed Carl's shovel still stuck in the snow and kicked his shoes clean before going inside. The moon dropped white rectangles on the floor, saving Dan from having to turn on lights. Before going to the basement to get his bag, he stopped in the kitchen for some food and remembered they'd meant to go grocery shopping tomorrow. All they had in the freezer were too few frozen dinners for one to go missing unnoticed, and the refrigerator held an unopened bag of apples, some loose tangerines, and a jar of pickles. He wished he'd thought about things like grocery shopping before trading in his car.

He snacked on three pickles and a tangerine, wiped his hands on his pants, and pulled his phone out of his pocket and dialed. As it rang, headlights shined into the dining room and kitchen. Dan went to the window and watched Carl, his wife, and their two kids pour out of the car. Kristie balanced three pizza boxes in one hand while shutting her car door with the other.

"You have a new phone," April said.

Dan pressed it hard to his ear.

"Are you there?" she said.

"Please tell me I can come over."

She said no, but she didn't hang up. Dan waited without speaking. April sighed.

"Are you going to keep calling and calling?" she said.

"I think so."

"Dan, it's been eight years. Wh—"

"Nine."

"Okay, nine. What are you doing? Can't you tell me what you want over the phone?"

"No."

She said "Fine" and told him to meet her at the downtown Marriott at six. "But don't expect anything.—Dan? Did you hear me?"

"I won't." It was twenty minutes to, which would give him just enough time to get there. He would come back for his things later.

FIVE

After a challenging five minutes finding a place to park in the hotel lot, Dan was still early to the restaurant. He waited at a small corner table and read the free publication he'd taken from a box in the lobby. Cars for sale, cheap vacations in the tropics, animals available for adoption. One of the cats, "Bear," was a long-haired tortoiseshell, two years old.

April liked cats.

Dan wasn't sure about calling from the table until he noticed how many others in the restaurant were on their phones. He left a message about the cat, then tore out the page and put it in his back pocket. The RV would easily accommodate two people and a cat. He imagined April cooking breakfast in the kitchen—"the galley," Wexler had called it—and the cat in a ball between the front seats. Dan would put a cup of water in the holder next to his coffee mug for when it got thirsty.

"Another refill?"

The server, young with hair that fell into his eyes, hovered at Dan's shoulder with a pitcher of water. Ice cubes tapped plastic when he jerked his head to toss his bangs.

Dan accepted the refill and unwrapped a slender breadstick from the canister on the table, bit off a dry and saltless end, and watched the elevator. Intentionally-dressed couples emerged with linked arms and styled hair. Children carrying plastic tubes dragged mothers and fathers to the pool, their sandals *flap-flapping* on marble. Several hotel guests came straight into the restaurant to sit under dirty amber lighting and sip from stemless wine glasses. Not everyone looked like someone who could afford such a place, and he wondered how many were, thanks to Farling, credit-splurging on dinner out and a night or two in a fancy suite overlooking the river. He couldn't be the only one trying to take it seriously.

The hushed conversations around him blurred into a collective murmur, making him aware of how out of place he was, the only single in the dining room. He bit another inch off the breadstick and looked around the room, boldly making eye contact when possible until he saw, at the next table, a girl of twelve or thirteen, stuck in braces, eating from a plate of French fries. She resembled a long-ago crush of his who'd worn a bright yellow headband to hold back thick brown hair. Brandi. She'd said yes to *Empire of the Sun* and they were boyfriend and girlfriend for three weeks after that, kissing for the first and only time in the stairwell between second and third periods. He'd have been all right to die then, standing in the hallway watching Brandi walk to her geology class after that kiss, but not later that year when he found out he would get to play drums in the school band. He wouldn't have wanted to die before learning to keep a rhythm.

There were so few perfect times to die.

The girl sucked ketchup off her knuckle. The word PRINCESS spelled in silver glitter beckoned from a tight t-shirt hugging her small breasts. Too many parents were in his database for having borrowed far too much to appease the children they'd spoiled early, unwisely using credit even after the nationwide security breach to present them with princess sparkles and tiaras, expensive sneakers, and all on loan. They didn't understand, or seem to care, that it wasn't really theirs, that they were living a fantasy.

A man's voice said, "Excuse me," and Dan blinked.

The girl hunched her shoulders and said, "Oh my *god*. Perv." Her father stared at Dan.

Dan opened another breadstick. "Try a hat if you want people to notice her head." He waved for the waiter and ordered a drink.

He had just waved a finger for his second when April stepped out of the elevator, eyes and cheeks bright. She didn't have to take a wind beating or exercise for it. It was just her. It was a quality Dan didn't doubt had contributed to her many pageant wins.

She said something to the host at the door and he pointed at Dan. Dan smiled. She walked toward him, her long, shapeless skirt kicking out at her ankles. He thought he could smell her from where he sat, something mint and floral or eucalyptus and grass or rose and cinnamon. He felt, in his skin's memory, her coarse, wavy hair tangled around his fingers.

He stood when she reached the table. She sat down, twisting to hang the straps of her bag over the back of her chair. When the waiter arrived with Dan's scotch, April asked for a drink menu.

"Wine list?" The waiter, JEREMY on his name tag, smiled slow at her, then looked at Dan. He tossed his hair and looked back at April with straighter, taller posture. "Or maybe—"

"I want your fun drinks. The ones with the pretty umbrellas. And those little swords stabbed through pieces of fruit."

"Right back," he said and walked off.

"Do you think he'd date me?" April said.

"Do you mean do I think he'd go out to dinner and a movie with you?"

She looked at him and smiled.

He said, "Anyone would date you."

She pointed her chin at Dan's glass. "A real power drink. When did you start drinking scotch?"

"When you left."

"Habitually?"

"No."

"Some effect I had. I couldn't even turn you into an alcoholic."

She sat back in her chair and crossed her legs, put a finger to her mouth and slid a nail between her teeth but didn't bite. Dan looked at her finger and her lips and the way her body moved with the swinging of her foot under the table. "I love you," he said. He picked up his glass and hoped the world would end the moment the alcohol touched his tongue.

"It's just so cliché, don't you think?" She deepened her voice. "A real man's drink for a real man. A *man's* man. Scotch. For men."

"Did you hear what I said?"

The waiter returned with the drink menu and April said, "Thanks, Jeremy," when he handed it to her. She went over the list, silently mouthing the names of flavored martinis and margaritas. Dan noticed that as Jeremy stood there, his attention never left her.

"Cheesecake martini," she said, pointing.

The red-lipped boy said, "It'll be right out," and lingered before leaving.

"He's twenty. If that," Dan said when they were alone.

"And teachable."

He pulled another breadstick from the canister and tapped it on the table. He watched April watching the waiter at the bar. When her drink arrived, she held it up, thanked him, and ate the cherry off the sword. To Dan she said, "So, what is all this?"

"Why did you want to meet in a hotel?"

She winked. "Why do you think?"

"I wish."

"Don't you like it?"

"I like it fine."

She dropped the sword on the table and stirred her drink with the hard red straw poking out of her thick pink cocktail. "I've been staying here. My walls smell like paint. Glue, too, I guess."

"Glue?"

"Yes. Glue."

"What's the glue for?"

"Oh, I'm just—You know. Hobbies."

He did know, but he wouldn't have had she not been drunk enough one night—the only time she'd ever talked about it—to admit that even in her twenties with her forced stage days years behind her she was still "hunting a talent." "You have to have something that makes you just a smidge better than the girl standing next to you who's just as pretty and special as you are," her mother had told her. As a child, April had been more interested in volunteer work than in performing. Some of her favorite hours, she'd told Dan, were spent on the rare days her father had time to drive her to and from food banks, soup kitchens, and shelters, dropping her off with a "Proud of you, Apie-baby" and picking her up with questions about what she'd done that day. Most days, she'd taken the bus. To prepare for the pageants, exhausted after a day of school followed by volunteer work and bus rides, she would stay up late practicing everything from ribbon dancing to blowing melodies into water-filled wine bottles, her mother observing and guiding her well past midnight. "No one can see you pouring soup into bowls," she'd say. "You need something people can applaud. If you can entertain them, they'll be yours forever."

April told Dan, when he asked, that her current project was something "artsy," a little bit like sculpture.

He squared his shoulders and lifted his chin. "Eh?"

April laughed, and as abruptly as she'd started, she cut it off and scratched at her neck. Dan wanted to kiss the spot she'd made red. Her skin had always been soft in a way he couldn't compare to anything else. Instead, he would compare other things to her skin. Something was as soft as her skin, or it wasn't. He leaned over the table to kiss her cheek—chances had to be taken—and when his mouth was close enough for her flesh to bounce his breath back at him, he saw her eyes, open and watching.

He said, "Do you not want me to?"

"When did that start to matter?"

He touched his lips to the hollow of her cheek. "I'm sorry."

"For what?"

"For the kiss."

"Liar."

He said, "Have dinner with me."

"I'm not hungry."

She sipped her martini and titled her head, looking at him so directly that he shifted in his chair. "Do you know," she said, "one of the reasons I never wanted to talk to you after that day is that I just couldn't believe you would do something like that on purpose, which—"

"I didn't."

"—which made me want desperately to stay with you. Up to that moment, you were … We worked so well. But who is so distanced from the person he says he loves, who cares so little for that person as a person, that he doesn't see what's happening right beneath him?" She put down her glass. "I was so in love with you. So in love, you know? The first time I saw you, I actually stopped breathing, you were so beautiful."

When he and April had met at the collection agency, he'd first been attracted to her scent. One morning, head in his hands as he tried to convince a debtor to make small monthly payments on a considerable bill, he smelled the air around him change from stale, forced air to roses and—as he remembered it—pinecones, or some kind of pine tree. When he lifted his head, she was gone. The next time she passed he watched her go to the break room and then back to her cube, entranced by the way her formless clothes danced around her body. After work that night he'd stayed long enough to make sure the elevator doors closed with her inside before visiting her desk. Hers was the only one without any personal effects thumbtacked to the walls or taped to the monitor, and he'd been intrigued. He later learned that she was the least sentimental person he'd ever known. Birthday cards went into the trash right after she read them, as did the little notes he would leave for her around the apartment or under her windshield wiper. She would read them, smile, and then ball or tear them up and throw them away. So he should have known better, now, than to look for hints of tears or other signs of emotional exposure.

He said, "Why did you let it go to collections?"

"It's just sitting there. It isn't hurting anybody. Is it?"

He finished his drink. Small chunks of ice hit his lips and face when he tipped back the glass. "No. But it might hurt your credit report."

She said she didn't care. She said the bill didn't bother her, but that if it bothered him, it would go away as soon as he paid it.

"I'm not paying for that."

"Dan." She closed her eyes and sighed. He imagined them well beyond this point, April asleep on the Pace Arrow's couch with her feet in fuzzy socks and her hair falling across her face, Bear the Cat curled against her ankle. Dan would listen to music turned low and wake her only when they passed something she would hate to miss. She would have forgiven him for making an error in judgment the way he had forgiven her for doing the same, and when she woke up from her nap, she would stumble up front with sleepy eyes and hug his neck from behind.

"April, I'm s—"

"Don't you dare tell me you're sorry again unless you're also going to tell me what you're sorry for," she said matter-of-factly. "Until then, I don't give a damn about your sorry." She waved at the waiter and held up two fingers. "But, what the hell. I still like looking at you, you devastatingly gorgeous asshole, and I probably won't ever see you again after today."

"What if you knew you wouldn't?"

"I already know. I was being delicate."

The drinks arrived, and as he left, the waiter touched April's shoulder with what sounded to Dan like an insincere, "Oops, sorry."

April said, "Is that what this is about?"

"What do you mean?"

"Is something wrong? Are you sick?"

"No."

"Why all the phone calls and this meeting if you're not dying?"

Dan picked at the scab on his thumb. Nina, when he'd told her about the end of the world, had at the very least respected him enough to believe that he believed it. There was no ridicule, just disappointment. April was so pragmatic that she would probably find herself having to agree that the world would end someday while confronting no barriers to an impulse to add that he was an idiot or a fool for imagining it could happen now, to him.

He said, "I don't think you'll unders—"

"You're not one of those dooms-dayers, are you?"

When he didn't answer, she laughed. April's laugh was part little-girl twitter and part throaty song, even and genuine and robust. He remembered her laughing frequently, and easily, when they were together. It was a sound he used to love much more than he did right now.

"Farling?" She used the napkin from the table to wipe her eyes. "You never think you're going to meet a real person who actually believes it. I'm sorry to laugh. It's just—Well, it's just that it's so funny. Do you believe it, though? You don't *really*."

"Just tell me what you'd do if you knew you were going to die soon."

"Why?"

"I'm interested."

"Oh, fine." She picked up a breadstick and peeled open the paper. Each strip she tore curled down over her hand. "Look, it's a wild paper daisy." She spun it and the strands fanned. She put it down. "How much time?"

"Could be ten seconds."

"That's not enough. Let's say three days."

"Three days."

"What would I do with three days to live?" She took a long drink through the tiny straw, swallowed. "Maybe I would spend it outside. Maybe I'd buy a tent and live in a field … Or at the edge of a lake, or the ocean, right on the beach. And I think I'd try a dandelion— they're supposed to be good for you, you know—and real tree sap, too, straight from the trunk. And … I don't know. I don't know what else. Whatever I wanted, I think. And I wouldn't waste time with second guesses."

"Why don't you just do that now?"

She bit the tip of the breadstick and shrugged. "Why doesn't anyone do the things they want to do? What would I do all by myself in a tent on a beach with no reason for it?"

Dan reached for her hands. They were small in his, her fingernails fine, sharp, and manicured, and immediately they were gone, yanked free. "When do you think you'll stop being mad at me?" he said. He slid out of his chair and got on his knees beside her. The floor, though carpeted, was hard on his joints. Low music played through speakers in the ceiling. It wasn't a song he knew, was maybe not a song at all but a series of light, bouncing notes, one after the other, arranged in such a way that they weren't intended to be heard, but felt, and he hadn't felt them before, but he did now. He told her he had traded in his car for an RV, that he planned to drive across the country, and that he wanted her to go with him.

She reminded him that he never traveled.

He said she could make hundreds of wild paper daises and scatter them all over the floor. He said he would sleep on the couch, if that's what it would take. He said he would be with her any way she could stand him. He told her he remembered all the places she used to want to see. North Dakota's Badlands, for one. And there was that picture she'd found in a calendar accompanying the month of November, a narrow country road dividing two rows of autumn-yellow trees—she had wanted to find that road. They would drive north to Fort Kent so she could finally travel Route One from where it began in Maine to where it ended in Florida, or they could go west to camp at the bank of a mountain stream in Montana, and then park at the base of the buttes in Utah's Monument Valley.

April whispered to him to stand up, go back to his chair, people were looking.

"Will you come?"

"Of course not. Now sit down."

Before getting up, he circled his arms around her. And then he let go, sat down, and took a sip of the fresh drink he hadn't seen the waiter leave on the table.

"I can't believe you remember," she said.

The hardness of her voice didn't distract him from the redness that had finally found its way to her eyes. He hadn't been trying for it, but that it was there encouraged him even if he knew better than to use it to his advantage. That she felt anything at all when it came to him was good enough for now.

"We went to Denmark because you wanted to," he said. "I always cared about what you wanted."

"Maybe. Or maybe you—"

"Do you remember the train ride?"

Her lips pressed into a flat, impatient smile.

"Esbjerg back to Copenhagen. Do you remember?" It had been stuffy. Hot. Crowded. Packed with school kids. They'd sat facing each other but hadn't talked, had instead alternated between watching the others on the train and making eye contact. One of the times their eyes met—somewhere just outside of Middelfart, they would both remember later—April's eyes were suddenly all he could see, everything else a blur while a deep, rushing, embracing *whoooosh* filled his ears and dizzied his brain and blocked out the sounds of the train. "Did you feel that?" he said when it ended, doubting it was possible. But she had. "Like star trails in a tunnel," she'd said.

"All gone." April made a fist, then spread her fingers. "Poof."

"I don't believe that." He pulled the free publication page from his pocket and set it in front of her. "Come with me." He tapped the cat picture.

"I don't know what you're showing me," she said.

"The cat. I called for it today. I'm taking it with me."

"In the RV?"

Their waiter, his voice behind Dan, said, "Get you another?"

Dan craned his neck. "Me or her?"

"Both of you, sir."

Dan asked April if she'd be having another. She said no. "No," Dan said. "For either of us."

Jeremy left them. By the time he returned with the check, April hadn't given him an answer. She hadn't said anything but had instead turned over the page and was reading the side with the vacation deals on it.

"I'll get the drinks," she said.

"You don't want to eat? Let's eat something."

She opened the bill folder and didn't look at the amount, but reached for her purse and pulled out her wallet. She slipped her hotel keycard in the credit card slot and closed the folder before handing it back to the boy waiter, who smiled, bowed, and said, "Ma'am." To Dan, the smile gone, he said, "Evening, sir."

Dan watched as Jeremy took out his own wallet on the way to the register.

"You should see your face." April stood up and pulled her sweater straight and said she had to use the restroom. "He's just a boy. It's not his fault."

Dan watched her walk away and then picked up her wallet and looked at her driver's license, memorized her address. He counted her cash. Fifty-three dollars.

He saw Jeremy tuck the keycard in his back pocket.

Dan pulled out the three singles from April's wallet and laid them on the table. When she returned, her wallet was where she'd left it and Dan had eaten half of another a breadstick. She didn't sit, but lifted her purse from the chair and slipped her arm through its long strap.

"How old is he?"

She raised her eyebrows. She picked up her wallet and dropped it in her purse.

"Legal, I hope," he said.

"Just."

"Doesn't he make you feel old?"

"I can tell you exactly how he makes me feel if you really want to know."

"That's—No, thank you."

"He's a baby, Dan. Of course he makes me feel older." She sat, but on the edge of the chair, not quite committing. "And powerful. Jeremy—beautiful, lean, hairless Jeremy—believes I'm complex. The awe in his eyes, sometimes … . It turns me on, Dan, and I don't even know why. Isn't that something? His perception of me has completely created who I am with him." She leaned closer, lowered her voice. "I find myself saying these ridiculous things. They make absolutely no sense. He thinks I'm being profound. It's just too much fun." She pulled away, put the distance back between them. "Haven't you ever slept with someone younger?"

"I've been with Nina."

"This whole time?"

"Sleeping around isn't one of the things I'm guilty of."

"Oh, goodie. At last." She tucked her hair behind her ears and plopped her elbows on the table. "Tell me. What *are* you guilty of?"

He swept at the breadcrumbs on the table. "When will it be your turn to apologize?"

April opened her mouth, then closed it. She slid back her chair, stood, and walked unhurriedly toward the door.

The waiter, no longer in his work gear but wearing a casual shirt and slacks, followed April to the elevator.

SIX

He hadn't been in the basement long when Nina's car pulled into the driveway, a faint glow from her headlights sending him scampering reflexively into a dark corner. His clothes were ready to go, but he hadn't yet gathered the things he would need from the kitchen.

Her car door thudded and she stomped up the stairs to the front door. He heard the key turn, heard the door open. He didn't hear the deadbolt unlock in between. He couldn't remember whether he'd locked it, or whether it had originally been unlocked and he'd left it that way. The door closed and he heard her walk into the kitchen and through to the living room, where the speakers popped on with the TV. Loud audience laughter marked a punch line.

A draft from somewhere tickled his head. He inspected the basement windows—closed tight—and then edged the room with his hands held to the brick while listening to her movements. She went back into the kitchen, opened and closed the refrigerator, and ran something in the microwave. Its loud hum rose and fell in an even cycle until the timer signaled and she opened the door, slammed it shut. Her footsteps to the living room were cut short by a ringing phone she answered with, "You're calling late." The couch creaked and the TV droned. Dan stood under the vent carrying sound, but little heat, from the living room. It was not a show they'd watched together.

After some time she said, "I did. He said to get back to him in a few days and he'd set something up. … I don't know. I don't know,

Sylvia. I would like to say I wouldn't, but I probably won't have to worry about that, anyway. I—Syl, I just can't talk about hi—Okay. Yes." She laughed.

He felt the draft again. He held his palm an inch from the wall and walked around the room again until he found it, a thin crack in the cinderblock that started at the floor and zagged up along the mortar, ending some inches over his head. He knew nothing about homes, foundations, or cinderblock, but thought a weakness in structure like that had to make the house more vulnerable. There was nothing he could do about it now, but he could at least stop the cold air from seeping in. He located an outlet near the shelves and plugged in the lamp, then shined it around like a flashlight until he found the tube of caulk next to the cooler. He sealed the crack as well as he could, using his thumb to flatten the goo into the seam.

The floor creaked above and her steps went one direction, and then back again. There and back. And again.

He wandered the basement. He straightened the boxes on the shelves. He centered the utility sink's faucet. He sat on his bag of clothes.

He imagined picking up the bag and taking the stairs to the main floor without masking the noise, letting her hear him come all the way up. She wouldn't open the door before he reached the top. She would either know it was him and wait for him to make that decision to come through the door on his own, or she would be afraid it was an intruder and run out the front door. When she saw him, whether she was standing in the middle of the kitchen with her arms folded over her chest or freezing in the snow without boots or a coat, she would hate him. In a single action, he would have admitted to denying her only request: that he not be in the house after leaving her for the woman who'd had him first. And he would have used the single return she'd said she would allow him.

There was little he could do but wait for her to go upstairs and fall asleep.

He slipped spoons and knives and forks into his bag one by one through the drawstring hole, packing them separately around the edges and tucking them into folds in his clothes. He froze when a fork hit another utensil as he stuffed it in his bag, but at just after eleven Nina was probably far past hearing anything.

The bowl, plate, and small saucepan didn't fit on top, so he would carry them in his arms. Food was all he needed, now, and he could buy that in the morning.

Over the breakfast bar he noticed the back of the swiveling recliner—his recliner, and he'd forgotten about it—partially hidden under the afghan Nina's grandmother had crocheted when Nina was seven or eight years old. Made for a child, it was too small to use as a blanket and had until recently sat folded on the shelf over the dryer. Nina was always good about remembering she shared the house, welcoming an even balance of her things and his. He'd tried to convince her to keep it out, because it was the one thing she hadn't packed away that would remind her of her grandmother. Hers was the first death Nina had experienced, and it had taken her years to get past it. The blanket, while not packed away where Nina could pretend the lost (grandmother, dog, cat) had never existed and therefore never been lost, had until now been visible only when the closet doors were open on laundry days.

Dan leaned his bag against the counter on the way to the living room and eased into the chair. He tugged the blanket from behind his head and tossed it on the couch, then swiveled in a slow circle and counted the other things that were his. His TV. His stereo. His coffee pot. The coffee table was his, too, left over from his relationship with April, as was the dining room table in the next room. They'd bought it together, and she hadn't wanted to keep it, or anything else the two had bought together, when they ended their short marriage. He had never told Nina about the furniture, had lied, in fact, and said it was brand new second-hand. It had been in good condition and not at all cheap, but she would have wanted to sell it for a fraction of the price and buy something else. Now it was all

Nina's, along with the walls he'd painted and the bathroom sink it had taken four hours, six beers, and three trips to the hardware store for them to replace.

He put all of his weight on the arm rests when lifting himself out of the chair (whose leather tended to squeak), and then tip-toed into the kitchen. His scotch—which he genuinely liked—wasn't next to the phone with Nina's gin, but he had a feeling she hadn't thrown it away. There was too much left, it was too expensive, and she wasn't wasteful. He searched the cabinets, opening each one just a crack to prevent the *click* of the hinge when the door swung beyond a certain point. He found it on an upper shelf with the paper towel rolls. She'd have had to use the foot stool to put it up there. On the days she didn't call out to him that she needed "someone tall," she would get whatever it was for herself and treat him to accidental poses—a stretch from the low stool that extended her back and emphasized her rear—or perform a clumsy climb onto the counter that had him running to spot her.

He pulled down the bottle and poured a glass (glasses were now in the cabinet that used to overflow with dry baking ingredients) and sat again in his recliner. He pretended there was a fire in the fireplace and tried not to remember the restaurant and tried not to imagine the boy waiter kissing her body in the same places Dan once had.

Less painful was to have another drink or two and think about Nina, until thinking about Nina and their unremarkable but very comfortable eight years together became unexpectedly painful to think about, too.

Nina had adored him. April had had many feelings for him, including love, but she had never adored him. April was not someone who adored people.

Dan stood over Nina and watched her eyes and listened to her breathing. Her lips vibrated slightly with heavy exhales that disturbed the sheet pulled high and close to her face. One of her arms was tucked under the blanket and resting on her stomach. The other was exposed, flat on the bed, her hand a few inches from a book with no title. He picked it up—the cover was soft leather, the pages thick and rough—and brought it to the window to read it in the light of the three blinding bulbs mounted on Carl's driveway lamp post, but the writing was too small and he was too drunk to make much sense of it. He identified "meet with Valbon" ("Bogdaaaaniiii," he mouthed), "empty," and "temperatures" before giving up. He returned it to the bed and looked outside, where nothing was happening. Carl's sports car sat in the driveway, spotless and shiny when most cars on their street had a salt and dirt film. A squirrel raced across the snow-scraped street followed closely by the neighborhood cat, both disappearing over Carl's backyard fence.

The view from the second floor was one he would miss. It was home beyond the walls of the house, the neighborhood characters and animals part of an extended, if estranged, family.

He had been watching Nina sleep from the window for what could have been one minute or ten minutes when she moved, inhaled sharply, and propped herself on an elbow to look at him.

"Iss juss me," he said. "Jus*t*. Just me, Nina. Nina, Nina, my Nina. It's midnight. We made it. One day."

She inched up under the covers, the sheet pulled over her chest and tucked tight under her arms. "I knew you would do this. I knew you would do it. Don't."

"You love me," he said, and Nina curled into herself, her knees drawing to her chin.

"I can't talk to you," she whispered.

"Neen …"

"I can't …" She pulled a breath. "I can't talk to you. Unless you're back."

When he said her name again she let her head fall back against the headboard and cried openly. She didn't dry her face, and every clutch her lungs made for air screamed to him to fix her. He went to her and wrapped his arms around her small body, warm from sleep. She rested her head on his chest and he held it there, felt the wetness through his shirt. He stroked her hair and smelled her shampoo, a smell that reminded him of the last eight years. Her body shrank into his and he absorbed her, curled an arm between her legs and pulled her out of the sheets.

His head hurt. Nina's cool breasts pressed into his back and her hand moved on his waist as her body inched closer. Last night had been good—possibly better than any other time, even after the drinking, which surprised him—but he wished the world would end, end now, before he had to face her, before she made him speak.

"Hi." The word fell warm on the back of his neck. He reached up to scratch where his skin now tickled, and she slid her knee between his thighs and traced his cheekbone with her finger. "I don't want to know why you came back. I don't want to hear about her, or about anything else. I just want this. I know it's—Where are you going?"

Her hand slid away as he bent over to grab his underwear from the floor. He did his best to put them on without standing, then shoved his feet into his socks and stood to put on his pants. Without looking at her, he covered her with the sheet and squeezed her shoulder, then picked up his sweater from the foot of the bed. He thought he heard her say something as he pulled it over his head.

"What was that?" he said.

She raised herself onto her knees and the sheet dropped down to the mattress. "I said you're not here. I thought it was just right now, this second, but you never were, were you? Last night."

He looked at her long neck, her small nipples, the pubic hair curling against the insides of her strong thighs. "I was here." He wanted to sit, wanted to take her hand, she was so small and so naked. "I drank too much. It's not an excuse." He wanted to tell her he had missed her, but that would do no good. "I didn't want to hurt you."

"What did you want to do?"

"I just mean there was no conscious—"

He stopped trying when she waved her hand between them in a wide, dismissive arc. She dropped from her knees and sat cross-legged on a mess of blankets, everything exposed to him. Dan picked up a corner of the sheet and held it out to her. "Take it."

"Why?"

He let it fall.

"Maybe it would be easier for you if this could be more like it is in the movies." She stroked her legs from her unshaved inner thighs to her ankles. "In a lot of them, one character kills another character, and then he just … leaves. And then, in the next scene, the killer is at an airport, and he's wearing one of those straw hats. We're supposed to know he's going to the Bahamas, or somewhere tropical, somewhere sunny and warm. But what did he do with the body? We don't see that part." She used one hand to wipe her eyes, and with the other swiped her index finger under her nose and sniffed. "How did you get in?"

He told her.

She said to return the key to the drawer on his way out.

SEVEN

Knocking woke him from his nap on the couch. He sat up and wiped sweat from his face and took a second to remember where he was.

A voice said, "Is anybody in there?"

He took off his coat and opened the door. The girl who worked the hotel's front desk smiled at him.

"Hi," she said. "Um—I'm so sorry, but you can't park here. It's not me. It's my manager."

When Dan had left his house that morning he'd meant to head straight to April's, but he hadn't felt quite up to it without more sleep. He'd only meant to stop in the parking lot for a few hours, which is what he told the girl while rubbing his eyes.

"I don't mean to be nosy, or anything," she said, "but you weren't sleeping just now, were you?"

"Should I not have been?"

"Not with this thing running. Are you crazy? Do you have a carbon monoxide detector?"

"I don't know. I'm sure it's fine." He smelled the air and noticed nothing out of the ordinary.

"You can't smell it.—Here, you have one there," she said, pointing at a box on the wall. "You need new batteries, though. See that light?"

"Got it. Thanks."

"You should use the generator," she said. She started down the stairs, and stopped. "So, do you live in this thing, or are you—Are you traveling, or … ?"

"Traveling. I hope."

"Lucky."

The door was still open and cool air flowed in. The girl wrapped her arms around herself and shivered. Her breasts were uncommonly large. Even under a coat, they were difficult to ignore. Harder still when she had them squeezed together and cradled in her arms. She was looking at him. He didn't know what to do, so he picked up his coat and held it.

"You know," she said, "we have all kinds of batteries inside. I'll go get you some."

He was about to tell her it wasn't necessary, but she was already gone, running across the parking lot in her big snow boots. He dropped the coat on the couch and closed the door, then turned off the engine and watched for her through the bedroom window. Within a minute she appeared again in the hotel's open glass doors, stopped to say something to a figure behind the counter, then waved absently over her shoulder and hurried back to the RV. She knocked and waited for Dan to say "Come in" before opening the door and stepping inside, pulling package after package of batteries from her pockets and dropping them on the kitchen counter. She'd brought six packs of double-A batteries and, just in case, three nine-volts. She told him she'd stolen them from the supply room, but said it was okay because the owner, Ray, had once accused her of stealing from the cash register so he could dock her check for the amount he claimed was missing and, in a round-about kind of way, steal from her. She told Dan she knew Ray was lying not only because she never took any money, but also because she'd asked to see the footage from the camera mounted in the corner behind the counter, and he'd told her there was no footage, that the camera wasn't on because it was broken. But it was always on, she told Dan.

Dan wasn't sure how he felt about having a possible thief in his RV who, under the guise of being a concerned citizen, could be casing his new home, but he supposed he didn't have much she would be interested in. What would she want with forks and knives, a few plates and bowls, or his doodads from home?

She opened the carbon monoxide detector's battery cover and nudged out the old AAs, replaced them with three new ones, and handed the old ones to Dan, who threw them in the trash can under the sink.

All finished, she bounced her shoulders and smiled at him. "It's funny being in an RV again," she said. "Even smells the same, in a way. This is a lot like the one my parents had before my dad died. The carpet was light blue, though, instead of brown." She bit her cheek and looked at him. "So, where are you going?"

"Right now?"

"No, I mean when you get on the road."

"I don't know."

She didn't seem anxious to leave. The way she slipped backward, away from the front door and deeper into the kitchen, made him think she was in fact anxious not to. He told her she could stay for a little while, if she wanted to, and that it was the least he could offer in return for the safety lesson. He sat in one of the chairs in the living room and apologized for having no soda or coffee to offer, but she was shaking her head before he could finish, saying, "Oh, it's okay. I'm fine."

She sat on the couch, her palms pressed together and tucked between her knees, and smiled again, mouth tight, eyes darting all around before settling on him. "What about California?" she said.

"What about California?"

"As a place to go. You can really breathe, there. It's so big and full of sunshine." She unzipped her coat, but left it on. "But you can probably breathe anywhere else better than you can breathe here."

"What's the matter with here?"

"Everything," she said. "There are too many trees, first of all. And it's crowded. And everyone is old and white. I mean old-old, not your—not, you know, normal aged."

"It is very white," he said.

"And haunted. Did you know we have a ghost called the White Lady? Even our ghosts are old and white. If I don't get out of here, in a hundred years I'll be one of those white ghosts wandering around the mills, or someplace, with a chain around my ankle. I'll probably have twigs in my hair."

Dan asked her name, and she said it was Jenny.

"And you're Daniel Palace."

"Dan."

She nodded, yawning. "So, who's—I mean, is anyone going with you?"

"Where?"

"Wherever you're going."

"I don't know, yet."

"Well, do you know why you're going, at least?"

He almost said he didn't, but the way she leaned into the space they shared, how genuinely she seemed to want to hear his answer, persuaded him to tell her. Not about the end of the world, but a truncated history of his experiences with April and Nina. She listened intently, undistracted, the way Nina always did.

"So," Jenny said, her face resting in her palm, "one woman left you, and another let you leave?"

"I guess so."

"Were they blind?"

He laughed. "Well, there's more to a per—"

"I know all that, but it's just … you're so nice. I can see that, and I've only known you for a minute." She put her hand over her mouth and yawned again. "I'm sorry. I swear you're not boring me. It's work that does it to me. My mom keeps telling me that if I just go to college I can quit the hotel and move out to live on a campus somewhere, but I don't know. I always hated school. I want to leave, but I don't want to leave to do that."

She would be eighteen this month, she said, but she was out of high school, having graduated early because she'd hated it that much.

He hadn't pinned an age on her, but he had thought mid-twenties, at least. Her eyes, deep brown and very round, looked much older than almost-eighteen. Darkness—makeup, he guessed, but still—filled in the small lines in the skin under her bottom eyelashes, and her mouth—wide, but somewhat downturned, as if molded that way more by experience than by genetics—had traces of lipstick around the edges that added a certain hardness. She closed her eyes and rested her head on the back of the couch. "This is nice. We had a couch like this in ours, too."

Her sleepiness and his hunger made him curious about the time. He checked his watch. Noon. (Thirty-six hours down, he thought.) He wondered whether she had a car. "Listen, do you want to—I see how sleepy you are. If you want to take a nap, for a little bit ..."

She sat up, her back straight, and stared at him.

"No, it's ... " He laughed. "I was going to ask if you have a car. I need a favor."

"Oh. Of course I have a car."

She sounded disappointed. Or maybe he was assigning an emotion that wasn't there. Something about that mouth. "Great. Good," he said, and went on to offer a trade: her car for the use of his RV so he could do some grocery shopping. "I'll pick up something for you, too, if there's anything you need."

Jenny jumped off the couch and rushed past him. She flew down the stairs and through the door, swinging it shut behind her. He thought about calling after her that there was no reason to be afraid, but wasn't that what any psychopath would say to lure a young woman? He went to the bedroom for his phone so he could call for a taxi, already feeling the silence now that there was no longer a second person filling the space. He was still searching for the number when he saw Jenny through the window, her big boots slapping in the slush as she made her way back. She didn't knock, this time, but opened the door and clomped up the stairs.

"My manager's gone for the day, and Andy said he'd cover for me," she said. "He used do it all the time when I took naps in vacant rooms. Until Margaret—that's my manager—caught me. Here." She handed him her car keys. The keychain was a red plastic ball with changing fortunes inside that appeared behind a dark window. "It's over there," she said, pointing at a blue hatchback parked at the far end of the lot.

Dan took the keys and put on his coat while she pulled off her boots and got comfortable on the couch, yellow socks poking out from the ankles of her pants and a pillow held over her head. He heard her muffled "Thank you" as he stepped outside.

The roads were slow with lunchtime traffic, and Jenny's gas tank was low. He pulled into a station (whose emptiness didn't necessarily speak to a nationwide panic over a coming Armageddon) and called again about the cat while waiting beside the pump, his armpits sweating in temperatures too warm for a coat. The cat was still there, the woman said, and Dan could stop by any time before three. She gave him her address.

He bought food and a few cases of water, cat supplies that included a cheetah toy like Paulie's, scotch and beer, sheets and a comforter for the bed, and, because he would try until she said yes, a new throw blanket, blue, from the seasonal section of the grocery store. He could see April wearing it around her shoulders or bunching it over her feet during their trip to the mountains.

The last stop was to pick up the cat, whose owner lived next door to the Willow Café, a restaurant he and Nina had frequented. He pushed the doorbell and thought he heard someone call "Gimme a minute." He took a sip from his water bottle and waited, turning to watch the street so he wouldn't have to stare at her door.

Two motorcycles slowed at the duplex and passed, their engines rumbling before turning off in front of the café. Dan recognized one of the drivers as a regular Nina enjoyed looking at but who they both suspected wouldn't be around long. How he kept his bike upright when he rode away at the end of the night had long been a mystery to both of them. They'd once tried riding their bicycles, now long gone, after a few drinks and had repeatedly slid off their seats to keep from falling over. A block from their apartment, laughing and shushing each other on the sleeping street, they'd turned around and walked them home.

The door opened behind him. When he turned around, a thirty-something woman in a soft-looking sweater said, "Oh, goodness, hello," and invited him in. She apologized for a mess Dan didn't see.

"She's in here," she said, leading him through a spotless living room and shiny kitchen to a closed door at the back of the house. She opened it, and Dan held his breath at the ammonia. A single litter box, the litter in dark clumps, sat in the corner on a rubber mat next to a worn cat tree, carpet shredded through to wood, dried vomit on the ledges and play tube. The two bowls at the base sat empty.

He didn't see a cat.

"She's in there," she said, pointing at the tube. She walked over and reached inside and pulled out a small brown cat with ears black at the tips.

"What's wrong with its ears?" Dan said.

"Frostbite. It looks like frostbite, anyway. I found Bear—that wasn't her name, I'm sure, but she did start to answer to it—last month in the back lot of the restaurant when that cold front came through. I'd like to keep her, but I really just don't have the time." She pushed the tip of her thumb between the pads of the cat's front paw and used her finger to stroke the tops of the toes. Her other hand supported the cat's hind feet.

Dan asked if she was sure she wanted to part with a cat she seemed to like.

"Just take better care of her than I can, and I'll let you have her for free. I've had that ad running since I found her, and you're the first one to call. You can have all her food, the bowls, and … well, I think you'll want to get your own litter box."

He asked the woman, who hadn't mentioned her name, whether she would mind if he had some lunch and stopped back in an hour.

She held the cat close, nuzzled its head. "Take your time. Just be back before three."

Before leaving, Dan poured some of his water into what looked like the water bowl and left the bottle, still a quarter full, on the floor.

He chose an outdoor table at the Willow, its space heater still useful even in the uncharacteristic, and only relative, heat. He slid his chair closer and held his palms, fingers spread, to the vent. A wave of warmth washed over his forehead and through his hair at the same time a breeze blew, the combined temperatures feeling like cool water dumped in a hot bath and with a smell and a feel that reminded him of some past winter … he tried to snatch it from where it danced around … maybe it was the one with April at Niagara Falls, the year they learned waterfall mist in November made a slip-and-fall layer of ice on the ground … or the one decades before, when he was a teenager, wet rocks and thick mud behind his house, a hiding spot to read a stolen book.

"That warm enough for you, Dan?"

The waitress with the limp and the fuzzy yellow hair, whose name Dan always forgot, dragged an unused heater across the stone patio and positioned it on the opposite side of the table. She said, "Where's your lady?"

"Not feeling well today."

"Oh, I'm sorry. She's a sweetheart. Hope she feels better. Get you somethin' to drink, or do you need a menu?"

He'd wanted to eat, but a drink sounded better. "A drink, I think. I'm celebrating."

"Oh, yeah? What're you celebrating?"

He didn't know what he should say. He wished he'd simply asked for the drink. "The nice weather," he said.

"Okie dokie." She gave him a scratchy laugh.

He ordered two scotches to mark time, half of each to be consumed in honor of memorable moments in his life:

The first half was for the stolen book. It was the only time in his childhood he'd done something out of character, something unexpected. Fourteen and a solid B student, he'd waited for the kind-eyed cashier with the nametag reading KATIE to be distracted so he could slip the latest Koontz novel into the waistband of his jeans. Nothing had ever been so exciting, nor so frightening, again—until April.

The second half would celebrate his third time with a woman.

Third half, his first date with the agent who'd worked with him at IP Collections, the one whose lack of material attachments and confident sway spoke to a spiritual freedom and sureness Dan had never known and was positive, at the time, was more than he could handle. But April—magnetic, sparkling—had asked, and he'd said yes.

Final half, the present, whatever it was and however long it might last.

When he finished, he ordered another drink for Nina and the last eight years.

The woman took too long to hand over the cat. She held her to her chest and looked sideways at Dan and asked if he'd been drinking. Dan said of course not, but that it was his to say if he should or couldn't be drinking and that he would get the cat home just fine, thank you, and she shouldn't worry so much about everything but go out and get what she wants, find her happiness in life—what was left of it, anyway—and "maybe don't take in any more cats, you know, if you can't water 'em or clean one litter little … one litter little … one *little* … *litter* box."

She told him she would watch him drive away and that she'd call the police if she saw him swerve even a little.

Dan put Bear—and it looked like one, brown and fluffy, even on the ears—in the back seat and got the food and litter from the woman, who didn't help carry it out. After closing the trunk, he got in the car and checked the backseat for the cat. It was in the sun on

71

the deck behind the headrest, licking its paw in the window and paying no attention to the woman outside tapping the glass and waving. Before putting the key in the ignition, he asked Jenny's keychain, "Will I get pulled over?" and shook the ball. The triangle that floated to the top read, IT IS DECIDEDLY SO.

He'd only managed a buzz, but drove just over the speed limit, anyway, and watched for police, the radio off for concentration. When he reached the hotel, he parked beside the RV and took Bear from the back seat and brought her inside. Jenny slept on the couch under a comforter from the hotel. Dan wanted to lie beside her and feel someone's arms around him, but instead he crawled onto the bed without getting the sheets from the car. He dialed April's number and murmured "April" when he heard her voice.

"No. Nina."

He said "Shit" and pressed the END bar and dropped the phone on the bed and closed his eyes.

EIGHT

Jenny had left a note on the counter, her neat, slanted letters written on a small piece of paper with CORNER INN printed at the top: *I hope you don't take this the wrong way, but can I go with you when you leave? I promise I'm not crazy. I looked through your things a little and I'm pretty sure you're not crazy, either. ☺ I have savings, and so I can pay rent or help with gas or anything else. It doesn't matter where you're going, because I'll go anywhere. You won't be sorry you brought me along. I'm fun! P.S. I brought in all your stuff from my car. Are you getting a cat?* She'd left her number under her name. Dan ran the water and drank some from his hands, rubbed some on his face, and then looked for the cat. He found it asleep under the driver's seat. Jenny had left his bags on the couch and the cat bowls on the kitchen floor. He filled one with water and the other with a can of food, but the cat didn't come out. He crouched on the floor to poke it and make sure it was alive. It made a noise that sounded like a question-song and stretched out its feet.

Dan looked out at the gray parking lot and the gray sky, the yellow light of the hotel lobby. Jenny stood behind the counter and appeared to be watching the RV. Cold air squeezed through the window seams, so he closed the curtains over the couch, where Jenny's hotel blanket lay folded and forgotten. He pulled his phone from his back pocket, pressed the CALL bar twice, and saw his own home number appear on the screen. He hung up quickly and scrolled to April's number. She answered after one ring.

"It's me," he said.

"And?"

"Did you take care of my dinner with that Jeremy kid, too?"

She hung up, and so did Dan. He picked up Jenny's note and dialed the hotel rather than the personal number she'd left. He planned to tell her she'd forgotten her blanket, but before he could say much of anything she sang "It's you!" and said she could be packed in half an hour. She offered to bring food from home—she wanted to contribute—and promised not to bring more than two bags.

"You forgot your blanket. The one from the hotel," he said. "That's what I was calling about." He thanked her for the use of her car and said he was sorry, but he couldn't take her with him. "Maybe if you were five years older." He laughed a little and added, "Or even a month older."

She moaned that she would be the walking dead in five years, her soul trapped in Connecticut's valleys or in pine needles scattered on the sidewalk. Before he could give into the temptation to reassure her with the possibility that nothing would be anywhere in five years, she hung up.

He called April again. He said, "I shouldn't have said what I said."

"Dan, I'm sick. Can you make yourself feel better later?" *Dand, I'b sick. Cad you bake yourself feel bedder lader?* "Besides. I would have said the same thing."

"Is someone there to help you?"

"Help me what?"

"With—Do you need anything?"

"I'm fine, Dan."

"I'll bring you soup."

"You don't know where I live."

One-nineteen Munson Street, apartment 5A. "So, tell me."

"I'm not telling you where I live."

"Chicken soup."

"Fine."

He drove the RV to the only grocery store he knew to have an uncomplicated parking lot with two outlets, picked up crackers and the soup brand he thought he remembered her liking, and drove to her apartment eight miles away. He parked on the street, blocking exit to the yellow Renault parked in front of the closed garage stall for apartment 5A.

Almost everything around him in the cold living room was red. The drapes, the walls, the ceiling. The furniture and throw rug and pillows. The only not-red decorative object was a rose quartz candle holder he remembered buying her at a gift shop in Denmark.

She had let him in with "It's oped" and had yelled from the bathroom after he came in that he should pour himself a cup of tea, if he wanted tea, and wait for her. "Ad I doh, dhe kitched is hod. It's dhe odly place the head works. I already called aboud id."

Utensils, cup saucers, measuring spoons, a soup ladle, a potted plant and more were glued—cemented—to the kitchen's yellow walls. "So this is how you art," he'd called. No reply. After pouring a cup from a small dragon-painted pot, he'd taken off his coat and wandered the kitchen and studied the walls, stopping to tug curiously at one of the stuck spoons. It had come loose in his hand, so he'd used it, teeth of hard glue clinging to the handle, to stir in some honey he'd spotted on the counter.

She had been in the bathroom for at least ten minutes, and his cup was empty. He bounced the spoon on the red rug. "April?" He closed his eyes and smelled whatever scent it was that filled her apartment. It smelled like her, the way she'd always smelled.

"Dan." Her hair fell in waves around her face. A sundress lay soft against her skin.

"April. Come here." He didn't have to open his eyes to know she was there. He kissed her. "April, I just—God, I missed you."

"What are you doing?"

"April. Come here."

"Open your eyes. Sit up." *Oped your eyes. Sid up.*

He opened his eyes. Sat up.

She squatted in front of him in a pair of blue jeans, her hair in a loose knot, her nose raw. "Where's the soup?"

He said it was in his coat pocket.

"In a can? You didn't get the good kind from the soup counter by the deli? What store did you go to?"

"I'll make it for you. Just show me where the pots are."

"I'm not hungry right now." She took the spoon from him and brought it to the kitchen. "But you can leave it here for later. And, thank you." She pulled a tube of cement glue from a drawer and stuck the spoon back to the wall where Dan had found it. She stepped away to look at it, then moved farther into the kitchen where he couldn't see her.

He heard pouring.

"April," he said. "When we were together, our walls were white. Weren't they all white?"

She came to the entry and leaned against the closed French door, red on the living room side. The other door, open and flush against the living room wall, was painted green. "I guess they were alwight." She moved into the room and sat on the floor, where she took a careful sip from the cup held delicately in one hand. In the other, she clutched a wadded tissue. Dan slid his foot toward her and she flung her cup at him. Tea splashed hot on his stomach.

"Jesus." He pulled his shirt away from his skin. "Fucking Christ, April."

"Well?" She coughed and blew her nose.

She brought out a bottle of wine and two sweatshirts, one for each of them, because neither wanted to sit in the hot kitchen. Both sweatshirts had once been Dan's. She tucked her hands inside the cuffs of the long sleeves, pushing them up only to blow her nose.

Dan recommended turning up the heat even more to drive the excess from the kitchen into the living room.

"It doesn't work. But if you're too cold you can put your shoes back on and go home."

He put on his shoes and sat back down, each of them now occupying opposite ends of her red couch. A wrinkle in the sweatshirt rubbed harsh against his tea burn. He yanked it away.

"You haven't asked me why I let you come over," she said.

"I thought it was the soup."

"It was the soup." She blew her nose. "It really was." She laughed. "But I'm also curious about you. It's been a long time. I want to know what you're doing, where your life has gone." She tucked a loose section of hair behind her ear with fingers that barely reached out of the sleeve, then leaned back into the couch with her feet on a coffee table painted cherry. She rested her glass on her stomach.

Dan told her a little bit about working collections and a little bit less about being married—"Kids?" April said, offering no expression when he said no—and didn't say much else, because there wasn't much else to say about his life. He had no adventures to share. All he could add, which he did, was that he'd thought about her.

"A lot?"

"Now and then."

She scratched her head, digging a finger under the base of her hair wad. "I thought about you, too."

"Dead or alive?"

"Yes. Neither made me very happy." She took out her bun to scratch again. Her hair fell over her hand and around the elastic band hanging on her finger.

"Jesus, you're beautiful."

"Oh, please, Dan. You're getting dizzy over some woman with a sinus cold?"

"You are not 'some woman,' April Periera."

April poured herself the last of the wine and stood and stretched before going into the kitchen. "More?" she called.

"Hold on a sec. I'll come out."

"Don't." She poked her head into the open space. "Stay there." She disappeared again, and Dan heard kitchen noises.

"Beautiful," she said from around the corner where he couldn't see her. "I used to think that meant something. Everyone makes such a fuss over it that it's almost impossible for a girl not to think she's somehow protected from everything bad in the world if she's lucky enough to get the right combination of genes." Dan heard a bottle sliding on the counter. "But how is she supposed to feel, and what will happen, if she gets in a car accident or, heaven forbid, ages?" The pop of a cork. The blowing of her nose. "So much fuss. Over skin draped over cartilage and a skull." She appeared in the doorway with a freshly opened bottle. A small piece of tissue stuck to her right nostril. "Do you remember that boy on the bus in Canada? It was years ago."

Dan said he remembered. Anyone who knew the story remembered.

"He was absolutely gorgeous. I bet he thought he was charmed. There he was, just sitting on a bus, seeing the world, and out of nowhere ... ." She set the bottle on the coffee table in front of Dan. "I actually wrote a story about it. Do you want to read it?"

He didn't remember her writing. He asked when she started.

She said, "Kindergarten."

When she came back from the bedroom with a worn folder, the tissue was gone.

"Were you going to tell me?" she said.

"Not a chance."

He filled both glasses while she rummaged through loose pages. She had started writing just after he left, she said. She stuck with it for three or four years and picked up photography when she couldn't get recognition from a publisher.

"I wrote one about you." She pulled out a sheet from somewhere in the middle and handed it to him. "This isn't it. I call this one, 'What We're All Doing While Someone Else Is Being Killed.' What do you think?"

"I don't know. Go away and be quiet."

During stabs one through twenty-four, she, in somewhere Oklahoma, was tearing the perforated cardboard strip from her frozen Lean Cuisine spinach and cheese pizza. One of the perforations wasn't deep enough, so she had to use her middle fingernail to poke through and loosen the strip, because if the tear didn't come out right, the whole box would collapse and the pizza would slide off the crisping tray and end up soggy, the way she didn't like it. Stabs twenty-five through forty-seven she was staring into the open refrigerator, thinking, "Milk or soda milk or soda I drink too much too much too much soda, milk milk milk," before pouring herself a tall glass of Mountain Dew. A hair clinging to her bare arm (they were always falling out of her head and landing on her skin, or collecting in the dark cup of her sweatshirt hood) made her twitch and shiver the way a spider would. It drove her fucking insane. Stabs forty-eight through fifty-five she eyed her arm for the hair she couldn't find, watched the microwave's green numbers time down, turned on the TV, and remotely punched the control's up arrow until she found a show to keep her company through her meal. She looked for that hair again (it was on her arm, somewhere near her elbow, but she couldn't find it, damn it, and she hoped it wasn't dipping into her cheese) through the something-odd strokes it took in those narrow Greyhound seats to saw off the boy's head while, on TV, a character screamed, "These *pretzels* are making me *thirsty*!"

"Jesus."

April, sitting beside him on the couch, said, "Jesus good or Jesus awful?"

"Do you have any sympathy for the poor kid?"

"Do you?"

"I do, now." He didn't want to think about decapitated people. He asked if she had some music they could listen to.

She looked at him. "Sure, Dan. Whatever you want."

He flipped through the CDs in her desk cubby until he found the one he knew she would still have. He put it in and Lennon sang, "You know I love you, baby. Please don't go."

"Least perceptive man I've ever met," she said.

"I chose it for 'Woman.'"

"Anyway," she said, "I was making a point. The point is that no one is special, and this brings us to you and your …"—She pressed her lips tight, not quite managing to hide the smile—"… your fear the world is going to … is going to end. What's silly about it, Dan, is that the world could have ended any minute since the time it began. Why shouldn't it? It's a planet in a solar system in a galaxy in a universe." She took a long drink and poured a refill. She was averaging two glasses to every one of his.

"And this is the year," he said. "Why wouldn't it be?"

"Doesn't every generation think at some point that they'll be the last one? What makes us special enough to be that last generation? We're nothing," she said. "We're just people on a planet in a solar system in a galaxy in a universe."

"You make me crazy."

She pulled her foot onto her knee and warmed her toes in her hand. "I can understand, in a way. I used to think I was special. As sure as I was that nothing bad would ever happen to me, I would also lie awake in bed at night afraid of being killed in my sleep by my mother, or a masked—and caped, don't laugh—serial killer. We all knew the JonBenét story. But, do you see? Even the death I invented for myself was extraordinary. I never imagined it would be something as everyday as being hit by a car, or…or choking on my lollipop. And I think that's not too different from believing your time is the time for something as magnificent as the ruin of the planet, or even that your planet is the 'chosen one.'" She used her fingers to make quotation marks in the air. "But what's really going to happen, Dan, is that we're all going to go on living, and most of us will eventually die average deaths." She coughed and blew her nose. "Look at what happened to me. What I suffered was as unspecial as it gets. I'm just … I'm one of millions."

"What you suffered?"

She uncrossed and re-crossed her legs and thumbed the curve of her wine glass. "Not apologizing is one thing, Dan, but pretending it never happened is insulting."

April's teeth were wine dark. He ran his tongue over his own teeth. "We hurt each other," he said. "I forgave you."

"No. You hurt me. I reacted."

"We had a misunderstanding. You were angry … sorry, hurt. But you didn't even tell me you were pregnant—"

She laughed at him. "You say that like it was a preexisting condition."

"I thought it was a fight. I thought you were taking a weekend to calm down."

"You are terrible at this conversation."

"All you left was some blood on the—the thing, the stool—at the end of the bed and a note in my shoe, and it didn't tell me where you were or how to get in touch with you. And I forgave you for all of that."

"When? Was it right away, Dan?"

"It was right away, because I underst—"

"What you understood or didn't understand is irrelevant. You don't get to forgive me for that blood. That blood was a consequence of something I never wanted."

"Then why did y—"

"Obviously I wanted it once you got me pregnant, Dan, but what I didn't want was to be pregnant in the first place. So you understand why I didn't have such an easy time forgiving you. You understand, Dan."

"No one made you do any of that. It was all your choice."

She brought her face close to his. "You gave me no choice." Her breath smelled of fruits and spices. "Don't pretend you don't remember."

He remembered everything, he said. They just remembered it differently.

NINE

The light in the room was muted. Shadows slid into corners, wrapped around curves. Dan noticed her wrinkles, deeper than they used to be around her eyes, and her lips had thinned just enough to make her look angry when she wasn't smiling. When she did smile, it was harder for her to hide the malice that he now wondered how often he'd missed in the past, or had mistaken for happiness.

"I wish I knew why you were still here," she said. "I don't know why I haven't kicked you out. I think I'm convinced that if you leave, you'll never see it. But if you stay, maybe I can get it out of you."

"Well, we can come back to it. Break? Just a few minutes."

They moved to the kitchen for a reprieve from the frigid living room, each taking opposite sides of the table. They pulled off their sweatshirts and tossed them through the French doors. Dan's hit the couch. April's missed and landed on the coffee table.

Over April's shoulder, green arms of ivy sprouted from a small terra cotta pot glued to the wall. Beside it, a tarnished brass watering can tipped eternally backward. Dan said he had never seen a plant on a wall.

"They grow out of a wall at the gardens in Pinellas, Florida," she said. "It was the most amazing thing. Right out of stone."

She began flying down a few years ago to visit estate sales, she told him. The auctions had supplied most of the pieces glued to her kitchen wall, but she'd stopped going after getting too excited during a bidding war. The items had been owned by an Alzheimer's victim whose mourning family sat in the back row.

"There I was, jumping up to bid, clapping any time I won, and these people … the way they looked at me … ." She reached up and fiddled with the ivy. "I thought it would, I don't know, redeem me, somehow, if I at least added some life to the things." One more tug and the pot came loose from the wall, bounced off the edge of the chair beside April's, and was ricocheted onto Dan's foot before rolling across the floor to the base of the stove.

"Fuck me!" he said, grabbing his foot. He took off his shoe and sock.

"Are you bleeding?"

He pressed his sock to a gash in the joint of his big toe. "A little."

April squatted by the stove and scooped up the plant. "Everything will be alwight," she said before losing her balance and falling over. She laughed, a crack of unrestrained amusement followed by an almost thoughtful giggle, and held the plant, still potted, over her head. "It's okay. I saved it!" She righted herself and pressed her fingers to the tile to gather the smaller clumps of dirt and rubbed them into the pot. "I don't like enjoying you."

"I like being enjoyed."

"I shouldn't have invited you. I shouldn't have told you where I live." She went to the drawer for her tube of cement glue and squeezed it onto the side of the pot.

"I already knew. You left your wallet on the table in the restaurant."

"Sneaky bastard." She held the pot to the wall with one hand and reached for her wine glass with the other. She looked above the kitchen door at a clock set inside a resin teapot mold. Dan looked, too. It was almost midnight again. Two days down. He yawned and saw April watching him from under the bangs that fell just to her eyelashes. He remembered trying to decide whether all or none of her features stood out, whether she was a combination of striking pieces put together or an exquisite mosaic of everyday parts.

She tested the pot with a finger curled around the rim. "Set," she said. She pulled a watering can from under the sink and filled it, then walked over to the ivy and poured in a narrow stream. Dan yawned again, this time using his voice to make her hear it. When he noticed a bare patch of skin between her raised shirt and the waist of her jeans, he slid back his chair, walked over to her, and touched it.

She twisted away and held the watering can between them. "Were you yawning?"

"I'm a little tired."

"Then you should go home."

"I am home."

She rolled her eyes. "Oh, please, Dan." She set the can on the counter. "You don't belong here."

"What about the break?" he said. "We never came back from it."

She told him it was extended.

He finished the small amount left in his wine glass and asked if she would walk him out.

"No."

He put on his coat, the soft lining reminding him of the cat. He told April he had picked her up, reminding her when she said "What cat?" of the picture he'd shown her in the restaurant.

"You've had a cat sitting out there this whole time?" She ran into her bedroom and came out in an oversized sweater and a pair of sneakers. He followed the squeaking of her rubber soles down the stairs.

Bear climbed into April's lap when she sat on the couch. Dan watched from the chair, his toe throbbing, and imagined the RV parked at the base of a gray mountain, stove-hot chocolate milk steaming away window frost, bread in the toaster for warm, peanut-buttered bread, and the cat purring and kneading April's stomach.

"You'd have been a good mother," he said.

April pet Bear. "You're lucky I've had as much wine as I've had. If I hadn't had as much wine as I've had, I would think you just said something phenomenally, unbelievably stupid, and I would throw this cute little cat at your face."

"I don't know why I said it."

"Because," she said in a coochie-coo voice to the cat. "You're The Accidental Asshole." She pulled Bear's paws to her chest and touched their nose tips together. "Be glad you're not a person, cat. You can't get any dumber than that."

"Her name is Bear."

"Perfect." She rubbed Bear's ears.

Dan wanted to feel her fingers on his own ears. He imagined them, then, on the waiter's ears and in his hair, her hands gliding down his neck and spine, her legs wrapped around his waist, and the noises she would make. He watched her fingers follow the cat's whiskers to the tips. "How long will you be sleeping with that kid?"

"It's so dark in here," she whispered. "I feel like we should be whispering."

"Sorry," Dan said. "I'll turn on a light."

"No, don't. I like the dark."

He got up to turn on the generator and then sat back down with his legs stretched across the space, feet tucked under the blue blanket he'd thrown on the edge of couch.

April pulled the other end of the blanket to her chest and curled up beneath it. "I'm so sleepy." She covered her yawn with straight fingers and laid her head on the pillow and pulled the cat close. "Ten minutes."

TEN

April's slumber, from what Dan could see in the rearview mirror, was peaceful, calm. Her hands lay loose and open. He tended to clench his fists. He had once, after lying awake and restless beside her, pressed his body to hers to absorb some of that calm mingled with the heat she'd amassed in sleep, so much of it that it had made the backs of his knees sweat. Within minutes he'd fallen away, and the next morning, rested, he'd told her about it.

"You can borrow my peace anytime," she'd said. "But only borrow."

Dan turned on the brights. Just forty-five minutes in, and he was tired. He slept in micro-seconds and dreamed brief, nonsensical dreams between strains to keep his eyes open. Even the cat slept, body in a C on the carpet between the two front seats, her back pressed against the cup holder. He touched his fingertip to his tongue and wiped saliva on both eyelids to cool them, fool them into feeling awake.

He passed a sign marking the next exit at twenty miles ahead. He would stop, sleep just long enough to be able to drive again, and get April as close to Maine as possible before she woke up. When she saw where they were, she would want to keep on. She was spontaneous like that. She had been the one to propose, greeting him after work with a flower, a kiss, and "Marry me," and she had been the one to begin their friendship with a coat-tug introduction in the break room while he'd stood in front of the vending machine deciding on a snack. After ten minutes of talking she'd invited him out for a drink, and sitting that night on a downtown patio under drifting clouds with the cold iron table grate under his elbows, she had been the one to initiate a kiss.

The couch springs creaked and the curtain rings clanked on the rod. "Why are we moving?" April said.

Fifteen miles had passed since she'd told him to pull over, but there had been no break in the narrow shoulder. April sat in the passenger seat with the cat on her lap and the window open. She wrapped her torso in her arms and Dan caught her shivering. Peripherally, he saw her mouth open and heard the intake of breath that usually precedes words, but she said nothing. And then she opened her mouth again: "I almost said this is the stupidest thing you've ever done."

Two miles to the exit.

A star ahead, low and large, blinked dim to bright. Dan imagined it expanding, exploding, propelling matter that would soon rain down. For a long time, now, he had tried not to think about stars and avoided looking at clear night skies. He would invariably wonder which of the points of light belonged to a star that was no longer there. It made him uneasy. He looked at April. The wind blew the hair away from her face, and the faint glow from the dashboard lights made shadows in the shallow creases in her neck. No one else—no one who hadn't known her for as long as Dan had—would take much notice. He wanted to touch the evidence of her aging. It didn't seem real that he had known her since they were in their twenties. "If you need me to say I'm sorry," he said, "I'll s—"

"I don't need you to say you're sorry." She slammed the dashboard with her palm and the cat sprang off her lap. "I need you to *be* sorry." She released a string of coughs into the fold of her elbow. Dan watched the cat's tail in the rearview mirror, saw Bear sprint to the back and jump on the bed. "Stop this thing and let me out," April said.

"You're drunk and you're sick, and we're too far away for you to walk anywhere."

"I'm not drunk."

"You are, in fact, *quite* drunk." He would turn around at the next exit, he said. One mile.

Gas station and fast food restaurant signs began to dot the horizon. April tucked her hands under her sweater at her stomach. She said, "Are you really sorry?"

He had lied plenty before, about things like eating the last piece of bread, whether he'd noticed the woman standing at the red onion bin in the grocery store, whether he'd used profanity with a debtor refusing to agree to a payment schedule. Why this time should be any different, he didn't know.

"Clearly, you're not." She rubbed her face with her hands and slanted her head into the wind. He reached over to touch her leg and she jerked it away.

"Are you afraid of me, or something?" he said.

She stared out the window.

"I asked you a question."

"No. I'm not afraid of you."

The shoulder ahead widened to a short inlet, tire tracks marking pit stops in snow-coated gravel. Dan pulled over, his toe throbbing on the brake, and let the engine run. The sunrise behind them was a piercing sliver of gold lighting the trees. "Don't you think you would be?"

"Dan."

"We had a misunderstanding. I—*I*—misunderstood. And afterward, you misunderstood. And you continue to misunderstand. But April, you have to know—"

"I know."

"What do you know?"

Her hands rested heavy in her sweater. "I want to go home."

"No. What do you know?"

"Damn it, Dan."

"It has to be my fault. Your leaving. Is that it? Maybe you believed it in the beginning, but you've known that I would never … How long, April?"

She rolled up the window with rapid turns of the handle and climbed out of her chair, leaving him up front alone. Dan spun the wheel and sank the gas pedal and pulled onto the road. He exited, crossed the bridge, got back on the highway, and headed for home. He checked on her in the rearview mirror. Her arms rested on the back of the couch with her chin propped on an elbow. The sky had lightened just enough to dim the stars behind them and the sun washed out the windshield, bright light filling in the tiny chips years of road rocks had scored into the glass. His eyelids started to fall. He passed a rest stop sign marking two miles and pushed the Pace Arrow to eighty-eight until he made it to the turnoff. He pulled in beside a tractor trailer.

"What are you doing?"

"Sleeping."

"But I want to go home."

He climbed out of his seat. "Keys are in the ignition. Try not to get pulled over." He opened the packages holding the sheets and pillow cases and made the bed while April watched from the bedroom door. He crawled under the covers and closed his eyes.

Warm air washed over his ear.

"You ruined Denmark for me." Her voice was just louder than a whisper. Dan kept his breathing even. He felt her adjusting herself to get closer and once felt her lips on his skin. An accident, because she pulled away. "You pushed, and you pushed, and then it was over. For you."

He remembered black lines from her makeup, the little bit she wore at the time, that would often be there afterward from heat or from kissing her.

"I did nothing wrong." Her words vibrated the fine hairs in his ear, warmed his neck behind his earlobe. He heard, just barely, "Oh,

Jesus Christ, Dan," before she tossed loose blankets over his pelvis. The mattress bounced when she left.

He kept still until he heard her going through the kitchen cabinets. A box opened and a bag crinkled and cereal poured into porcelain. Dan got up and took out a bowl. He sat at the booth and invited her to join him with a jerk of his head, but she stayed where she was.

She looked at her spoon as she dipped it into her bowl and brought it to her mouth. "Any dreams?" she said. She chewed.

"Sure. I dreamed you didn't hate me. But you had to believe you did."

April took her cereal to the couch and pulled the blanket over her folded legs. "That would be lovely for you. Convenient, too. Maybe you should have a writing phase so you can share these little stories with people."

He reminded her of their conversation up front. He told her the thought she almost shared still needed finishing. She said she remembered no thought, unfinished or otherwise, and accused him of taking advantage of her drinking. The last thing she remembered, she said, was telling him to turn around and then going to sleep on the couch.

They ate the rest of their breakfast without speaking. When they finished, they rinsed their bowls and April returned to the couch and blanket. Dan picked up the cat from where she waited for scraps on the kitchen floor and set her on April's lap, then climbed into the driver's seat and started the engine.

Rain beaded on the needles of short evergreens standing guard at the entrance to April's building. Dan, looking up at her window, made his hand a visor to keep his eyes dry. She opened her curtains, pushed up the window, and shouted down, "I got in okay. You can go, now. You're soaked."

"I know."

She rubbed her hands together but didn't move away from the window. Hard, cold drops pelted his head and cut trails down his scalp.

He said, "Is there something else?"

"You didn't try very hard. I might have gone with you if you had tried a little harder."

"I drove away with you unconscious on the couch. How much harder could I have tried?"

"An unconscious person is hardly a challenge, Dan."

"You said you wanted to go home."

"I know." She shrugged. "So you took me home."

"Well, come down here, then. We'll go right now."

"No. I don't think so. But you should go, anyway. Go … see things."

It was not a lie or an exaggeration when he said, "I can't go without you." Without her, he didn't know where to go, didn't even know why he would go.

She held up a finger and disappeared from the window. When she returned, she slid up the screen. "Catch."

Something dark came down and he reached for it. It hit his hand and slipped away. He grasped at it, catching mostly air, and then his pinkie hooked a loop of thick string. A camera dangled from the other end.

"Take pictures," she called down. "It's better than the one on your phone. If you survive Farling's asteroid, you might be one of the few with photographic evidence of what the world was before." She laughed. "Bye, Dan," she said before closing the window.

ELEVEN

Mist fell from low clouds skimming the water of Narragansett Bay, Dan's favorite place since childhood. The Point's winter-hard sand pressed into the bottoms of his feet. He pressed back, then picked up some of the loose grains and rubbed them between his fingers, held them under his nostrils. Their wet-rock smell mingled with the salt and fish breeze rolling off the water.

He thought about taking a picture—April's camera was still in his pocket—but he had never been interested in photographing things. The images never seemed true. They were collapsed versions of an experience, nuanced colors reduced to a surface layer. Every bit of natural depth was flattened, horizons chopped and sectioned. Nowhere in the image would be the sound of water pushing through the space between the rocks he'd played on when his mother would bring him on hot summer weekends. It wouldn't capture the slow, graceful bending of tall grasses he would hide in when he was still brave enough to want to explore, or the decades-later dimensions of twenty-something April visiting his spot, lying on the sand without a towel, her hair falling into the dips of deep footprints and her arms spread out from the shoulders, stretched straight all the way to her fingertips.

His phone vibrated against his leg and the jarring, classic ring of an old rotary blared into the quiet. When he answered, Nina said, "Hey." He waited for more, but nothing came. He asked her why she called and she said she didn't know.

"Do you need someth—"

"I saw a dead dog on the interstate yesterday. I think it was a black lab. Later on I saw a beagle. I think people abandoned them, left them there to die."

Since Dan had known her, Nina had gone through sporadic periods of sadness that would inevitably lead to distress over abandoned or mistreated animals. Animals more than anything else, she'd explained to him one day, revealed the depths of humanity's innate rot.

"You don't know they were left there," he said. "They could have run away."

"They were between concrete construction barricades."

"They could have jumped. Over the barricades, I mean. They could have escaped the house and gotten lost."

"We can do better, but we don't. We kill everything, Dan." Her voice was low and flat, the way it sounded after they'd argued too long. "I don't know why I called you." The line clicked.

His "Nina?" came back hollow. He dialed his old number.

"Hello?" she said.

"You're not going to do anything … I mean, you're not … "

"Dan."

"Yeah?"

"Do you really think I would kill myself?"

The line clicked again.

He put the phone in his pocket. Something tapped and squeaked behind him. Bear, he saw when he turned, on the back of the couch and pawing at the glass. The ringing began again and he dug out his phone.

"I remembered why I called you," Nina said. "The mortgage. Any time today is okay. You can just leave a check in the box." She waited and then said, "Okay?"

"Okay."

A little over an hour later (three days and fifteen hours down), Dan wedged the Pace Arrow into a back corner of the hotel's parking lot not visible from the lobby. Tree branches pressed against the side and darkened the wide living room windows. If memory served, the nearest highway rest stop in either direction was no fewer than sixty miles away. Driving to one or the other could be a waste of gas and time if he didn't know where he was going, or might want to go. He would stay close to home until he had a plan.

He turned off the engine and saw Jenny coming at him in a fast walk across the empty parking spaces, her hair bouncing away from her full and smiling face. She knocked when she got to his door. He heard the handle jiggle and then her voice. "It's locked. Can I come in?"

She slid past him to the couch and sat with her legs crossed, her back hunched, and her arms folded together. She looked around. "Oh, there it is." She snapped her fingers at her ankles, but Bear didn't go to her. Dan took one of the chairs and folded his hands on his lap. Bear rubbed against his leg.

"Are you back for good?" she said.

"Do you mean am I going to live in this parking lot?"

"I guess not." She bit the inside corner of her mouth. "I mean, are you here for a while?"

"Not too long."

"Where're you going next?"

Dan wasn't sure, so that was what he told her.

"It's not fair. You could go anywhere, but you stay here by choice, and I'd kill to go anywhere, but can't."

"Why can't you? Just get in your car and go."

"And do what?"

Bear had by this time left Dan's ankles for Jenny's. She lowered her fingers to Bear's nose and let them be sniffed. "Have you thought about maybe going to California since we talked?"

"I haven't."

"Women are in their bathing suits all the time, you know. I know I would be if I lived there, anyway." She stood up and walked over to him until she was very close. She lifted her shirt. He was about to protest when she stopped just above her belly button, under which curved a tattoo in Old English stencil still irritated at the edges. It read, "live huge sleep etc." A thorned, budless stem underscored the words. She let her shirt fall down and returned to the couch. Her cheeks were red. "You're the first person I showed. I just got it yesterday."

"What does it mean?"

"What it says, I guess." She wedged her hands between her knees and looked around the RV. "Are you going to decorate at all?"

"It's just a place to sleep."

"But it's where you live," she said. "Don't you want it to be cozy? You could put a little rug here in the middle, or put up some better curtains."

"I guess I like things simple."

Jenny seemed to consider, then nodded. "I get it. I guess that's why I have the job I have, if I think about it. It's boring, sure, but it's simple. I stand behind the desk, I say hi to people coming in and bye to people going out, and when they leave their rooms, they're just gone, and they're not coming back." She rested the back of her head against the window. Her nostrils were small and dark. She said, with a quick look at him and then at the ceiling, "Sometimes I work extra hours, or go in even on my off days. It gets kind of crazy at home. When we're both there—me and my sister, I mean—my mom … she doesn't really know what to do with both of us around. She's mad at me a lot for, well, for having good legs, or being me, or something. Or maybe the house is just too small for three people."

Dan was reminded of Nina's request for his part of the mortgage. He excused himself and got his checkbook from a drawer in the kitchen. One check left. The last had been written two months before on a day he'd forgotten cash but had the emergency checkbook in his glove compartment. He'd made it out to Moxie Joe's for five dollars and twenty-eight cents. Coffee and a slice of apple coffee cake to celebrate another substantial bonus.

"Do you have a pen?" he said.

"I can get one. We have tons at the desk."

She sprinted out the door and across the parking lot without her coat. Her feet kicked to the sides a little bit when she ran.

He considered giving Nina three months' worth of mortgage payments, but he didn't know what would happen in the next three months or how much money he would need. More practical to pay as the months came, assuming they did.

Jenny bounced back across the lot, tight gray sweater clinging to her arms, the rounded slope under her belly button, her wide hips. She knocked on the door, but didn't wait for an answer before opening it. "I brought you two," she said with heavy breaths. "One blue and one black, because I wasn't sure. Do you like blue or black?"

"Either is fine.

"You can have both." She handed them to him. "A lot of guests come in with their own pens, and once they sign the room register they just leave them on the counter. Not the nice ones, though. The people with the nice pens always remember to take them. I always figure people who have nice pens must have important things to write."

Dan tested the ink on the back side of the note Jenny had left him, still on the counter because he hadn't bothered to throw it away. "People with nice pens like to spend a lot of money on pens." He filled out the check and tore Jenny's note in half for some blank paper. He wrote, "Please sell the house. Keep whatever you get for it."

"I don't care too much for money," Jenny sang, standing beside him and reading over his shoulder. She waited with a smile and a look that made Dan feel like her boyfriend.

He didn't offer the next line. "I have to drop this off," he said. "Shouldn't you get back to work to help … well, to help?"

"His name's Andy. And it only takes one. They just like us both to be 'a presence' at the desk. Me more than him, it seems like."

"Girls at counters attract customers," Dan said.

"Not me. I repel them." She stretched, fingers wiggling at the ceiling. "I'm just not a people person." Her sweater crept up and Dan wondered about her tattoo, what her life up to this point would mean to her in a look back at it in the final seconds. He imagined her with a boy at the base of a tree in a cherry blossom orchard, saw her walking through the pink flower bursts with flyaway hairs catching sunlight. Saw the bright fire of burning trees and Jenny curled and petrified like a Pompeiian ash figure.

He said, "Do you think you've lived huge?"

She sat on the couch and pulled her coat onto her lap. "No. Why do you think I want to get out of here?"

Bear climbed onto the couch and Jenny lifted her. She pressed her face into her fur.

He said, "What does living huge mean? To you."

She leaned back and plopped Bear on her coat. "To me? I don't know. It's like—Well, my cousin goes rock-climbing probably a couple of times a month. One time, something happened with his rope, or something, and he fell two hundred feet. He bounced a few times on the way down and broke both legs and his collarbone and punctured one of his lungs. But he still does it. I guess I just think you must be missing a lot of the little things in life if the only way you can get a thrill out of it is to try not to kill yourself."

He found he was looking at those eyes, big and unwavering. He didn't want to be the one to break contact. There were too many messages his looking away could imply, and he didn't want her to think he was sending any one of them. He wore an expression that he hoped convincingly communicated nothing more than his conversational interest. When she moved her head, just so and just a little, he saw the woman she might or might not have known was there. She blinked and looked down at the cat.

He could invite her to bed. She would say yes.

He saw himself inching the sweater up, revealing her tattoo, her belly button, the vulnerable triangle between her ribs, and coaxing it over her head, static snapping at her hair.

If April could sleep with a child, so could he. And Jenny was hardly a child. Maturity counted, and in that regard he had no doubt she had years on Jeremy.

"All I know is that I need to start now," she said. "I'll be old, twenty-*seven*, in ten years, do you know that? No. Twenty-eight. I'm eighteen in two weeks." She uncrossed her legs and left the smallest space between her thighs. Her chest rose and fell with a deep breath. His phone rang in his pocket and he put his hand in there and pressed buttons until it stopped. "By then, I'll be away from Connecticut forever.—I'm serious. Forever. She'll be glad. I don't know where I'll be, but I know I'll have an apartment somewhere in California with my own furniture and TV, and maybe a bakery around the corner I can go to every morning for a Danish or a loaf of French bread, or something." She pressed the balls of her palms to her forehead and yawned. Bear jumped down, and Jenny put on her coat. "I have to go back to work. Andy'll kill me." She stood up and walked toward the door, stopping just short of touching his legs with hers. She bent over and her hair grazed his cheek when she lowered her mouth to his ear. She said, "Please, please don't leave without at least coming in to say bye," and walked down the stairs and through the door.

He watched her cross the lot while checking his messages. Nina's voice came through quiet and flat. "There's a spider on the wall. I can't kill it. They must have respiratory systems. They breathe, so they must have little lungs." She paused for a long time, and he pressed the phone to his ear to hear what she might have been doing, but the only noise was shifting or movement. When she spoke again, her voice sounded hollow, the airflow distorted. He imagined her standing near the wall, her neck arched, staring up at the spider. "I would trap it in a glass and throw it outside, but what if it freezes? But I really do hate it up there on the wall. I'm sorry to call you with this, but you're the only one who understands me and won't think I'm crazy."

The message ended. Dan folded the note to Nina and put it in his back pocket with her check. Bear, now on the passenger seat with her cheetah toy under a paw, rolled onto her back to warm her belly in the sun. Dan ran to the hotel lobby and asked Jenny if he could borrow her car.

TWELVE

Nina's car was in the driveway, but she didn't answer the door when Dan knocked or rang the bell. Bear squirmed against his chest. A claw caught his skin and paws pressed at his stomach. Her head, ears back, nudged and jabbed at the hand Dan used to keep her tucked inside his coat.

"Nina." He kicked the dented brass kick plate and waited, then backed down the stairs and looked up at the windows. No shadows moving across them, no lights, but it was daytime and unless the sun was shining directly through the glass, he'd see nothing but the glints on the small, crystal star stuck with a suction cup to the upstairs hallway window. It was there when they'd moved in. Nina had kept it, she'd said, because it was happy.

A dull *thud* came from the back yard, and then another. Dan walked around to the side of the house and stopped when he reached the fence, now secured with a rusted padlock, unused for years, that he thought he remembered as having been in their toolbox in the basement. More thudding—pounding, cracking—and he couldn't see what it was. He called her name again, but the noise covered his voice.

He carried Bear to the other side of the house, used his foot to push open the basement window, and nudged her inside. The drop was five feet, maybe six. Nothing that could hurt, but to be sure she was okay he watched her sniff the carpet for a few seconds after she landed. When he saw her jump onto the shelves he closed the window and walked over to the Belowskis' house, hoping someone might let him in so he could see his back yard from one of their windows. No one answered the bell. Kristie must have been out on a walk with the kids. It was almost warm enough for Dan to take off his coat, and he was starting to think so much warmth in January was probably a sign of the end, that something related to global warming might be a more likely scenario than Farling's asteroid. Were that the case, they would all have a little more time to do and say the things needing doing and saying.

He walked back over to his fence and listened to the pounding. He called Nina's name again, but she didn't answer. He climbed the fence and, pressed flat to the side of the house, inched his way to the corner. Nina, in sweatpants, a t-shirt, and sneakers, crouched in a wide patch of flattened, faded grass where the snow had either melted or been shoveled away, or a combination of both. She pushed something into the ground with hard shoves that made her body bounce.

"Nina?"

She stopped.

Dan took a step forward. She looked at him sideways over her shoulder. She rested her fingers on the handle of a mallet lying at her feet. Hair wet with sweat clung to her face. It was a wood plank, he saw now, that she'd flattened into the yard. Two more of similar width and two or three others of varying sizes were stacked on the patio's gray brick.

"What are you building back here?" he said. "Aren't you cold? Let me go inside, get you a sweatshirt."

She peeled the hair from her cheeks and neck. She stood with the mallet and raised it over her shoulder, brought it down on one end of the piece of wood, and then slammed it down on the other. The sharp cracks made Dan wince. She crouched to eye the board.

"There's a level in the tool box in the basement," Dan said.

Nina crawled to the other side of the board. Dan walked up to it and tapped it with his foot. "What is it, anyw—"

"*Don't touch it!*"

He staggered backward, stepping in a bowl of food left out for the neighborhood cat. He scraped the heel of his shoe on the patio while Nina scampered around on her hands and knees, ripping bunches of grass from the yard. Her hands full of soggy stalks still clinging to wet soil, she crawled to the board and scrubbed at the spot his foot had touched until it stained green and the grass was crumbled pulp in her hand. She ran a finger along the grain, then wiped her eyes and sat cross-legged in front of it. "Ruined."

"I'm—"

"*Go away!*"

"I can't," he said. "Nina, you—You're acting a little strange."

She pulled herself up and stumbled onto the patio.

"Here," Dan said. He took the check and the note from his back pocket and held them out to her, but she wouldn't accept them. He set them on the short wood stack. "Don't throw away the note without reading it," he said. "Okay?" He'd added a post script about Bear: *I know you never wanted to replace Paulie, but Bear needs a home, and I think you need her. She likes canned food, sunbeams, and having her front paws massaged.*

She picked up the check and the note put them in her pocket.

"Look at the note. If not while I'm here, then right after I leave. Okay? Nina, okay?"

She went up the stairs and reached for the doorknob.

"Don't give it too long," he said.

She opened the door.

"There's a cat in the basement," he said, spitting out the words as fast as he could while the door was still open. "I'm leaving her litter box on the front stoop. I forgot to bring food."

She closed the door.

Dan looked at the stacked wood—two boards of one length, two shorter boards, and a few sturdy, small pieces—but couldn't figure them out. He walked over to the window and cupped his hands to the glass. Nina stood at the open doorway to the basement, looking down. Her cheeks dented in a whistle. The breakfast bar was bare, even the lamp was gone, and a small saucepan sat on the stove's rear burner.

He was hungry.

He climbed back over the fence, got the litter box out of the trunk, and dropped it at the front door before ringing the doorbell and rapping a series of knocks. "Litter box!"

Jenny introduced Dan to Andy, a tall blond boy with a long narrow face. He stood in the doorway behind the counter. Dan nodded a hello and told Jenny he needed to make one more quick trip, if he could use the car a bit longer, and Jenny said he could, but that she was on her way out for food, so she would drive. Andy, watching Dan, told Jenny not to be too long.

Dan loaded the trunk with the case of canned food and the extra litter he'd bought. They stopped at a drive-through on the way and ordered hamburgers and French fries, with an extra order for Andy. They ate in the parking lot, Jenny with one knee on the steering wheel and the window open. She threw out her pickle slices.

"The birds'll eat it," she said. "It's not litter."

He shrugged. He crumpled his hamburger wrapper and opened his window and tossed it out. After a reflexive desire to jump out of the car and pick it up, he did the same with the extra napkins and the empty bag. He told her about Farling, whose name she said she'd heard, and about the NPR program she said she hadn't heard. Dan gave her as much of the show as he could remember, sounding as convincing to himself as the host had been when explaining the likelihood of an asteroid, whether Farling's or some unnamed meteorite, someday striking the planet.

If the world was ending, what did litter matter?

Jenny balled up her own wrapper and tossed it out the window. She smiled.

Jenny's trash sat on dirty snow at the curb. His crumpled waste had landed in the neighboring parking spot.

They were deep into day three. He reminded himself the end could come at any time, and that "any time" could be a time just like this, squawking seagulls buzzing the parking lot for French fries, the only smells hamburger grease and spoil from the nearby landfill, and possibly a hint of Jenny's apple-scented hair. His litter on the ground three feet from a trash can.

He flung open the door and scooped up their trash around the car. He stuffed it past the outdoor receptacle's swinging flap and got back inside the car and closed his door and window.

"Why did you do that?"

He felt her hand on his leg, squeezing, heard her say, "You okay?" He put his hand over hers, soft and plump, and curled his fingers around her fingers and felt her skin against his skin. "Dan?" she said. He opened his eyes. She leaned over the emergency brake, one side of her white shirt collar tucked inside the neck of her sweater and the other folded out, a thin gold chain with delicate loops kinked over her collar bone. He touched her hair, slid his fingers through it at the roots, and waited until her eyes were closed before kissing her. She opened her mouth first, and he followed, slid his other hand upward along her other arm, the fabric and all of it so soft, her lips, her breath, the smell of the makeup she wore. He touched her side at her waist and her body jerked, the subtlest twitch. He pulled away.

She cleared her throat. "Sorry."

"For what?"

"I don't know."

Dan adjusted his pants and sat back in his seat.

"I said I'm sorry," she said.

"But what for, Jenny?"

"Quit asking me that."

"I should apologize," he said.

"It's okay."

"What's okay? Do you know what I'm apologizing for?"

"Oh, my god." She laughed. "Everything's okay, all right? We kissed. It's not a big deal, or ... anything." She looked at her hands in her lap. Her eyelids, their lashes heavy with black makeup, moved with the darting of her eyes, and her lips tightened and softened.

"Let's get me to the RV so you can go home," he said.

"Why?"

He told her she was too young, that they—he—had no business doing any of that.

"I'm not that young." She started the car.

"Seventeen is young."

"Well, maybe seventeen—and anyway, I'm practically eighteen—isn't what it used to be. You know, in the old days."

The sun was down when Jenny knocked on the Pace Arrow's door at the end of her shift. He let her in. He didn't tell her to lock the door behind her, but she did, and he didn't object when she tugged his sleeve to stop him from turning on the light. She put her fingers on the highest of his closed shirt buttons. Parking lot light fell through the open curtains and cast Dan's shadow onto her torso and arms, but he could see her face as she tried to push the button through the hole. It was one of his more difficult shirts. He heard her swallow, and as he watched her, patiently waiting for her to work it open, he never saw her eyes. He stilled her hands with his and said, "Look at me."

She slid out of his loose grip and tried again, eyes down, this time succeeding. "Got it." She moved onto the next one. "If I look at you I can't see what I'm doing and I'll never get your shirt off." She unbuttoned the rest of his buttons—"See? Told you."—and untucked his shirt from his pants. She pushed it off his shoulders. He let his arms hang straight and felt the material slide past his elbows, wrists, and hands before it landed at his feet.

She pressed her sweatered chest to his skin and wrapped her arms around him. She squeezed him and breathed onto his collar bone and he stood there, made himself simply stand there, until she let go. Finally, she tipped back her head and gave him her earnest, achingly transparent, dark brown eyes. "Could you please kiss me, or something?"

He said, "Are you sure this is what you want?"

"Sure I am." She put her lips to his chest, moving sideways toward his nipple. She stopped before reaching it, and he saw her looking at it. She instead slid her hands to the button of his jeans.

"It's okay," he said. "Some men like that. I like it."

"Like what?"

"What you were about to do."

"I don't know what you mean."

He smiled. "You were going to either suck, lick, or bite my nipple."

She fiddled around near his zipper. "I—I just stopped because some guys think it's weird. But now I know you like it, so … ."

He helped her with his button. She said thank you, lowered his zipper, and got on her knees to tug his pants and underwear to his ankles. She had crouched so close to the ground that her eyes were level with his knees, and he didn't catch her stealing a glance any higher. He stepped out of his clothes, and she picked them up and folded them.

"Have you done this before?" he said.

She set two perfect squares of cotton on the arm of the couch. "Of course."

"With boys—men—people your age."

"Well, no one as old as you."

"And you're sure you want to now? With me?"

The softening was visible. Her shoulders dropped from military attention to a casual slope. "You really are a nice guy."

"I don't know about that," he said. "But I am a guy who's getting a little cold, so if you don't want to do this …"

She smiled, then, an easy smile that was much older than seventeen-almost-eighteen. "If you keep asking me if I want to do this, I'll think it's because you don't." She crossed her forearms at her waist and pulled her sweater up and over her head. "Besides. If

Tucker Farling is right, it's the end of the world, right?" She dropped it to the floor and took off the rest of her clothes.

Her body looked different uncovered, her proportions more balanced. Dan took her in, not moving toward her but waiting for her to come to him.

She folded her arms under her chest, then dropped them and held them behind her back. "We're going to need to go back there, now," she said. "I'm … I'm cold."

He told her to go first, and when they got there, he continued to let her go first.

She held onto him under the comforter, her forearm resting too close to his bladder. He lifted her hand from between his legs and brought it to his ribs. She made a fist and said, "I'm sorry. That was … I was too … I shouldn't have just thought I could do that."

"It's fine, Jenny. Relax."

She pressed the side of her face against his chest and he stroked her hair, then eased onto his side, his back to her.

She touched him, then pulled away. She said, her voice loud for so much darkness, "Did I do something?"

"Only the right things."

She snuggled closer. "We should spend all day in bed tomorrow."

He pushed off the covers and went to the bathroom, and then reminded her as he got dressed that he still had an errand to run. He said she could stay behind in the RV, if she wanted.

"And do what?" she said. "You don't even have a TV."

THIRTEEN

Dan drove, the wipers on high, and parked behind Nina's car. He and Jenny stepped out into cold puddles. Dan carried the fourteen-pound bucket of cat litter, and Jenny carried the food because she said she wanted to help. The front porch, an oversized stoop with a railing around it, was uncovered and wet and neither of them had an umbrella or coat hoods. He rang the bell and waited only a few seconds before kicking the brass plate. He apologized to Jenny. She blinked at the water dripping into her eyes and Dan used a finger to push back her bangs.

Jenny had just finished saying "Who's house is this, anyway?" when a pound on the door—Dan thought it sounded like a kick—made them both jump. Jenny looked at Dan and he told her not to say anything. When Nina opened the door, Jenny stepped back and Dan held out the litter bucket. "For the cat."

Nina looked up at the sky and then at each of them. "Your name?" she said.

"Jenny. Sheer, ma'am." She adjusted the bag in her arms.

Nina tucked her hands in her sweatshirt pockets.

Raindrops tapped their coats.

Jenny sniffed and her mouth puckered, pulled to the side. She was biting the inside of her cheek. Dan wanted to tell her not to.

Nina reached into the rain and took the litter and set it inside on the floor. When she straightened and turned back to them, her hair, long and messy and full, had fallen forward over her shoulders and around her face. Dan thought he should want to kiss her, looking like that. He thought maybe he did want to. He blew on his hands.

Jenny sniffed.

"How old are you?" Nina said.

"I'm … um—"

"Take the food," Dan said, and Jenny tucked the flat case to her chest. He nudged her forward. "I meant Nina. Nina, please take the food."

The wind shifted and rain fell at a slant against Dan's bare neck. Nina took a step inside, away from door, and looked again at Jenny, then Dan. "I don't even know who you are."

He grabbed the case of food. As he set it inside the door, he heard Jenny running down the stairs behind him.

"She's leaving," Nina said.

He looked past her inside the house. To the right was the dining room, whose walls used to be beige. Now they were the color of milk chocolate. Except for a drop-cloth in the corner and an open paint can on the built-in shelves Dan had painted, the floor and the walls were bare. Nina said, "She's in the car," and stuck out her foot when Bear walked toward the open door. She pushed her back, away, with gentle force, losing her balance and falling sideways and down, her arms flinging out for support. Dan caught her and steadied her.

She pushed him away. "Why would you bring her here?" she said before rushing down the hallway to the bathroom and slamming the door. He checked for Jenny and saw her wave from inside the car. He held up a finger, *Wait*, and went inside, closing the door to keep in the cat. He listened outside the bathroom and heard heaving and spitting. "Are you okay?" He knocked.

Nina screamed, the syllables stretched on a wail, "*Get ouuuuuut!*"

Jenny's hand looked young on the gearshift. At red lights, she rested it on her thigh. Night colors traveled over the dashboard, the steering wheel, Jenny's coat and face. Without much trouble, she'd accepted his apology for not preparing her for Nina, for not giving her "at least a fucking heads-up" that she would be face to face with his wife.

"So," she said, "I've been thinking about that Farling guy since you brought him up. I mean, what if the world is ending? I suddenly realized I don't even know what I would do. Sure, California would be great, but what if I only had a single day? I can't even think of anything I want to say to anyone. Except maybe my mom, but I don't really think I'd feel good about it if I did, and I think I'd want to feel good in that last minute."

Jenny was right. He pulled the phone out of his pocket. "You should do whatever you want." He had every confidence April remembered what she'd said in the front seat. Even if she didn't, it was there. It was in her. Which meant she didn't, couldn't, hate him. And hadn't her teasing from the window been a challenge? He tapped APRIL followed by the CALL button.

"What if what I want is to be with you?"

"That's not what you want."

"It might be what I want."

Three rings. "I might have been misleading about … things. I'm sorry if I gave you the wrong idea."

She changed gears, missing the clutch. The grinding noise made Dan jump. "That's not what I meant, anyway," Jenny said. "I just meant as fr—"

Dan held up his hand when April answered the phone with "No," and Jenny shifted hard into fourth.

"Are you at your residence?" he said to April.

"I'm not alone."

"Ah?"

"Jeremy.—No, not you, Jeremy. I was telling Dan you're … never mind."

He wondered what the child waiter was doing at that moment. Jerking away the bangs that seemed to be eternally in his eyes. Waiting to get her attention.

"I'd like to meet with you again," he said. "To—To settle the, uh, the agreement."

Jenny pulled into the hotel lot and parked beside the Pace Arrow.

"Dan, what are you talking about?" April said. "Wait, are you still in town? And why am I surprised?"

"Ah, yes."

April laughed.

Jenny looked at him, and then she smiled. "What's so funny?" she whispered. She touched his mouth and Dan grabbed her hand, set it on her lap, and stopped smiling. He held onto her fingers.

"Are we just going to sit here until someone says something?" April said.

"Issue resolution," he said. "And in person would be best. It would be inconvenient to have to call repeatedly."

"Mm. Okay." She sounded like she was smiling. Then she murmured something to the boy, words he couldn't make out delivered with the singsong-sweet inflection she used when she was feeling tender. Or horny. To Dan she said "Five o'clock tomorrow" before hanging up.

He returned the phone to his pocket. Jeremy wasn't a permanent obstacle, if he could be called an obstacle at all. Dan had made progress. She might have gone with him, if. If. If he had done it just right, if he had been just a little more forceful.

Be forceful. Don't be forceful.

"All I meant was that I'd like to travel with you," Jenny said. "I don't want anything from you or expect you to be my … my boyfriend … or anything. I mean, what we did was just—It was just … I know what it was, I mean. I'm not naïve. —Hey, ow!" She pulled her hand out of his. He hadn't been aware that he was still holding it.

He said, "I don't think—"

"What do you have to worry about, anyway? If the world is ending, so what? We'll just live our last days having fun, right? Oh! We should go to Las Vegas! If we win a ton of money, we can … I don't know. I think I'd like to help people with it, give it all away. I've always wanted to walk around with a stack of one-hundred dollar bills and just pass them out to people. No assholes, though." She drummed her fingers on the steering wheel. "And if I lose it all, it doesn't matter, because I won't need it, anyway. I have two thousand dollars saved, and you must have a lot of money saved up, too. We can get one of those penthouse rooms with the remote-control blinds. You buy the alcohol, and we'll get wasted and then go to the casinos—the Venice or New York ones—and play some slots, and then … and then go back to the room and eat room service in a giant martini glass." She grabbed and shook his arm. "We can leave tomorrow. It's a slow day, anyway."

"I just made plans for tomorrow."

"We'll leave after."

"The appointment isn't until five."

"Oh." Jenny looked down at her hands. She picked at blue polish on her left thumb nail. "Well," she said, "we can still go after. It's just night. It's just dark."

"It'll take days to get there," Dan said. "Let me think about it." If his meeting with April failed, what else did he have to do? He had the RV, and now he had a place to go and someone to go with.

"What's to think about? Come on." She leaned over her knee and into his side of the car. "Let's just do it. Who knows how much time we have?"

"I'll think about it," he said again, and he let her kiss him, a quick kiss with hard, pursed lips.

FOURTEEN

The engine ran for heat and to melt the freezing rain. He watched April's windows for moving shadows behind the blinds in case she'd been hiding when he knocked. Aside from the light inside there was no sign she was there, and because she always left on a light, home or not, it wasn't much of a sign. He watched the building's front door, but no one had come or gone since he'd pulled up in Jenny's car at ten to five. Radio voices warned against road travel.

He left her a voicemail: "I'm here. Something tells me you know that."

He opened the window an inch for fresh air, immediately closing it when the rain came in. He flipped the vents, wiped dust off the dashboard with a flat palm, and picked up a balled piece of paper from the passenger side floor, its edges coated with dirt grit. Jenny's work schedule, her days marked in calendar boxes.

He opened the glove compartment. A tight stack of repair receipts and other papers left enough space on the sides for a pen and a tire pressure gauge. Dan pulled out the pen and went through her papers until he found something he didn't think she would miss.

Icy rain pelted his head when he opened the door. He ran through shallow puddles to the building and up the stairs to her door. He knocked, said "April," and waited. He knocked again. The stairwell was hot and smelled like dinner. He pulled his coat collar away from his neck and put his ear to her door, then lowered himself to the gap on the floor and looked inside. Light fell on a blue throw rug in her hallway. He folded the paper in half, pushed it under the door, and went back to the car. He asked Jenny's keychain, "Will April let me in?" and shook it. IT IS DECIDEDLY SO, the floating triangle predicted.

Jenny called to ask Dan when he would be back with her car and if he'd given any more thought to Las Vegas.

"I haven't had much time for that today," he said.

"Everyone has time to think. Come on. Let's go. Seriously."

He stared up at April's window, but still, no shadows, no movement in the curtains. He'd waited forty-five minutes. He started the car and pulled away from the curb. "You're not legal, yet."

She said in a near-whisper, "I have a fake ID, and Andy says I look twenty-three."

A male voice in the background said, "Who are you talking to?"

"A guest." And then silence. Her breathing.

"Hello?" Dan said.

She whispered, "Just a minute."

He waited.

She whispered, "Do you really, honestly think that Farling guy is right? Do you think the world is going to end?"

It was an inevitability. He said, "Yes."

After a minute she said, "Yeah. Me, too. I believe it, too." She whispered, "If you come now, I can fake sick, go home, and you can pick me up on the way out."

"You have money and you have a car," he said. "Why don't you go ahead?"

"I don't have a car. You have it."

He didn't respond.

"I don't want to go alone," she said.

"I have things to do here." But he supposed he probably didn't. Not right now. She would find the note when she came home, and she would contact him when she was ready. If she didn't, he would try again, but he would have to give it time. April had never responded well to aggressive persistence she didn't want.

"I'm scared, okay?" she said.

"What's that?"

"Scared. I'm scared."

"Of what?"

"Of—I don't know. Breaking down. Getting a flat tire. I've never driven farther than New Haven by myself. What if something happens and I don't know what to do?"

"Don't you have insurance? A lot of those companies offer roadside service."

"It's not like they get there right away. I could be on that roadside waiting for service for two hours."

A gust blew against the car and the wipers at high speed did little to keep the windshield clear of rain. Streetlights swayed on overhead wires.

April would take her time. It could be weeks. Until then, he had nothing to do but sit at a rest stop. Las Vegas would move things along. April would be surprised, and Nina, too, but that was more a byproduct than a goal. He never went anywhere, and he found himself looking forward to—even getting excited about—going to a place he'd only seen on a screen.

"All right," he said. "We'll go."

"Go? Really?"

"Invite your boyfriend."

"I don't wan—I—what boyfriend?"

"The one you work with. Andy, right? If you can get him to come along, you can go."

"Why?"

"Because I can't get pulled over with a teenage girl."

"I'll say I'm your niece. Plus, I have fake ID, remember?"

He said either Andy came along or he would go alone, which he wouldn't.

She said, "Fine." Louder, she said, "Andy. *Ann-dyyyy*. Want to go to Las Vegas?"

Dan heard Andy say, "What?"

Jenny said, "Whatever. He'll go."

Dan parked as close to the doors as he could get and ran with his coat pulled over his head to the hotel entrance. He opened the door to the lobby and stepped through a wall of warm, dry air. Jenny and Andy sat at a table in front of a TV mounted high on the wall. She saw him and stood up and looked at Andy.

"Your keys." Dan tossed them to her.

Andy slid back his chair and got to his feet beside Jenny, the center of his chest level with her chin. He was shorter than Dan by a healthy inch.

"Can you be ready tomorrow morning?"

"Ready for what?" Andy said.

"I already said," Jenny told him. "We're going to Las Vegas."

"I didn't know you were serious."

"Well, I was."

Andy said, "But, why? I don't get it."

"Because of the end of the world," she said.

"The—?" Andy looked from Jenny to Dan and laid his arm across Jenny's shoulders. "Really?"

"It could happen," she said. "Tucker Farling."

He kissed the top of her head. "I guess you never know." He picked up the remote control turned off the TV. Dan noticed that his black slacks were pressed.

Jenny pulled the key from the cash register drawer and taped a note to the counter beside the bell. *Back in one hour. If checking out, please leave key cards on counter.*

"We're not leaving until tomorrow," Dan said.

"Maybe we can get to know each other before we spend a few days driving across the country together. Or something like that," Andy said.

FIFTEEN

Andy called the manager. He and Jenny were both sick, he said. He would leave the register key locked in the office.

Margaret would be there in ten minutes, he told Jenny.

The three walked as steadily as they could across the glazed parking lot. Dan let them into the RV and gathered their wet coats and laid them on the shower floor, then positioned himself in the kitchen so they could choose the spots that made them comfortable. Jenny sat on the couch, and Andy sat beside her with his arms limp at his sides, his knuckles touching her thigh. Dan took a chair.

Rain fell hard and loud on the roof.

Jenny bent over to pull up her socks and Andy touched the ends of her hair, pressed flat and damp to her back. She moved her shoulders in shrugging circles until he took his fingers away. "Tickles," she said.

"I'll start," Andy said. "Why did you invite us to go on some road trip with you? You don't know me, and I don't think you really know her. What are you, fifty?"

Before Dan could answer, Jenny said, "He invited us just because. Why not? He came in that one time and he was talking about driving around the country, and when he said he was going to Las Vegas I just thought—I don't know, I thought it sounded like fun, so I asked him if we could go, too."

"You met a strange man and thought it would be fun to go with him on a drive across the country?"

"Well, I'm not stupid, Andy. We talked more than once before I made any serious decisions. You're not always around to see everything. If you don't want to go, just say so." She looked at Dan. "I mean, I want you to go. That's not what I'm saying. I'm just … . Don't you think it sounds like fun?"

"I never said it didn't sound like fun. I just wanted to know. Wouldn't you want to know a little more if some strange woman invited us to go somewhere with her?"

The rain fell harder and they had to raise their voices to be heard. Dan got up and went into the kitchen and opened the window over the sink. He stuck his fingers out and touched the side of the RV. Still ice. "You two might want to stay in one of the hotel rooms tonight instead of driving home."

"Why don't we just hang out?" Andy said. "You have anything to drink in here?"

"Won't your mom worry if you don't go home?" Jenny said.

"I don't have a curfew, Jen."

"I meant she might worry because of the weather."

"She won't."

Jenny leaned back and crossed her arms. Dan said he had to go to the bathroom and asked Jenny to grab a few glasses.

"Why me?"

"Your friend doesn't know where anything is."

Jenny said, "Well, *I* don't know where anything is," and leaned into Andy.

Andy scratched under his nose and looked down at the top of Jenny's head.

"Right," Dan said. "Well, give me a second and I'll get the drinks."

On his way to the bathroom he heard Jenny say to Andy, "It's because I'm a girl. How is it my job to fetch just because I have a vagina? It's like you guys think we use them to carry things."

Andy and Jenny were still sitting on the couch when Dan came out of the bathroom, but farther apart. He poured two very short tequilas and filled his own glass halfway. Andy took the drink Dan handed him and rested it on his lap. Jenny drank hers.

"I *said* I've been here, before. It was just for a second, and it's not like I went through the cabinets. Come on, Andy," she said. "Just drink. Oh! And then we'll all say what we'd do if thought the world was ending."

"I thought we were doing it, and I thought you said it was."

"It is."

"You said 'if.'"

"You know what I mean. I hate it when you pay attention to my words instead of listening to what I'm saying." She set her empty glass on the floor and Andy did the same with his, still full. Jenny reached for it.

He grabbed her wrist. "It's not yours."

"You're not drinking it."

"It's still mine."

Jenny sat back.

Andy said, "If I thought the world was ending—*really* ending—I would take you out of here and lock you in a hotel room with me until we died," he said. "I would take off your clothes and look at you.—Not like that. I wouldn't touch you, and it's not—Not everything is about sex, okay, Jenny? I just want to look at you and I want you to see me looking at you." He picked up the glass, didn't drink, and set it back down.

Jenny's cheeks were pink. "Can I just have it? Please?"

Andy said, "Dan—Right? Dan?—What would you do?"

"He's doing it," Jenny said. "He's taking us to Las Vegas."

"I wasn't talking to you."

Dan said Jenny was right, that he supposed he was doing it, even if he hadn't envisioned it quite this way. "I like the idea of going with people who seem to want to have fun. I haven't had a lot of fun."

"I guess I would want to do that too, then," Andy said, but Dan didn't think he was talking to him. "If you wanted me there." He drank his shot.

"Of course I do, mister drama," Jenny said. "I wouldn't have asked you otherwise."

The rain still sounded like wood screws dropping down.

"I think we should leave, now," Andy said. Ignoring Jenny's protest that it was only seven o'clock (four days and nineteen hours down, Dan thought), he brought his glass to the kitchen and set it on the counter. "Thanks for the drink." He stopped in the bathroom for their coats and brought Jenny's to her. He put his on and said, "Coming?"

She slowly slid her arms into the sleeves and pulled the zipper to her neck. "We'll see you in the morning, Dan?"

He said they would, as long as the weather cleared.

Andy went down the stairs and opened the door and stepped into the downpour. "Come on, Jen," he said from outside.

Jenny stayed where she was. She fingered her zipper tab. "I don't want to."

"What?" Andy said. "What are you talking about?"

"I don't want to go home."

"You can come to my house, then. Come on. It's cold out here."

"You know I can't. Your mom."

"I'll sneak you in. Damn it, Jen."

She unzipped her coat.

Dan moved deeper into the kitchen so he couldn't see Andy standing outside in the rain.

"What the hell—What's going on with you?" Andy's head appeared in the door, his blond hair dark and wet. "What's going on?" He looked at Dan, at Jenny.

She raised her arms at her sides, then let them fall.

"What's that, again?" Andy said.

"I don't want to go. That's all."

Andy used a hand to shag the water from his hair. He started to say something, then shook his head, backed himself outside, and slammed the door.

Jenny took off her coat and laid it on the couch. She said, biting her cheek, "Sorry."

Dan sat down across from her. "What for?"

"I don't know. The awkwardness, I guess."

He said, "Why do you do that to him?"

She shrugged a shoulder and tilted her head, raised her eyebrows. "What do you mean?"

Dan went to the kitchen and put away the bottle of tequila beside the white rice. "You forgot to bat your eyelashes."

"Are you mad, or something?"

He called April, a last effort before morning. She didn't answer. He listened to the first part of the "leave a message" message and hung up. He asked Jenny if he could use her car.

"You want to drive in this? My car?" She twisted on the couch and pointed a finger at the iced trees tapping against the glass. "Are you crazy?"

"Yes or no."

"Well, okay. But I want to go, too. And I'm driving, because I know my car. And anyway, it's my car, so I get to say who drives it."

The parking lot had them sliding sideways. Jenny played the clutch and the gas for traction and said she wasn't sure it was a good idea for them to drive, but the roads outside were salted and clear. "I guess we could have left tonight," she said.

At April's, Dan asked Jenny to wait in the car and stepped onto crunchy, frozen grass dividing the curb from the sidewalk. The sidewalk itself was salted, and the building's front door was not only not locked, but open a few inches. He would have to tell April that with her money she could at least live in a secure building.

He took the stairs to her floor two at a time, favoring his hurt toe. With just three stairs to go to her door, his wounded foot caught on a buckled edge of a rubber strip and sent him into a twisting dive. His right wrist took the bulk of his weight when he landed with a thud on her welcome mat.

A woman's voice from behind one of the four closed doors circling the landing area said, "I heard a—Oh, you're on the floor. Are you okay out there?"

"Fine."

"You want me to call an ambulance?"

"No. Thank you." He used his unharmed hand to feel the wrist at the joints and in the soft flesh between the bones. Painful all the way around. He moved to knock on April's door from where he sat on the floor, thought better of it, and stood up first. When she didn't answer, Dan heard, "She's home," from the woman who had asked if he needed an ambulance. Her floorboards creaked, the sound quieting as she moved deeper into her apartment. He pressed his ear against April's door and heard faint music. Etta James. "April." He knocked again, returned his ear to the door and heard voices, hers and another. Male. He punched the door with his good hand and waited, then kicked it, hard, and dropped to his knees to peer underneath. The note was gone. He saw the bottom hem of a white bathrobe, a set of narrow ankles, round-toed slippers pointed at him. The hem got closer to the floor until it touched, and his view of her feet was suddenly blocked by her eye staring back at him.

"Get your face out of there," she said.

"Why do you do this to me?"

She stood up, but her feet didn't move. Another set joined hers, white sneakers with jean cuffs falling over the laces.

"What're you doing to him?" the sneakers said.

Her slippers went left into the kitchen. He heard her stirring something in one of her pots. The sneakers stayed put, but the jeans cuffs raised with the squatting of the body. A sideways face looked at him through the crack under the door. The eyes were brown and the hair was long in the front. The waiter, the boy, Jeremy, stood up and his feet went into the kitchen.

"What's he want?" he said.

"Me."

Dan lay on his back. A steady draft of warm air from her kitchen blew against the side of his face. He rested his damaged wrist on the plump softness off his goose-down coat and traced his fingers over the skin. When his phone rang, he let it. At the fourth ring he heard footsteps nearing the door and April saying "Leave him, Jeremy." The steps stopped, went back into the kitchen. Dan's voicemail signal chimed. He smelled someone's dinner again. Tomato. The ceiling creaked with someone walking, or with age, and wind beat the high stairwell window and pushed and pulled at the loose-latched entry door. He turned his head and smelled sage or soap or both coming from April's apartment, the scent of her pillow or her hands or her hair after a shower. Plates tapped and the refrigerator opened and closed. Glasses were set on a surface and something poured. The downstairs door squeaked high and long, then slammed shut. Dan listened to his ex-wife and her young sex partner comment on how good everything tasted. He had to strain to hear them over the sound of feet drag-stomping up the stairs. He thought instantly of teenage girls in their summer flip-flops, their heads hanging, their backs curved from slumped shoulders, their feet so low to the ground that sandals just barely clinging to their toes would *shhhhhk*, *shhhhhk*, *shhhhhk* across the floor.

Chair legs slid in April's kitchen and he heard her ask Jeremy to please check the hallway. Dan turned his head and waited for Jeremy to kneel and look. When he did, Dan smiled. "Still here."

"Yeah, hey, man. Or dude. I don't know what guys your age say," Jeremy said. He stood up and his feet went away. "He's still out there."

Dan flexed his fingers, then heard a noise and looked down the stairs at Jenny, standing on the half landing, shoulders hunched, eyes wide.

"What are you doing? Oh my god, are you okay?" She rushed up the final set of stairs and sat beside him. "Are you hurt?"

"I'm okay." He asked for help and she held out her hand. He stood and used the good hand to brush dirt from his pants and jacket.

"Who lives here?" she said.

"No one."

"Someone does."

"A friend."

"Fine." She hurried ahead of him, down the stairs and through the door. Afraid she might leave him there, he ran down after her. He found her waiting behind the wheel, raindrops on the windows fragmenting her face. She didn't look at him when he opened the door. He took his seat and pulled the door closed.

"The other one was Nina, so this one must be April," she said.

"Yes."

"Oh." She put the car into gear and pulled away from the building. "Her loss, I guess."

The rain had stopped sometime in the night. Jenny slept in Dan's bed. She'd taken off everything but a t-shirt and her underwear, blue with pink flower buds and narrow strings that sank into the flesh of her hips.

Dan reached out from under his blanket and pulled open the curtain over the couch. Jenny had reminded him it was a fold-out before he went to sleep on it the way it was. He pressed his palm to the window. Cool. He held his bad wrist against the glass until the temperatures seemed to match, then picked up his phone from the floor and called Nina. When she didn't answer, he left a message telling her he would come by soon with the money she needed to help pay the electric bill, which—she'd said in the message she'd left while Dan lay on the floor outside April's apartment—was over two hundred dollars, and "I need assistance, because half of the income that used to go toward expenses is no longer available."

He woke Jenny and told her to get dressed and come up front to direct him to Andy's house. "It's time to go."

Jenny had bought a drugstore bandage on the way to pick up Andy and wrapped it around Dan's wrist, making driving a little less painful. He pulled up to a two-story house on a still suburban corner and honked the horn with the bandaged wrist. He switched to the good wrist for the second push of the horn.

"I'll get him," Jenny said.

Dan watched as she rang the doorbell, then knocked. A woman not much older than Dan, her hair wrapped in a towel, invited her inside. Ten minutes later, Jenny climbed into the RV and took her seat. "He's not coming."

Dan said, "I'll drop you off."

She heaved herself out of the seat and went back outside, slamming the door behind her. She knocked on Andy's door again and picked at the grout in the stone façade while she waited. Dan turned off the engine when the towel-headed woman opened the door again and invited Jenny inside, then closed his eyes in the warm sun brightening the massive windshield.

The opening door and Jenny's loud "Got him!" woke him. Dan turned to find Andy standing in the living room in a light shirt and shorts, a baseball cap hanging from a strap on the backpack slung over his shoulder. He tossed his bag on the couch and avoided looking at Dan.

Jenny jumped up and down as well as she could under the low ceiling. "I can't believe we're actually going to Las Vegas! In English it means 'the meadows.' Did you know that?"

Dan and Andy said they did not.

Daytime driving was quiet, with Jenny sleeping on Andy's lap and Andy not going out of his way to talk to Dan. He would sometimes catch Andy looking at him in the rearview mirror. Other times he would see him stroke Jenny's hair or leg or hand and whisper something to her. Sometimes Jenny would catch Dan's eye in the mirror before smiling at something Andy said or did.

When Dan bored of the endless trees alongside the interstate, he called Nina again and left a message. He would drop off the money in a couple of days. After another hour of trees he called April and left no message, but listened to her recording. He called twice more just to listen and, unsure why, half hoped she wouldn't answer. She didn't.

They parked at a truck stop parking lot somewhere in South Bend at the end of the first twelve-hour shift. Jenny and Andy, in the bedroom, were a mound under the blankets when Dan made up the couch.

Their second stop was in North Platte, but Dan couldn't sleep. There were enough stars out there to coil his soul. While Jenny and Andy slept in their clothes in the back bedroom, he ate vending machine pretzel snacks in the driver's seat and watched the miles of sky from behind the windshield. At ten minutes to midnight, movement caught his eye and had him pressing his face against the glass to see. Just a shooting star, but it stopped his breath for the long seconds that passed before it blinked out somewhere in space. Shooting star sightings were rare at home, where all of the sky but a wedge directly overhead was blocked by trees. He and Nina, early in their years together and before the stars had started triggering anxiety, would bring an old comforter out to the rectangle of grass behind their apartment building and lie on their backs on clear, crescent-moon nights. All they could see were the brightest stars and the strongest constellations that happened to hover in their small, visible block of the universe.

At midnight, six days down, he called Nina to check on her, but again she didn't answer. When a tone prompted him to leave a message, he asked her to give him a call if she decided it was too soon to have a Bear. He would pick her up.

Andy drove when they got going again. Dan slept through the one-week marker, and twelve hours later they pulled into BITCHIN' HITCHIN.' Dan paid the fee, and Jenny showered and changed her clothes. They ate some hamburgers and French fries at the campsite's restaurant before taking two buses to the north end of the strip, luggage in tow because Jenny had persuaded both men that they couldn't visit Las Vegas at the end of the world and not stay in a hotel on the strip.

Jenny and Andy bought their own bus fare and sat together in a two-seater on the packed bus. Dan stood in the aisle and held onto the bar, swaying forward and back with the stops and starts.

PART II

SIXTEEN

Men looked at Jenny in her black pants and button shirt open along the dark line between her breasts, the imbalance caused by her rolling suitcase exaggerating her sway. Andy blended with the tourists crowding the sidewalks, bag strapped over his shoulder and his baseball cap turned backward, a hand reaching out to press his fingertips to the small of Jenny's back. She spread her free arm to the side as if to catch the wind and said she was never going back to Connecticut.

Dan walked behind them, scuffling through the crowd of mostly young men wearing what he guessed was the uniform for partying twenty-somethings: dark jeans and a tightly tailored, dark-toned button-down over a white t-shirt. Someone slapped a flyer into Dan's hand advertising a forty-nine dollar special on prostitutes. He didn't see a trash can, so he stuffed it in his back pocket.

Jenny turned around and said to Dan, her fingers linked with Andy's, "I thought people would be dressed up in nicer clothes, like jewels and tuxes. Suit jackets, at least."

"Only on TV," Dan said. He wore jeans and hadn't showered since the day before. He used the center pocket of his sweatshirt to cradle his wrist.

"Or at the high-rollers' table," Andy said.

Jenny matched her step with Andy's. Dan lugged his bag on his left shoulder, awkward because he was used to carrying loads on his right. His foot, thankfully, didn't hurt anymore. Jenny pointed up ahead at a tall building with mirrored windows. "Hotels already."

Andy said there was no way he was sharing a room with Dan.

Jenny reminded him it was the best way to save money, and besides, they'd already talked about it. They'd made a deal.

"Fine," he said. "But we're getting a suite, or something. Something with separate bedrooms. I'm not staying in the same bedroom as him."

"I told you nothing happened."

"And I told you I'm not a fucking idiot."

The hotel Jenny had heard the most about was the Bellagio, and that was where she wanted to stay. The Palazzo looked "boring," she said when they passed it, and the Venetian like it was "trying too hard." The Mirage had a "tacky" band crossing the high floors, and Caesar's Palace was "too obvious." She walked fast. Andy had let go of her hand somewhere near the Trump Hotel, which she had said was "gaudy, just like Trump."

When they reached the Bellagio, Dan's shoulder hurt and his wrist throbbed and his hand sweated in his pocket. Jenny asked the man at the front desk for a suite.

"Presidential, executive, penthouse, tower, lake view, or—"

"Oh my god," Jenny said. "Any one of them. Penthouse. No. Presidential!" She said to Dan and Andy, in what she must have thought was an aside, "If it happens this weekend, we'll have died in the Presidential Suite," the last two words part whisper, part squeal.

"I want the tower," Andy said.

The man, LEE on his nametag, typed on the keyboard until he was able to inform them there was one room available, a lucky-for-them cancellation. Not a suite, but two beds and two arm chairs. It was the best he could do.

Lee handed them off to a concierge who took them to the fourth floor and a room with the promised bed and chairs. Jenny dropped her suitcase inside the door and claimed the bed closest to the window.

Dan and Andy set their bags on their respective beds, and the three of them followed the concierge back down to the front desk. Dan and Jenny paid cash in an even split for the room, and Dan supplied the credit card. He and Nina, like most, had held onto theirs, but they used them only for emergencies—and for hotels, which still required them. He was down to one, now, the one granting access to his checking account. He'd thought it best before leaving Connecticut to bend and mutilate the card to the account he shared with Nina.

They returned to the room when Jenny said she wanted to change after the sweaty walk to the hotel. While they waited, Andy sat on his and Jenny's bed, legs spread with the excessive width Dan had seen used to show full possession of a bus or subway seat. Andy kept his eye on the bathroom door.

"She's lucky to have you," Dan said.

"I know."

Dan passed Andy to get to the window, intentionally not using all the space available to him. His pants brushed Andy's knee. Andy watched him, but didn't move. Dan looked down at the pool, an unrealistic blue, and at the straight line of chaise lounges shaded by blinding white umbrellas.

"I didn't bring a suit," Jenny said, suddenly next to him.

"I think they might have a store here," Andy said behind them.

Jenny wanted to go straight to the highest paying slot machines. Andy said he had some change in his pocket he could play in the quarter slots.

The machines' screens glowed and ticked with the rolling displays of cherries and lemons and single, double, and triple bars. Many chairs were taken, but just as many were unoccupied. The rhythmic, graceful reach, play, wait, reach, play, wait of men and women with bagged eyes held Dan captive for a good half minute before he felt Jenny's nudge to keep going.

He had always imagined a Las Vegas casino as having more energy, with electric sparks and disembodied laughter, an ever-present server with a drink-heavy tray and the ongoing *ding! ding! ding!* of lucky winners. Instead, it was a larger version of any number of the smaller casinos he'd seen, like Foxwoods in Ledyard but with less expensive rooms. He remembered that April had once told him to appreciate the excitement of an idea. "When does reality," she'd said, "whether good or bad, ever live up to the idea?"

SEVENTEEN

Somewhere, a bell. Somewhere else, the reproduced sound of change clanging in a tray. Jenny and Andy stood on either side of Dan as if waiting for him to lead. He recommended that they go their own ways and meet up later.

"Oh, oh, at Le Cirque!" Jenny said. She stood on her toes and held a shiny black purse against her bright pink shirt. "Please?"

"We all have phones?" Dan said. "Andy? Phone?"

"Who doesn't have a phone?" he said as Jenny grabbed his hand and yanked him away.

Dan pulled out his wallet and counted seven one-dollar bills among the fifties and twenties. He found a dollar slot machine and slid a bill into the narrow, sucking hole and lost it. He pulled another from his wallet and let the machine take it. The rolling images stopped in another losing combination.

It took less than two minutes for him to lose the rest of his singles.

He found an ATM and withdrew his five-hundred dollar cash limit, exchanged it for chips, and wandered over to a twenty-one table occupied by just one other player. Dan sat with an empty chair between them. He ordered a drink from a woman with curly orange hair and matte pink lips.

His game companion ordered a house wine and laughed when the dealer scooped his chips. He looked at Dan. "Never lost a dollar in my life before today. Feels fantastic."

The man, around Dan's age, had shaggy brown hair cut thin over his ears. His black suit was worn into comfort, and his loosened tie revealed two freed buttons at the collar of a starched white shirt. A brown satchel on the floor next to his chair stretched at the top zipper seam.

The shaggy-haired man said, "You here to lose?"

Dan said, "I might not have a choice."

The man reached his hand into the space between their chairs. "Larry."

His fingers were hard and dry, his grip tight enough to make Dan squeeze a little harder than he normally would. "Dan."

They placed their bets and the dealer laid the cards. Dan turned over twenty-four.

Larry pulled his winnings only as far as the betting circle and took a few long swallows of wine.

The noise in the casino elevated as the hours rolled by, developing into something of a discernible pattern that included clicking heels, the rise and fall of excited conversations, and at one point a crescendo: a high-pitched scream Dan thought sounded a little like Jenny. When all of the noises stopped in one of those moments that occurs for no reason other than perfectly timed chance, the faces of the steadfast gamblers continued to flicker in the glare of spinning pictures.

Larry took all of his losses with a raised glass and a smile. Anything he won, he bet. Dan lost as often as Larry won. He'd played enough to know the rules but had never developed a feel for the game, didn't know whether to hit or stay on a sixteen. When he tried to mimic Larry's winning method, the cards would still fall in favor of the dealer. The more Larry won, the more he drank, and when he ordered for himself, he would also order for Dan. Dan was drunk. No matter how far he tilted his head to correct it, the wall slanted right, and when he tried to pay close attention to Larry's words and sentences because it was the polite thing to do in the company of someone with so much to say, he could not keep straight who was the wife or the sister or the name of the wine, or for which one Larry had left Tennessee on what he called his "quest."

"Already got my feet," Larry said. He tapped a heel on his bag.

"We've all got them," Dan said. He looked at his own. His shoe was untied. He reached for it and his head poured forward, so he sat up straight and reminded himself to remind himself it was untied when he stood up to walk somewhere.

Larry leaned over to unbuckle his bag and pulled out a bottle just far enough for Dan to see the label. "Chateau Lafite," Larry said. "Cost me eight hundred because it's past its prime. No telling how it'll taste, but I had to have it. You know how it is. The eagle, I'm chasing down. Used to be it was all over the place in California, but no one has it there, anymore. Sold out. Found a guy in Kentucky, though. It should only cost three thousand, but he knows he can take me for four."

"For an eagle? What'll you do with it?"

Dan turned over his cards and Larry did the same. The dealer played his hand and lost to them both.

"Wine," Larry said. "Screaming Eagle. It's a wine."

Larry said he'd come down from Nashville to play what he had and then disappear, "Get rid of everything but what I need to get my Eagle, and then go somewhere to enjoy the bottles. Not sure where, yet. I may stay in Kentucky. It's a nice enough state in some places."

"Why didn't you just give the money away?"

"Gambling scares the shit out of me. Figured I'd better do it."

Larry ordered another drink for each of them. Both pushed forward their chips and the dealer laid the cards and waited, hands at his sides. Larry folded up a corner and tapped the table. The dealer gave him a king and Larry made blackjack. "Well, damn," he said.

Dan stayed and lost three hundred dollars.

"Did you say three thousand dollars for a bottle of wine?"

"If I'm lucky."

He asked what Larry did for a living.

"Not a thing, now."

But he used to own a furniture sale and delivery business, he said. It had originally been a regional moving company, but once it started making enough money he'd scaled down to COMFORT CONSIGNMENT & DELIVERY. ("You can't count on people, movers. We had some issues with intimidation for tips.")

"Anyway," he said, "my wife's sister started up a trade website and we collected from businesses changing out their furniture. Got deals at garage sales, cleaned it up, put it online."

"Good money?"

"Not too bad. Not too bad at all. And then my wife—well, Lisa and her sister—they got a nice chunk of change when their mother died. Both of them stuck it straight in the bank and went on with making more. Didn't spend a cent of it. Lisa wanted to retire a millionaire. Put away every nickel. Every goddamned nickel." He looked at his cards. "I don't think that plan'll work out too well for her, now. Even if we *are* all still here come July." He smiled, said, "Hit me," and wiped his mouth with his fingers.

The dealer, MIKE, hit Larry. He said, "Farling?"

Larry said, "Ayup," and, "Just another dumb southerner waitin' out the end of days, that's me."

"I was a Mayan Calendar man, myself," Mike said. He assured Larry that he wasn't alone, that there had been more than a few like him who'd come through over the last couple of months.

"Dan!" Jenny raced toward him. "Dan!"

She jumped into the seat between his and Larry's and plopped her purse on her lap, palms pressed tight against it. "Are you almost ready?" She wore a carnival ride smile and the manic bounce of her ankles shook her thighs.

"For what?"

"Anything I want." She made a noise that was part squeak, part squeal. "But first, I'm starving. Me and Andy want to eat, so I came to get you."

"How long has it been?"

"I don't know. Three or four hours, I guess. It feels like ten minutes."

"Where's Andy?"

"He wanted to buy new clothes for the restaurant, so I gave him a little bit of money." She looked at him and waited, but he didn't know for what. She said, "I came to find you in case you forgot we were supposed to meet or didn't know how to get to Le Cirque."

Dan looked at his watch. It had been four hours. "I'll find it."

"I just mean—It's just that I've walked around the whole place, so I know exactly how to get there. That's all." She looked at Dan's chips. "Oh! Look what I bought." She dug around inside her purse and pulled out a light blue, shiny leather circle with a smaller circle hanging from it by a gold chain. With pauses for effect between each word, she said, "Four hundred and fifty dollars."

"What is it?" he said.

"A change purse!"

"For a kid?"

"For me. You don't like it?"

"Those aren't your initials."

"It's the designer's initials." She handed it to him.

"I know." Dan held it. "Why?"

"Look." She reached inside her purse again and pulled out some coins. She took the blue circle from Dan and tucked in four quarters and a dime, then closed the zipper. "See?" She dangled it in front of him.

Dan asked her if she knew how many people went into debt, compromising their ability to get home or car loans, for overpriced vanity items.

"Yeah, but they can't afford it. I can." She dropped it in her purse and folded over the handles. She smiled.

He asked her how much she won. She held her purse tighter and said, "I don't know. A lot." The carnival smile again. "Once you win here and there, you lose count and just keep going." Her feet swung out and back. "Oh my god, okay. So, it was like I was sitting down at every slot machine right at that moment when if the last person sitting there all day would have stayed for *one* more chance, they would've won. And this was at the big-givers, thousands and thousands. I hit two! Well, Andy hit two, because he's twenty-two and there was no way I was trying my fake here, so I would tell him where to play next and what to do. I just kept winning and winning and winning. Even at roulette, and I don't even know how to play it. I watched people putting their chips on random numbers, so I had Andy stick mine on eighteen for my birthday, and the little ball bounced around and around until it landed right on it. Then I thought, well, there's no way I can pick another number and expect to win, so I just put half the chips I won on black. And the ball bounced into a little black number. It just kept going on like that. I mean, I won *so much money.* So much that spending four hundred and fifty dollars is, well, kind of like nothing." She leaned close and whispered, "*Seventy-six* thousand. No joke. I never have to go back. I can go to California. I can stay here!" She hugged him and said into his neck, "Thank you so much for bringing me."

"Better quit now before you lose it all," Larry said.

She spun her chair to face him and said, "Oh, I did. Believe me, I'm not losing any of this unless it's on purpose, like if I'm buying something." Swiveling back to Dan, she said, "That's why I wanted to find you. I was waiting, but I knew if I waited around too much longer I'd be tempted to go back and put everything on red, this time. He's probably waiting at the restaurant now. Are you coming?"

Dan looked past her at Larry and asked if he wanted to come along. He shook his head, waved Dan away. "Appreciate it, but I've still got a lot to lose, here."

Dan told Jenny to go ahead and that he'd catch up later. She squeezed his sore wrist and slid off the stool and tucked her purse under her arm. "I'll walk around some with Andy, then. Should we meet in an hour? I really want to buy you dinner. You're the one who got me out of Connecticut. Forever. Please," she said, her hands at prayer between her breasts.

"An hour."

Jenny kissed him on the cheek and raced away. Dan rested his wrist on his thigh where no one else would reach for it.

Good hand after good hand increased the size of Dan's meager chip pile. He had enough to keep himself drunk all night *and* take April away for a few days without any need for her to use her own money. It wouldn't matter to her, but it was something to him.

Larry, red faced and sweating, was losing, his bets getting smaller and his fingertips rapping the green felt so hard they turned white. "What is this bullshit?" He flipped his cards at the dealer and his wrist knocked his glass, spilling the drink on the table. The dealer signaled over Larry's head while mopping the stain. Escorts arrived and Larry scooped up his chips. Dan counted a little over five thousand dollars before they were gone, stuffed in Larry's bag. "I'm a guest in this hotel," he said as they led him away.

Dan gathered his chips and concentrated hard on walking in the direction of Larry's forced exit. He found him standing under the glass-domed ceiling in front of a jewelry store.

"I might want that dinner, after all," Larry said. "But I'll have to buy a suit. This one's an embarrassment." He eyed Dan's clothes. "You ought to get one, too. Hey, be a doll and cash out my chips for me."

He took handful after handful from his bag, and Dan transferred them to his front pants pockets until he had two sizeable bulges. When he returned with the cash, he followed Larry to a white-lit shop with dark suits hanging from floating rods.

Dan unwrapped his wrist and put on the store's least expensive suit in his size, along with a bright pink tie recommended by the in-house stylist. He smoothed down the jacket and combed back his hair with his fingers in front of the mirror. It had been a long time since he'd worn a suit. The collection agency had allowed khaki pants and polo shirts, and that was what he had worn every day. Jeans on Fridays, but only with a button shirt. He turned sideways and rubbed the growth on his cheeks and neck. He could pretend it was on purpose, just like the hair shadows on the jaws of the framed suit models on the walls.

It felt good to look good.

It felt good to spend time with another man, someone outside of work, someone somewhat more interesting than Carl. Dan didn't have many friends.

Any, really.

After paying, he waited at the register for Larry, who emerged from behind a curtain in an equally (relatively) inexpensive, but equally well-fitting, gray suit and bright green tie. "Never once wore a tie this neon."

As they walked to the restaurant, carrying their old clothes in bags provided by the store, Dan felt like one of the well-dressed people Jenny had hoped to see. Women looked at him more openly than usual. They looked at Larry, too, whose posture and gait were more poised than what Dan had expected from the slouching man at the card table.

"We walking funny, or something?" Larry slurred.

When they reached Le Cirque, its ceiling draped in broad silk strips of red, orange, and yellow, Dan spotted Jenny's hand in the air waving them over.

Larry introduced himself when they sat down.

Jenny stared at Dan.

Andy see-sawed a knife between his thumb and finger. "It's been an hour and a half," he said. "We figured you weren't coming. We already ate."

"We did not. I was about to call you," Jenny said, still looking at Dan.

Andy put down the knife and leaned back in his chair. "She has a thing for old guys." His cheeks and neck and mouth were red.

"Oh my god, am I staring?" She covered her face with her palms, then opened them like shutters and said to Dan, "I'm sorry. It's just … you just look *really* good."

No one spoke again until their drinks were in front of them. Andy took a swallow of his—"Mmm"—and set it down beside Jenny's water. "Sure you don't want to try using your ID just once?"

Jenny picked up Andy's glass before he had time to react, emptied it into her mouth, and put it back down. "I can't believe we didn't need reservations here," she said. "I guess it's a slow time of day or week, or something. Andy didn't even have to wear a jacket and tie, but when we came in everyone else was wearing them, so … ."

Andy pulled his tie away from his throat.

"What is the matter with you, all of a sudden?" Jenny said. "I don't know why you came if you're going to be like this."

"I don't either." He loosened his tie some more and opened his shirt collar. "The whole idea behind this trip was dumb. You'll be out of money by next year —by next month if you keep buying all that shit—and I'll still be at the hotel because I won't go to college to qualify myself for something that'll have me in ties. The world still won't have ended, like it hasn't any of the other times just like this, and you'll be stuck having to face it. Then what?"

"All I know is that tomorrow I'm getting another room. I don't even care if it means going to another hotel. I want French doors that go out onto a balcony. "

"Where you'll butter your breakfast baguette," Dan said, and Jenny smiled.

"What's he talking about?" Andy said.

"Nothing."

Dan rubbed his forehead and his eyes and looked around for a menu, but there were only napkins and candles.

"You said you two already ate?" Larry said.

"We didn't," Jenny said. "Andy was just being a jerk."

Larry raised his hand and asked for menus.

Salads started at twenty-five dollars, and the prices only went up from there.

Jenny said, "Sole manure? Yuck."

"Meuniere," Larry said. "It's a, uh—it means the fish—the sole—it's seasoned, and then it's cooked in a butter sauce."

Dan said, "How do you know that?"

"How d'you not?"

"Well, I don't care what it is. I'm not getting sole manure."

"It's mighty tasty, the meuniere. Mighty tasty."

When the server arrived, Jenny ordered half shell oysters. Andy asked for the butternut squash soup, Dan the rack of lamb, and Larry ordered a salad and complained about the price.

EIGHTEEN

Dan's chips were low, even after some—too many—sizeable cash advances. The deal before, Larry had lost everything he had left to gamble with a nineteen to the dealer's twenty-one.

"Goddamn it," he'd said before getting up to use the bathroom. Dan had reminded him he was there to lose.

"Yep. I did say that."

Larry returned to his chair as the dealer swiped Dan's cards and chips.

"Holding steady?" Larry said.

"Losing steady." Dan ordered two drinks, the last he'd be able to afford, and bet twenty-five hundred of the twenty-seven hundred on the table. Before walking into the casino, Larry had reminded him that "living the end shouldn't be done half-assed." Dan had agreed and had immediately gone to the restroom to change back into his comfortable clothes.

The dealer gave him a five, and then another card face down.

"I saw your girl," Larry said. "At the craps table with the boyfriend. He rolled a winner."

Dan lifted the card's corner: a seven. He tapped the felt.

Twenty-five hundred shrank to two hundred. He pushed his last chips forward.

Larry shook his head. "If you're not holding some back, I hope you got somewhere free to stay."

When those chips, too, were gone—dealer, twenty: Dan, seventeen—he considered pulling from what remained in his account, six hundred dollars that had begun as a thousand-dollar safety cushion.

"Well, I guess I'll be on my way," Larry said. "Nothing left to play with."

Dan turned to look at him and felt sick with the movement. "Where're you going?"

"Told you. Kentucky. Got to get my Eagle. The perfect wine, they call it. Perfect. You ever have anything perfect in your life?" He spun his wedding band around and around his finger. "Should never have done this. Should never have. Don't know what I was thinking."

"I'll give you a ride," Dan said. "Kentucky's on the way."

"To where?"

"I'm going back. Tomorrow. You'll come with me."

"Go with you where?"

"Kentucky. Connecticut's on the way. I mean, Kentucky's on the way. To Con—"

"Naw." He shook his head. "I don't want to put you out."

Dan told him he'd be doing him a favor, that he'd welcome the company. Jenny would be staying in Las Vegas, and he'd bet everything he had left in his account that Andy would follow. It was a long trip to be alone. "How were you going to get there?"

When Larry said "Bus," Dan warned him against it and told him the story of the decapitated boy. "You never know who'll be sitting next to you," he said.

"Well, I want no part of that."

"Then it's done."

Larry insisted on paying what he would have paid in bus fare, and they shook on it. Larry stood and said he'd take Dan over to where he'd seen Jenny and Andy, but when Dan slid off his chair his body didn't hold up. Larry helped him through the tables and slots and through the bright, airy hallway to the elevator. He asked Dan what floor he was on and took his room key.

He opened his eyes. He was alone in the room on his bed. Bright lights from outside lit the window. He remembered Larry guiding him there, sitting him down, and saying "See you later" and "There's a trash can next to you on the floor" before walking out diagonal. He didn't know how long ago that was.

Something poked him through his jeans and he reached back, took it out of his pocket and uncrumpled it. He looked for a long time at the picture. At her smile. At the little green stars hiding her nipples.

He'd never done it before, but he'd known people who had. It wasn't a morality issue, he just hadn't been available. Hadn't thought about it.

He had never had any kind of anonymous sex, even for free.

He imagined a paid stranger lying beneath him, saying yes to everything, making him feel good and right because there was no reason to feel bad.

He pulled out his phone and dialed.

She had short brown hair, and legs nearly fully encased in high black boots with skinny metal heels. She looked nothing like the girl on the coupon, but she smiled when he opened the door and stepped inside without waiting for him to invite her.

She sat on the bed.

She left, her boot heels thudding on the hallway carpet, when Dan came up with nothing after searching his pockets and bag for the cash she wanted up front on top of the card payment he'd already made.

NINETEEN

Movement came from somewhere. Dan opened his eyes. It was late, still, but not dark. No one had closed the curtains and the lights from outside reflected off the walls and silhouetted Andy rummaging around near the bed where Jenny slept. He picked up a bag and carried it out to the hallway, the door clicking quietly behind him. Low snoring came from the far side of the room where the two chairs had been pushed together to make a sort-of couch.

Dan felt his phone in his hand and had a sense of April. He couldn't remember what they'd talked about but he had a feeling she'd answered her phone and that they'd talked about something.

It was the frantic muttering that woke him for good. Jenny, in a t-shirt and underwear, sat on her knees on her bed, purse between her thighs. The sun had come up and the room was a mess of clothes and water bottles. Larry slept on the chairs with his bag under his head, blankets on the floor. Jenny's hands were stuffed in her purse and moving around hard and fast.

Andy lay in the bed on the other side of Jenny, closest to the wall. Dan saw him open his eyes and then, when Jenny turned to shake him, quickly close them.

"Andy," she said. "Wake up."

He made a sleep noise.

She slapped his arm and told him again to wake up, that the money, all of it, was gone. She opened pockets inside the bag and felt around the lining, turned the whole thing upside down and dumped it out. Some change, a pen, lipstick, and a brown makeup disc dropped out. The small blue plastic change purse bounced off the bed and onto the floor.

Andy sat up and yawned, and then slid away from her until he'd backed himself against the headboard.

"It was all right here," she said. "I remember cashing out and putting it all in here and zipping it up. We came here right after that." She looked at Andy. "I remember. It was all in here."

She looked inside again, ran her hand along the bottom.

Larry rolled over on the chairs. He hadn't taken off the suit jacket before going to sleep, but he had taken off his shoes and socks and tie. One of the chair's arms propped up his bare feet.

"If you did anything with it, Andy." She swung the bag hard at him and he blocked it with his wrist, then yanked it from her. She grabbed for it and he pulled it away and dropped it on the floor.

"Where is it?" she said.

Andy said, "Gone."

"What do you mean, 'gone'?"

"It's gone."

"*Gone?*"

Dan had never known someone with such big eyes.

"I don't know what that means," she said.

"It's gone, Jen."

"Like, you hid it?"

"No."

"How much of it is gone?"

"Um ... well, all of it. I mean, I kept some for gas so we can get back."

"Back? I don't want to go *back*," she screamed. She jumped off the bed. "What did you do with it? Where did it all go? Did you just give it away? How do you make seventy-six thousand—"

"I bet it." He bent over for his pants.

TWENTY

Sun fell on them at the bar, and on two middle-aged women tanning on white chaises who, during conversational pauses, would absently watch an old man in water goggles swimming breaststroke laps in the center of the pool. The bar pressed cool into the underside of Dan's forearm and the breeze smelled like chlorine. Larry stirred green juice in a tall glass with a straw. His suit jacket was off, folded and placed on top of his bag on the stool beside him.

The bartender brought Dan another orange juice.

After he walked away, Larry said, "Green juice and sunshine. Goddamn it."

Dan licked a piece of pulp off his upper lip and chewed it. The acid and sweetness helped settle his stomach. The space between his chair and Larry's was not enough to take away the smell of Larry's shirt, slept and sweated in and stained tan at the armpits.

The sun made Dan tired. When Jenny and Andy showed up he would ask Andy to drive the first stretch. He hadn't had as much to drink as the rest of them, had seemed in good condition when he'd chased Jenny—her arms wrapped around her shoes and her empty purse—out of the room.

Dan closed his eyes. The wind up high pushed through the palm trees. He liked the sun but not the heat. It was too hot for so early on a winter morning. He missed the cold.

"How much longer you think it'll be?" Larry said.

"She said eleven-thirty."

"I'm not talking about that. I mean in general. Think there's time to get to Kentucky? A few days?"

"I don't know," Dan said. "Nothing's happened, yet. Maybe nothing will until later this year. We could have plenty of time."

"All I want's just enough time. What am I supposed to do with plenty of time?"

"You could always go home."

Larry pulled the straw from his drink and set it on the bar and took a long swallow straight from the glass. He stroked a thumb across his mouth to wipe away the juice.

Dan heard Jenny's shoes before he saw her. She wore torn jeans, her Las Vegas t-shirt, and flip flops that dragged. Andy trailed behind, walking tall with his shoulders back. When Jenny got close, she shifted the bag on her shoulder and the purse on her arm and her mouth made a small, tight circle before she said, "Well? Let's go, I guess."

"Everything okay?" Dan said.

"Are you serious?"

Andy said, "She wanted to try to win some back, and we lost a hundred of the gas money I saved."

"Isn't he so thoughtful and responsible? He saved gas money."

"I've got the gas," Larry said.

"Oh, goody." Jenny dropped her purse on the ground and let her bag fall beside it. "We can still go home, then." She stepped between Larry and Dan. "Sir? Are you serving alcohol?"

The bartender didn't ask for identification. While she waited, she pushed back from the bar so Andy could see her and smiled at Dan and Larry, her bust pushed farther forward than could be considered natural.

Dan hadn't thought about it before, except to notice the difference between Larry before and after the new suit, but he guessed he could see what a girl would find attractive about him. His eyes were light blue, and his hair, which Dan had thought greasy or dirty, might be something a girl Jenny's age would like. Grunge had been out of style for decades, but things had a way of coming back.

Larry said, "When does high school start up again for you? You on holiday break about now?"

Jenny's face turned red before she said "I graduated" and turned away. When her drink came, she walked with it to the edge of the pool and stood under the sun.

Larry said, "Kids."

Andy took one of the bar stools and swiveled to watch her. "She'll get over it."

Larry laughed. "You sure hope so."

Jenny had her face turned just enough so that, Dan imagined, she could see them out of the corner of her eye. She shifted on her feet, a self-conscious behavior that endeared him not to her, but to a different time when such a contradiction in a woman's character could make him fall in love, had made him fall in love. He had thought he loved April when she asked him to marry her, but until that train ride, and until the next morning when she stepped out of the hotel bathroom in the dress she'd bought for their wedding, he'd not experienced anything close. She'd held the material—separated from her skin by a shaving of air—at her thighs, one hand inadvertently pulling up the loosely ruffled seam to reveal a bare knee. "What do you think?" she'd said.

Jenny slipped off a shoe and touched the water with her toe. Andy started to get up. Jenny, still watching sideways, gave him a look that said he'd better not. He settled back onto his stool. Jenny took off her other shoe and sat down with her legs dangling in the wind-rippled water. Her head turned slowly, matching the speed of the old man swimming by.

Andy continued to watch her, reminding Dan of himself, of April. He wondered what she was doing. It was cold there, today, even for Connecticut, the morning's television's weather forecast had said.

A vision of Nina, just her face, came to him. He didn't know why and wasn't sure he wanted to. He replaced her with the first thing that came to him by way of association, which was the basement, and then the exterior of their house, and then the yard, and then farther out to the driveway where he could see Belowski's red sports car next door, and from there to the parking spot near the trees in the hotel parking lot, and then roads east to April's sidewalk.

April had been right. The idea was better than the reality. He wanted to go home.

He said to Andy, who was watching Jenny kick her feet in the pool, "You're driving first, so we'll go whenever you're ready."

TWENTY ONE

Dan and Jenny sat on the couch and Larry slept in the back. He'd dozed right away in one of the chairs, snoring, head flung back and his body twisted sideways. Dan had woken him to tell him he could use the bed.

Jenny sat with her bare feet wedged under Dan's thighs, her elbow on the back of the couch. She maneuvered her wrist to make her watch face catch sunlight.

Dan watched the brown countryside and tried again to remember the conversation he'd had with April the night before. All he could recall was having heard her voice.

"I hate him," Jenny whispered.

He said in a way Andy wouldn't hear over the sound of the engine, "I don't think I'm the one you should be telling."

"I can't tell him. I need my job, now, and if I make him too mad he could convince them to fire me. They love him. It's disgusting," she said. "But what do you do when you have so much hatred for someone and you have to be around them, anyway?"

You fake it, he told her.

"How?"

He thought of his parents, who had only recently ended their hyperbolically civil marriage. Afterward, his father had rented a downtown apartment and met an attorney he called "the one" while getting breakfast at a nearby café. His mother had bought a small house on a high-traffic country road where she now sold used books

159

and other things she liked—candle holders, old picture frames, framed prints—out of the attached garage. Both of his parents laughed more during a single visit or phone call from Dan than he could remember having heard in the eighteen years he'd lived at home. Even their hair seemed freer. In what Dan guessed was an effort to cover up the lack of laughter, his parents had refined their ability to be courteous, never forgetting to help each other with coats and doors or to say "please" and "thank you."

Dan said, "You do the things you did when you liked him."

They stopped at a rest stop for food and a more private restroom experience. Andy said he was good to keep driving, but Larry took the keys and said he'd had enough sleep, was bored, and wanted to take over. Andy followed Jenny to the back, to the bedroom, and Dan sat up front. Larry drove in suit pants and rolled sleeves with hunched shoulders and his hands at nine and three.

A few hours passed with no one talking up front. Jenny and Andy fought in the back, their voices carrying through the RV. Andy shouted at her to be quiet for one second, please listen, and Jenny screamed long and loud, a wail meant to make a point. Dan and Larry had opened their windows to mask them with wind, but it wasn't enough. Larry slammed his foot on the brake and Dan's seatbelt gripped his chest.

Andy called "Sorry," and Jenny screamed that Larry should do it again, but kill her, this time, because the end of the world wasn't coming fast enough, and "I'd rather die in some old van than spend one single day back in Connecticut."

"Keep it down, back there!" Larry said. He asked Dan, "What's she got against Connecticut, anyway?"

Dan's phone rang. He pulled it out of his pocket and checked the number. Nina. He set it in the empty cup holder.

"Wife?"

Dan didn't know how to answer that, so he didn't. He listened for the message chime.

When it came, Larry said, "Message."

"I'll get to it."

"I never did get a cell phone," Larry said. "Lisa had one and always took it with her. It would ring during dinner."

"Did she answer?"

"Nope. But it rang, and even if she didn't answer we'd get pestered with that other ring when there was a message. Hated that damn thing." Larry looked in the rearview mirror and yanked Dan's shirt sleeve. "Take a look."

Dan twisted around and saw them kissing. The stove's overhead light just reached Jenny kneeling on top of Andy, their clothes still mostly on and their faces wrapped up in her hair.

"Keeping on," Larry said.

"She asked my advice. I said to fake it."

"Good for her."

Dan wasn't sure. He said so.

"What do you care about some little girl? You jealous?"

He wasn't, and he said that, too. He told Larry what he knew about Jenny's life at home and what it had meant to her to get out. He said he didn't think she deserved to have to fake it.

"Maybe she isn't. Maybe happiness is keeping on." Larry drank from a bottle of water and dropped it in the cup holder. "People have to do what they do. We're diggers."

"Diggers," Dan agreed, not knowing or really caring what Larry meant by it. Beyond the chipped windshield, black mountain silhouettes cut into a wide, full moon sky.

Nothing's going to happen, he remembered Nina saying.

He relaxed his hands. They passed a sign for SNOW COLLEGE, RICHFIELD CAMPUS.

"It's like this," Larry said. "Say you round up some people and put them out by a real high wall, give them all shovels."

"Why?"

"Just listen, now. You put those people out there—the wall's too high to climb, even if they boost each other up—and you tell them there's no escape. Even with the shovels. You tell them to test the walls, go ahead and dig down." He paused to look in the rearview mirror when Andy made a noise from the bedroom. Dan peered around the side of his chair, saw more than he wanted to see, and kept his eyes on the floor as he got up and walked back to close the curtain. When he returned to the front he buckled his seatbelt and Larry went on.

"So, now you get two more people and put them out there. Except, these two have guns. You tell the ones with the shovels that the ones with the guns are going to take one step forward, toward the wall and toward those people with shovels, every ten minutes, or so. And when those two gun people get to a certain point, they're going to shoot all the shovel people in the head."

"Wouldn't they just run in the opposite direction of the wall?"

"It's a closed-in wall like you'd see in a bullfighting ring, or maybe a gladiator arena. So it's certain death, see. But they can choose. They can end it early, ask to be shot. Save themselves some anxiety. The poor souls are going to die, anyway. Or they can dig up to the very second one of those gun people gets to the shooting marker." He whapped Dan's thigh with the back of his hand. "What do you think they'll do?"

"I don't know."

"Come on. Sure you do. They're not going to say, 'Kill me now, mister, please.' Not unless they're suicidal already. No, they're going to take all the time they can get, however many steps it takes for those guns to get there, to try to find a way out. Hell, some of them will strike bargains with other shovel people and try to get help digging. One of them'll even knock another one out if their hole looks deeper. But either way, they're going to live the only way they know how and use those shovels to dig. Like those two back there. Like you. Like …"

Dan followed his attention and saw, up ahead, an SUV heading straight for the wide open door of a Volkswagen beetle stopped on shoulder. A head popped out of the SUV's sunroof and his scream—

"The end is near! Woohoo! Say hi to Jesus!"—rode the airstream into their windows. The head slipped inside just before the SUV crossed the white line and slammed into the open door. It flung loose from its hinges, spun over the hood of the Volkswagen, and landed hard in desert grass.

The SUV drove on. A beer can shot out of the window and bounced on the pavement, clanked along the RVs undercarriage.

"We've all got our ways," Larry said.

They listened to the radio. Little music was available, so Larry had found a news and talk radio station. Commentators debated the latest flare-up between North and South Korea.

"Surprised the North Koreans didn't use this year as their chance to launch a missile or two. They've been waiting on it since oh-nine," Larry said. "Maybe they have a different end of the world date in mind."

An orgasmic cry came from the back bedroom. It was Andy.

Larry said, "Sure took his time," and then much louder, "Keep it to yourself, you kids!" He sucked some air and made a whistling sound. "That's what girls are taught. 'Use that pussy.' It works well enough, but that Jenny—if we don't get lucky, if this world doesn't end—when she gets her senses about her and thinks about the money, and about how that Andy kid should've been better than to let her think the only way to save herself was to get into bed with him, she's going to find that boy and beat him senseless." He sipped from his water bottle, plopped it back in the holder. "I hope she does, anyway."

Dan followed the river through Louisville until Larry pointed him off at the North Twenty-Second Street exit. Dan followed Market Street and took a left toward the river, past Slugger Field, and kept on until Larry told him to stop when they saw a sign for a park. Dan said he would be happy, really, to drive Larry into the city. There were more transportation options, phones.

"The park'll be fine," Larry said. "I think I'd like more chasing time. You get me?"

Andy gave Larry a half empty box of crackers from the kitchen cabinet. Larry stuffed it in his bag, packed for the last few days with his new suit jacket and bottle of wine. Jenny hugged him and wished him luck. Dan recognized the Jenny of Connecticut. From what he could tell, she'd come to like Larry.

"You be careful with that thing, Jenny girl," Larry said.

"What thing?"

"Never mind," Dan said. He shook Larry's hand and asked him if he needed anything else.

Larry held up his bag. "Got all I need." He pulled out the jacket and put it on, then walked into the park, stepping off the path into muddy grass.

TWENTY TWO

"I think Larry's killing himself." Andy sat in the passenger seat with his elbows on the armrests. "I think he's jumping in the river."

Dan had already considered turning back to get him. Not because he thought Andy was right, though now he did wonder about the possibility, but because Larry had been the only other adult on the trip and he'd genuinely enjoyed his company. But Larry knew what he wanted to do, whatever that was, and whatever it was was none of Dan's business.

He checked the mirror for Jenny and saw her half-curled against the back of the couch, knees tight together, blank eyes looking out onto dead fields sliding by. She wore sweatpants and a thin t-shirt. Her sex hair hadn't been brushed, but fell in knotted waves to her shoulders. She reminded him of Nina, and for a second he missed her, missed her so much that the thought of never going home again made his head hurt.

He dismissed it as a consequence of not having fully caught up on his sleep.

He thought about the cat.

He missed the cat.

Andy said, "I told her we should get a place. I know how much she hates living at home, and since she's eighteen soon, she can move out. The apartments back behind Pine Street are pretty cheap."

"Safe?" Dan said.

"Oh, yeah. It doesn't get bad until you cross to the other side of Pleasant Street."

He looked at Andy.

Andy laughed and shrugged. "It's true."

"At least someone's having a good time," Jenny yelled.

They pulled onto Andy's street at seven-thirty on a dark morning. Fresh snow covered mailboxes and tree branches, stoop stairs and sidewalks. No plows had been through. Dan rolled down the window and took a deep breath of cold, thin air.

"Stupid snow," Jenny said from the couch.

Dan parked in front of Andy's house. Jenny sat with her arms crossed and let Andy kiss her on the lips. He touched her cheek and strapped on his backpack. "I'll see you later. Tonight?"

"Why not," she said.

He sat in one of the chairs and said something too quiet for Dan to hear. He waited with the engine running and checked his voicemail for the message Nina had left while he and Larry were talking. She said, "I ... I think I dialed the wrong number." Dan deleted it. He heard Andy say, "... don't understand why you won't—"

"I'm just really tired, okay?" Jenny's voice was high. Happy. Chipper and cheerful. "That's all. I'll call you later. I *promise*."

Andy said, "Okay, then," and adjusted his backpack before standing to leave. "Thanks for the trip, Dan man." He flipped his hand in a wave on the way down the stairs. Jenny hopped off the couch to run to the door after he closed it. Dan heard the latch lock. She walked up front and sat with her brown slipper-booted feet on the dashboard.

Dan pulled onto the road and stopped at the intersection, waited for the light to turn.

"God, I don't want to be here," she said.

"You have a car."

"But I don't have any fucking money, thanks to that fucking fuck." She picked at tan fuzz coming out of her slipper. "Green," she said, and Dan hit the gas. "I'm just going to steal it. From the hotel." She rolled the fluff between her thumb and finger. "Why not? They accused me of it when I didn't do it, so I may as well. They owe me."

"Because it's wrong."

"But who'll suffer? They won't even notice. Not right away. Besides, it doesn't really matter, anyway. Right?"

He said, "Where am I driving you?"

"The hotel, remember? That's where I left my car. It's like—It's seriously the only thing I have left that's mine." She stretched a foot to his side of the cab and nudged his thigh. "What do you think I should do? To Andy, I mean. What would you do if someone stole that much money from you and you couldn't leave the stupid town you grew up in, and you had to go back to living with your mother and sister? Oh, yeah, and they hate you."

She left her foot on his leg. He raised his elbow to keep his arm from resting on her shin.

"I don't know," he said.

"I could kill him."

"No, you couldn't."

"I really think I could." She took her foot from his leg and propped it back on the dashboard beside the other. "I don't mean it." She moved the toes of her boots together, apart. Together, apart. "But I could do it," she said. "Not to him, but to someone. I've always known that about myself. I could kill someone in self-defense and not feel a thing."

"In self-defense," Dan said.

"But, you know what? People kill people all the time for robbing their houses and call that self-defense. I don't see how what he did is any different. With that money I could have done anything I wanted until we all died from the asteroid, or from the Korean missiles they were talking about on the radio before, or whatever. I could have bought a brand new Mini Cooper."

"You would have thrown away that much cash on a car?"

She lifted her shirt halfway and pointed to her tattoo, then covered up again. She yawned. "No. I probably would have bought a cheap used one. But I was going to have fun, at least. I mean, I won *seventy-six thousand* one hundred and three dollars. That's more than what I'd make in four years at the hotel. It was the chance of a lifetime. Instead, he basically decided my life for me. I hate him."

Dan wondered if eliminating Jenny's escape cash was worse than kidnapping a woman passed out on red wine. He decided it was. "He did it because he loves you."

She looked at him, and then she laughed. "*That's* what love is?"

"Sometimes. Maybe. When it's passionate."

"Passionate about your loser, selfish self, maybe." She looked out the window. "If that's what it is, I don't want it."

Dan didn't know how to make her understand the complexities of desire and need, the power of impulses. He tried again to remember what he and April had talked about on the phone.

"Where are you going now?" Jenny said. "After you drop me off, I mean. You don't have any money, either, right?"

He said he didn't know what he was doing.

He didn't know what he could do. The tank was less than a quarter full, and he had nothing left. All that prevented him from incapacitating himself with panic was the possibility that tomorrow, or the day after, or the day after that, would never come. He reminded himself of that whenever he felt sweat threatening.

"We can go back together," she said. "After I get the money we need, I mean. We'll even take my car to save on gas. I don't want to go back alone." She smiled small and blushed and said not to take it the wrong way, but she liked him. Wouldn't it be fun, she said, to live his last days on the run with someone? "We'd be like Thelma and Louise. My mom watches that movie all the time."

He parked beside her snow covered car and let the engine run. Small flakes fell past the RV's flat windshield. Jenny unfastened her seatbelt and counted the cars in whispers. "Ten, eleven, twelve … . God. Busy today. Do you see Andy's car?"

"I don't know what it looks like."

"I don't see it. He's not here for his regular shift. I was sure he'd come straight here after you dropped him off. 'Hi. I'm back, Lovely Margaret, Super Ray. I'm so sorry. So sorry I did anything wrong or anything that you would disagree with even a little, tiny bit.'" She tucked the bottoms of her sweatpants into her slippers. "They'll let me back in if I apologize and they haven't hired anyone else, which they probably haven't." She leaned over the center console and kissed him, the tip of her tongue wetting his upper lip. "Will you think about it? It'll only take a few weeks for me to get the money." She jumped out of her seat and ran to the back, grabbed her bag, and said "Bye" before the door slammed. She sprang across the lot and pushed through the doors to the lobby, stomped the snow from her slippers, and said something to the woman behind the counter, her hands together. Pleading. Nodding, nodding, *Yes, yesyes*. She carried her bag past the counter and disappeared. The bathroom, Dan remembered.

The RV's engine knocked and rumbled. He turned it off and watched the manager walk through a doorway into the office behind the counter. When Jenny reappeared—sweatpants replaced with black slacks—he put on his coat and used the path to the hotel Jenny had made and went inside. Jenny looked back at the open office doorway and then beckoned him close with a curled finger. "You won't be able to park there unless you pay for a room."

He told her he would find somewhere else to go but that, first, he needed to borrow her car. She reached under the counter and brought out her keys. "You can brush off all the stupid snow." She whispered, "You should see the reservations. We only have two rooms left, the handicapped ones. I really think I'm—Dan. Wait. Come here." He leaned closer. She said, "I know I asked you this before, but do you really, honestly think we're going to die? I mean, really?"

"We're only eleven days into January. It could happen any time," he said.

"Okay. Then I'm definitely doing it. When I have enough, I mean it, I'm leaving." She listened for a moment, ear toward the open office door, and went on: "Are you coming with me or not? We don't have to go to Nevada, or even California, if you don't want to. We can go to Arizona. Or Mexico. Anywhere there's desert. It'll be so much fun. We'll take the same road they took in *Thelma and Louise*." Her eyes shined. She used her fingertips to push away hair falling close to her eyes and smiled. Dan wanted to squeeze her to him. What was it women had that could do that to a man?

The manager, Margaret, emerged from the back office carrying a deposit bag. She smiled at Dan. Her nametag read MANAGER. She walked behind Jenny, opened the register, dropped in a roll of quarters and slid a stack of ones under the spring-loaded arm, and pushed the drawer closed until it clicked. She said, "Evening," and went back into the office.

"We'll talk about it later," Dan said. "Okay?"

Jenny bit her cheek. "Mm … okay."

"How much gas do you have?"

"I filled up before getting Andy the day we left. Don't use it all."

TWENTY THREE

Dan turned onto his street and saw their house, then stopped short when he saw Nina's small figure in the driveway with a shovel. He hadn't expected her to be home at eight-thirty on a weekday morning. He crept closer and watched her push the snow across the driveway and heave it onto the lawn. He waited for her to look up and recognize him, and then realized that even if she did look up she wouldn't recognize the car. Unless she remembered it.

She stopped shoveling to push back her hat and Dan waved. She looked at him, yanked her hat back down over her ears, and after a moment waved back. She made a face Dan thought might be a smile, of some kind, and then wedged the shovel under a high pile of wet snow.

He lowered the window. "Hi."

She sniffed, wiped her nose with her mitten. "Are you lost?"

"I shouldn't be here. I know. I just—How's the cat?"

"What do you know about my cat?"

"Nothing. You're right." He turned off the engine. "It's none of my business." He opened the door. Nina took a step back. She adjusted her grip on the shovel and brought the handle to her chest.

"Would you rather I stay in the car?"

"Yes, please."

He closed the door. "I wouldn't have come if I didn't have to," he said. "I need—I need a little bit of money."

"You want to borrow money from me?"

171

"I don't need a lot," he said. "A couple hundred. Two. Three. Maybe four." She had it saved, he knew. And she could have used it to pay both the mortgage and the electric bill—she would probably have to, now—but they'd both agreed that savings shouldn't be used for bills unless absolutely necessary.

She squinted at him. "Do you just drive around neighborhoods looking for people you can ask for money? Is this something new you people are doing?"

"'You people'?"

"I'm sorry I can't help you. Maybe you'll find someone standing outside on the next block."

"Nina."

She did something with her eyebrows. It wasn't a look he remembered seeing before. "That's my name," she said.

"What?"

"Go away." She used the shovel to stab the air between them. "Go on."

"Nina, I don't have anywhere to go. I don't have any money. I lost it all in Vegas, and now I'm—"

"You went to Las Vegas?"

"Yes, and—"

"I—I just meant that if you're someone who has a gambling problem, you should probably stay away from those places, or … but there's nothing I can do for you. I don't have any money for you." She took a few backward steps and planted the shovel's blade between her feet. "Please go away."

"Nina. I can't. I told you. I have no money. Not five dollars."

She blinked, tightened and loosened her grip on the handle. "Wait here. Don't get out of the car or I'll call the police." She tossed the shovel on a snow mound and went inside. The woman who lived in the little white house salted her driveway. Dan wondered where her husband was. He looked across the street at the Belowskis' house. Carl watched her from an upstairs window.

Dan heard his front door slam. Nina walked down the driveway with her wallet held in front of her like a full glass of something. She brought it to the car, stopping short of his reach. "I have twenty-five dollars. You said you didn't have five." She pulled out a time-softened five dollar bill and held it up for him to see. "Now you do."

"Nina."

"Stop saying my name. And … and stop reading people's mailboxes."

"What? What are you talki—"

"Do you want it or not?"

"I want the twenty."

"Beggars can't be choosers."

"Oh, for Christ…" It was another debtor line, one collectors hated even more than blood and stones, and one he'd complained to Nina about over many dinners.

"Take it or leave it."

"Give it to me."

"Give it to you? Who do you think you are? You drive up out of nowhere, ask me for money—"

"I'm sorry, Neen. I'm just … I'm hungry. I'll take the five." He added, "Please."

She held it between them. He snatched it and set it in the passenger seat. "Thank you."

"You're welcome." She picked up the shovel and walked toward the house. "I really will call the police."

Dan closed the window and pulled away.

He bought a hamburger and ate in the restaurant's parking lot, staring over the hood at branches bending under snow and enjoying the quiet. When his phone rang, he hurt his wrist trying to get a look at the number but forgot about the pain when he saw that it was April.

"I don't know if this is the right thing to do," she said.

She told him she didn't enjoy the conversation they'd had when he called from his hotel room, but that she appreciated his honesty. She stammered, and she was not a stammerer. She laughed, sounding nervous, like a quiet girl being smiled at in English class by the boy in the back of the room. She said she appreciated the note. She wanted to talk again, she said.

"When?"

"How do you feel about tomorrow?"

"I have very strong feelings about tomorrow."

Before dropping off Jenny's car, he stopped at a gas station and used what was left of the five dollars for a candy bar and a small bag of chips for later. When he pulled into the hotel lot, Jenny was standing behind the glass doors with her purse over her shoulder, her puffy, coat-arms folded. Dan put the candy bar and chips in his pockets and brought Jenny the keys.

"Where've you been?" she said. "I've been off for half an hour."

"It's the middle of the day."

"For lunch," she said. "I only get forty-five minutes, so now I only have fifteen."

Dan apologized and told her he'd make it up to her. When she asked how, he asked her what she needed.

"A place to stay," she said.

"Sorry?"

"I won't bother you. You won't even know I'm there."

Without thinking, he said sure, she could stay in the RV.

And he knew immediately that he would have to find somewhere else to be.

In the many days in a row between leaving for and returning from Las Vegas, he'd learned that being bombarded by Jenny's emotional youth combined with her youthful energy and equally youthful passion for all things upon which passion could be heaped was more than he could handle.

He also had to think about the consequences of being discovered with a minor.

All that aside, even if he wanted to, he couldn't afford to stay in the Pace Arrow without her—or anyone's—help. But Jenny was getting a paycheck, and she could manage it while working her way up to long distance gas money.

"Really?" she said. "I was kidding. I didn't think you'd say yes. Really? I—I would just have to grab my stuff tonight. I never even unpacked. I could be there tomorrow." She stood on her toes and smiled, looking happier than he'd seen her since the casino. "Really?"

"Really."

Using the same cheerful tone she'd used with Andy earlier, she said, "So, we'll be, um, *living* together, or …?"

Her smile softened into one that was real and easy when he said he'd find another place to stay for a while. Until that moment, he'd been afraid he would have to be the one to let her down at some point, so her reaction surprised him. His expression must have revealed it, because she said quickly, "It's just—It's just that I've never been by myself, and I like you so much, more than I know I should, but …"

She went on to explain the difference between traveling to a destination together and living together. It would be a parallel move from one adult's house to another, she said in more words, all of them designed to soften the difference in their ages. When he told her that she could relax, that he understood, she asked if he would still come by.

He said, "I'll be around."

She tugged his sleeve and pulled him along until they reached her car. "Look." She opened her purse and showed Dan a cluster of tens and fives. "It's only about fifty dollars, but it's only been since Margaret left, and if I do this for two or three months … but I don't know, that seems too long. I was watching TV in the lobby this morning after you left and there was this show on the alien channel about that Farling guy. I wasn't sure I was going to do it—because what if I got caught?—but then, I mean, I can't just keep standing behind that computer. Not now."

"Right," he said. Something about what she'd said triggered the edge of a memory, one that may or may not have had anything to do with his phone call to April. It was becoming increasingly important to know before meeting with her what the two of them had talked about, or, more accurately, what he'd talked about. She had been open to seeing him. Eager, even.

"Dan? Hello? Something wrong?"

He told her.

"All you have to do is get drunk again. I read that somewhere," she said. "Anyway, I'll call Margaret and get her to let the RV stay one more night. I'll be here in the morning, okay?"

Dan took off his coat and twisted open the bottle and poured a glass. He wasn't in the mood to drink. He sat on the couch and put his feet up on the chair.

Cold.

He turned on the generator, checked the thermostat, and pulled the curtains closed. He saw, through the small wedge of glass not covered by curtain, a familiar car parked at the opposite end of the lot. A white exhaust stream poured from the tailpipe. Dan inched the curtain aside and looked hard. Nina. He waved, but she was looking down, leaning forward, possibly playing with the radio.

Dan put his drink on the floor and ran outside, stopping when she looked up. "Hey," he yelled, still some distance away. "What are you doing?"

The car lurched out of its spot and sped across the parking lot. As she passed, she looked at him—like he was crazy, he thought, or like he had been the one following her—and then she was gone.

He called her three times and left three messages: What was she doing? What did she want? Was she okay?

He called again and listened to her voice, the same recording they'd always had on one of the answering machines nobody used, anymore. He imagined her sitting in his chair with her grandmother's blanket on her lap while she watched TV. If he were there he would stack some logs and light a fire. He would lie on the couch—which was long enough at home for him to be flat on his back without his feet hanging over the edge—and listen to the crackles filling in the quiet pauses of sitcom conversations, silence neither of them had ever felt pressured to fill.

Three tall scotches and a packed duffel bag later he was no closer to remembering his and April's conversation. He let the counters and narrow passage guide him to bed.

As he dangled on the precipice of full sleep, a thought appeared behind his eyelids as words, capitalized and loud, and wouldn't dissolve to let him fall until he agreed, until he believed: the RV would become a replacement crutch if he retained ownership of it. He would stay, even with Jenny, who would let him. He would hide out in it for as long as he needed to because it was safe.

TWENTY FOUR

Bang. Bang.

"Dan? Hey, are you in there?"

Bangbangbang.

He pulled open the curtain. Light snow fell again, or still, on the parking lot. Headlights from the busy main road blinked through bare trees. The sky was a yellow-gray haze, part clouds and part parking lot lighting. He called out "Just a minute" and felt himself for shirt and pants, zipper zipped, before getting up to unlock the door.

Jenny's suitcase, not the same one she'd brought to Las Vegas but a bigger one, blue and shiny, wedged her in the narrow doorway. "I know I said I would wait until tomorrow, but it was one of those nights when the two of them decide to get together, and I'm the—I just didn't want to be there, anymore. I hope you don't mind that I came early."

Dan helped yank in her suitcase and threw it on the couch.

"I took everything I could fit." She sat down. "I'm sorry I woke you up so late. She said I couldn't go because I'm not eighteen, yet, so I had to wait until she was sleeping." Jenny brought her feet together and put her hands on her knees. "I should feel bad, right?" As she wriggled out of her coat, he saw her noticing his duffel bag on the kitchen floor. "Margaret said you have to leave tonight," she said. "I told her you would."

Dan sat in the chair across from her. He told her she could take the RV wherever she wanted to take it. It was hers, if she wanted it, and it was fully paid for. All she had to worry about was upkeep.

"Mine?" she said.

Yes, he said.

She launched herself off the couch and onto her knees in front of him. "Oh my god, of course I want it! This is the most perfect thing that has ever happened to me." The last of her words were muffled by his armpit as she squeezed him in a hug. When she pulled away to go back to her spot on the couch, he asked that, in return, she leave the keys to her car where he could find them whenever she wasn't using it.

She asked where he planned to stay, and he reminded her of the apartment building where she'd found him on the floor.

"With April?"

"Yes."

"Oh." She bit her cheek. Tucked her hands between her thighs.

"You're different here," he said.

"Here where? What do you mean?"

"Here. Connecticut."

"I know it. Why do you think I didn't want to come back?" She played with the zipper tab on her bag, sliding it an inch one way and back, *zipzip, zipzip.* "I just want to be like the women in celebrity magazines. What lives they live. Everything they do is interesting. Nothing for them is average."

"You think their lives are interesting because they aren't yours. To someone else, your life would be fascinating."

"Ha." She wiped her eyes and rubbed her hand on her jeans. "Anyway, it's hot. Can I turn down the heat?"

"It's your RV."

She squealed, hopped off the couch to adjust the temperature, and then sat again, legs and arms crossed. She made Dan think of a licorice whip.

"So you'll just come and take my car while I'm working?" she said.

"Only on the days I need it."

"I'm not going to be around for very long."

"No one will," Dan said. He smiled.

"That's not what I mean. What are you going to do for a car when I leave?"

He asked what her plans were. Was she taking the RV? Her car? Towing the car behind the RV?

She pulled at her hair. "Hm," she said. "Yeah. You're right. You know, all I thought about was gas, but I'd actually save money by traveling in this thing instead of my car, right? No hotels or apartments or anything. Oh my god! Deal. You can have my car after I leave."

"Let's just say I'll take care of it for you. Keep it running until you need it again."

Dan parked the Pace Arrow beside Jenny's car at the interstate rest stop outside of East Willington following a round-trip driving tutorial that had taken them three exits down the road. Jenny had watched him drive, leaning over to see how close he was to the lines on his side, observing the speedometer and expressing frequent surprise at how slow sixty-five felt.

"Think you can handle it?" He handed her one of the two keys Wexler had given him.

"Had you ever driven one of these before you got this one?"

"No."

"If you could do it, why couldn't I?" She climbed out of her seat and went to the couch for her bag. Dan, hungry, passed her on his way to the kitchen. She wedged past him and dropped the bag in the bedroom doorway.

While Dan microwaved a dinner, Jenny sat at the kitchen table and pulled loose bills from her purse. She carried them to the kitchen—maneuvering around Dan, who spun out of the way and sat at the booth—and opened drawers until she found the silverware. She spread the bills flat across the floral liner under the tray, which reminded Dan that Nina still needed money for the electric bill.

On her way out of the kitchen Jenny grabbed the half-empty bottle of scotch on the counter.

"Oh," she said, stopping. "Can I have some?"

Dan learned the two-step. Jenny said Andy had taught her on their first date. She held on tight to Dan's sides and giggled. When she took off her shirt and her body was absorbed by the darkness of the bedroom, he stood in the kitchen until she told him to follow.

TWENTY FIVE

The next morning, Dan rode with Jenny to the hotel. The lot was still abnormally full. She pulled the brake and gave him her keys and said any time he returned the car he should put them on the passenger-side front tire.

She rested her hand on the gearshift. "Hey, are you sure about … well, that woman? I don't *have* to have the place all to myself, you know." She paused. "She wouldn't even let you in when you were hurt, so if you really need to, you can stay with me."

"It's complicated."

"I hate it when people say things like that. I'm not ten. I probably understand more than you think."

"I know you're not ten." He moved her hair away from her eyes. "But you're not thirty-nine, either."

"So why do you keep fucking me, then? If I'm such a kid, I mean."

He had no answer, and she looked at him long enough for it to become uncomfortable before she got out of the car. He waited as she walked toward the entrance, reflections on the glass layered over the figure of Andy standing behind the counter. When he was sure she wouldn't turn back, Dan drove out of the lot.

Jenny had taken mostly tens. Dan pulled out all the bills and counted them. By the end of the first day, she'd stolen one hundred sixty dollars. It was nowhere near what she would need to start her trip. In a day or two, once he and April worked things out, he would return the money, but Nina needed some of it now. He folded two twenties and six tens into his wallet and returned the silverware tray. He wished she'd taken more twenties so the pile's thinness would be less obvious.

He brought the car back to the hotel, put the keys where Jenny had said to store them, and walked home.

Nina's car wasn't in the driveway. He considered leaving the cash in the mailbox, but he had no envelopes and didn't want some random mailbox thief to get it. He tried the front door, just in case. Locked, and too well sealed to slip the money underneath.

They had envelopes inside.

He walked around to the side of the house and pushed open the basement window. Bear stared at him from the floor, her brown eyes wide. She meowed, "*Rau-WOW*," the voice so oddly pitched and loud that Dan winced. "Shh!" He poked his hand inside and flapped it around until the cat ran across the room and around the corner to the stairs. He took off his coat and pushed it through, then climbed in and closed the window.

The basement looked the same. Nothing had been moved, added, or taken away.

He wondered where she kept the litter box.

One of his black socks lay small and crumpled in front of the water heater. He picked it up and put it in his back pocket. The refrigerator's ticking sounded through the floor. The furnace blasted on and the pipes whooshed air. These were the sounds that had kept them both awake their first week in the house. Later, he couldn't fall asleep without hearing the echo in the kitchen or the tapping of the furnace.

He followed the cat up the stairs. Dirt, dust balls, and some litter hugged the corners. He noticed his shoes were tracking wet prints, so he took them off and left them on a step before opening the first-floor door, a fresh hole sawed into it for a cat door. Without the litter box downstairs it didn't make sense. To let Bear catch cellar mice, maybe.

She had also finished painting the dining room. Not Dan's taste, but not offensive. For the living room, she'd bought more books—legal suspense thrillers, one on understanding cat language, and one on business and management—to fill the shelves. As he had suspected she would, she'd more fully moved into his recliner. A new floor lamp in the corner would, when turned on, drop light over it for reading. A thrift-store side table, edges worn and the top scratched and dented, pushed up against the arm.

She would set coffee or wine on the table while she read. And food, most likely.

A sandwich and a glass of milk. Grilled cheese, probably. Maybe a hot bowl of soup.

He went to the kitchen and opened the cabinet for something to eat, but she'd put the dishes where the chips used to be. He remembered the baking ingredients cabinet and opened it for glasses, took one out, and filled it with water. While he drank, he opened the glasses cabinet and found an open box of crackers. He grabbed a handful and re-rolled the plastic bag the way she had it, tucked the tab inside the slot the way she did, and returned it to the shelf between the rice and the stuffing. He looked over the breakfast bar into the living room. The TV had been moved to the opposite corner and she'd arranged knickknacks in front of the fireplace where there used to be a grate.

It didn't feel like his home.

The phone rang on the counter while he filled his glass with more water. He turned off the faucet and heard Nina's recorded voice saying to leave a message, and then a beep. The line clicked and a dial tone followed. He saw writing on the pad beside the phone and picked it up.

Howie for Dan Palace. Work? Jan. 9. Beneath that, *Thurs., Jan. 12: Valbon, 9a,* and *Syl, 10 a.*

The microwave and his watch said ten o'clock. He didn't understand how Nina would have time to meet with Sylvia at ten on a weekday.

He was halfway up the stairs, curious to see what changes she'd made there, when he heard a car in the driveway. He ran back down, taking the steps two at a time, and looked through the peephole. Nina. He hurried down the hall and picked up his shoes on the way down to the basement. He'd made it to the bottom of the stairs by the time he heard the front door close. Bear meowed—"Rau-WOW?"—and Nina said, "Hi, kitty," and, "Ooh, itchy face. Nix has the face itches. Ooh, scratch, scratch."

She'd renamed the cat.

Dan didn't like the name Nix.

He still held the water glass. He set it on a shelf beside a dusty shoebox. Across the basement, morning sun dropped through the high window and onto the utility sink, lighting up beige and white paint smears left over from when she and Dan had painted, in every room of the house, over her parents' mint-green walls and trim. "On the upside, we're really getting a head start on making the place ours," Nina had said from the floor, where she scrubbed paint dots from Dan's over-saturated roller off the tile.

He considered climbing out the window and knocking on the door to give her the money, but fitting through the window wasn't easy and the frame left such violent scrapes on his hips and spine that Jenny had asked if he'd been in a fight. If, instead, he called her and told her he was at the closest gas station, she would leave, and he could exit through the front door. He would run to meet her.

He dialed and heard the ringing upstairs. Her footsteps went into the kitchen and stopped. He picked a thick blob of latex paint off the faucet and rolled it into a ball. The machine picked up and Dan listened to her recording echo through the kitchen. At the beep, his mouth close to the phone, he said, "Nina."

The floor creaked overhead.

"Pick up. I know you're home."

The cat meowed and Nina's footsteps moved out of the kitchen, down the hallway, and up the stairs. Dan followed the sounds from below. When she still hadn't said anything, he hung up, put on his coat, climbed quietly to the main floor and slowly turned the knob. He poked his head through the opening to the kitchen and listened, hearing only soft noises upstairs.

"*Rau-WOW?*"

Bear watched him from the small foyer, where Nina could see her if she looked down. Dan froze, listened, and rapidly waved his hand at the cat until she skittered away. "C'mere, Nix!' came from upstairs, and he inched down the hallway to the door without breathing. He knocked on it twice, opened it loudly, closed it hard, and called "Nina? You left the door open, so I came—"

Her scream cut him off. He looked up and saw her leaning over the railing at the top of the stairs, one of her nicer necklaces dangling at the open neck of a new blouse. He held his hands out to show her they were empty, a reflex. "It's just me."

"Get out!" Loud and shrill, squirreling her eyebrows. "Who are you?" She gripped the twisted iron. "Get out! Get out get out get out!" She ran halfway down the stairs, then stopped, turned around, and ran back up until she reached the top. She stumbled into the bathroom and slammed the door. "Go away now and I won't call the police," she yelled.

The cat ran past Dan, up the stairs and into the spare bedroom. He went up, himself, and knocked on the bathroom door. "Nina."

"Go away," she screamed. Her voice shook. "I don't have anything you want."

"What are you talking about? Open the door."

"I'll call the police if you don't leave."

"And tell them what? My name is on the deed. This is my house, too."

She screamed again, louder than before, until it died out and was replaced by coughing.

"Are you okay?" He put his ear to the door. "Neen."

He heard another car pull into the driveway. From the narrow window at the end of the hallway he saw Sylvia closing her car door and tucking her keys in her coat pocket. He went downstairs to let her in.

Short brown hair curled out from underneath the folded-up flaps of her winter hat. Her eyes, dark and deep beneath a wide brim of golden sheepskin, were like Jenny's, big and brown. And alert, but with skepticism instead of Jenny's wonder. She didn't ask what he was doing there, even if she seemed surprised. Dan stepped aside to give her room to pass and asked if she'd noticed anything strange about Nina.

"Why? What's going on?"

He told her about the screaming, her threats to call the police.

"What did you do to her?"

"Nothing," he said. "I knocked, and she didn't answer. So I opened the door and came in." He told her again about the screaming.

"Is she mad at you?"

He was sure she was, he said, but this was bizarre. "She doesn't seem to know who I am."

Sylvia raised an eyebrow at him. She had done the same in what had seemed to Dan like a constant, hours-long arch when he'd first met her. During the dinner he and Nina had made in their small apartment, Sylvia had eyebrowed him over her glass. Every one of his gestures, every word he'd said, she'd treated as a cloak hiding a lie. She had with that eyebrow made him wonder whether there was something about himself he didn't know.

"Talk to her," he said. "You'll see. Or maybe she'll come out of it."

Sylvia climbed the stairs with Dan behind her and knocked on the bathroom door. "Nina."

They waited. When Nina didn't answer, Sylvia pounded on it. "Nina. Say something."

"How do you know my name?" she said. Her voice was even and low. Dan thought she sounded bored.

"What are you *doing*?" Sylvia said.

"I don't know what you mean."

"Okay." Sylvia sighed. "Well, are you ready to go to brunch?"

"With you?"

"Yes, with me."

"I don't even know who you are."

In a small voice that made Dan feel sorry for the woman he could never have imagined would inspire pity, Sylvia said, "I'm your sister."

Nina didn't answer. Sylvia looked at the door. Dan whispered in her ear that the lock was broken, and she reached for the knob and turned it. A sound of surprise came from inside the bathroom and Sylvia put her foot in the open door just in time to keep it from slamming shut.

Dan said he would wait in the living room.

Instead, once Sylvia was inside with the door closed, he sat at the top of the stairs and listened.

"You're faking," Sylvia said.

"I don't know what you mean."

"How did you get amnesia? Did you bump your head on something?"

"How would I know?"

The bathroom fell silent, and then Sylvia said, "What are you looking at?"

Nina said, "Your necklace. What does it say?"

"Damn it, Nina, you know what it says." Dan heard the window open and the flick of a lighter. "Is this because of Dan?"

"Dan who?"

"Dan your husband. The one sitting outside the door." A pause. "I hate to break it to you, but you can't pretend it away, Nina Lee."

Nina's "I don't know any Dan" barely made it through the door. She asked her sister for a cigarette.

"When did you start smoking?"

"I don't know," Nina said. "Didn't I always smoke?"

TWENTY SIX

Dan fingered one of the crackers he'd stuffed in his pocket before the three of them had set out together with Sylvia driving. Fishing boats bobbed in the choppy harbor and flag chains clanged their poles. Small white clouds, puffed, almost cartoonish in their perfect cloudness, moved fast across the sky. Dan pulled up his coat collar to cover his ears and stomped the pier to warm his feet.

"Remember this, Nina?" Her sister stood a few feet in front of her, arms spread wide like a game show host showing prizes.

Nina held blowing hair away from her face. "Sorry."

Sylvia swore and Dan stroked Nina's back, torn skin from where he'd picked at his fingers snagging on her fleece. "It's okay," he said.

She stepped away.

"I don't know what you two did, here, or where you went." Sylvia sniffed and flattened her hat's flaps against her ears. "Is this a good spot? Is this the part she'll remember, or was there somewhere else? You're going to have to take over."

He and Nina had been there once, and it wasn't for anything special. He'd offered it as a "memorable spot" when Sylvia had asked for one because he thought he and Nina should have one, and because—both of them homebodies who rarely traveled anywhere—it was the closest to one of those they had.

They'd come on an autumn Saturday. Not a birthday, not a celebration. Just a weekend Dan had been unusually restless and had wanted to get out of town. They'd had a room with a wall of windows overlooking a narrow, restaurant-heavy street.

New England really capitalizes on its quaintness, Nina had said over a bowl of restaurant chowder. Their table gave them a view of Bowen's Wharf. *Sixty dollars for that t-shirt with the boat on it? But I really want it.* She'd smiled and looked out the window between bites of white soup. *Too many people feed French fries to the seagulls. It's not good for them.*

Later that night, Dan had popped the champagne, a small, jolly bottle, and they'd toasted to Saturdays. Nina had taken a coaster from the coffee table and packed it in her bag the morning they left.

"We came here for our first anniversary," he said to Sylvia, but loud enough for Nina to hear. He watched her face, but she gave nothing away. "We'll bring her to the hotel," he said. He led them across the street, past the docks. Three seagulls bobbed on the ripples of the harbor. "Wait," he said, and Sylvia and Nina stopped. He pulled out one of the crackers and tossed it in the air. All three seagulls lifted off the waves and their wings beat against the wind. None caught the first one, but one of them spotted it on the ground and snatched it up and flew away. Dan threw another cracker in the air and a different gull caught it on the way down.

Nina watched silently.

"I love feeding the gulls," he said. "It's easier with French fries. They don't blow around as much."

Sylvia pulled her coat tight around her middle. "Are you finished?"

He held one out to Nina. "They look hungry, don't they?"

She took the cracker and tossed it in the air, watched as it was caught in an updraft by a yellow beak. She looked at him. "What fun." She smiled.

They walked through Queen Ann Square. "Nina loved it here," Dan said.

Nina used the thumb of her mitten to pull clinging hair from her eyelashes. "I don't see why."

"No memories?" Sylvia said.

"No."

When they reached the hotel, they stood in front of it, stomping and tightening in the cold, until Nina said nothing looked familiar.

Sylvia yawned. "I guess we leave, then," she said, already walking. "That was a productive two-hour drive."

Sylvia and Dan ate sandwiches in the kitchen. Nina ate hers in the living room in front of the TV. Dan had said he thought he should leave, but Sylvia had whispered that she thought he would do more good if he stayed.

Nina took slow, small bites of her sandwich and watched the screen. Dan made a second sandwich for himself and slipped it in his coat pocket.

"That's a leopard," Sylvia said. "That cat on the screen."

"Oh?" Nina said. "How do you spell it?'

Sylvia shrugged. "L-e-o-p-a-r-d."

Dan saw Nina smile and filled his mouth with sandwich to hide the one he felt sliding into place. Sylvia raised her eyebrows at him. *Faking*, she mouthed.

"What's the cat's name?" Sylvia said.

Dan said "Bear" and Nina said "Nix. N-y-x. Come here, Nyx." Bear kept drinking her water. "She's thirsty," she said.

Dan finished his sandwich and pulled the milk out of the refrigerator. He took a glass from the cabinet and set it on the counter.

"How long has it been since we've lived together?" said the side of Nina's head. "She—Sylvia—said you moved out."

"It hasn't been very long."

Nina took a bite of her sandwich and set the rest of it on the plate. Dan saw her jaws work while she chewed, the joints flexing. "That must be how you know where things are."

He tried to remember what used to be in the cabinet that he could have been looking for: not flour, not baking powder or baking soda, not sugar. Salt. "I was looking for salt. It used to be up there. Do you want some milk?"

She shook her head. Slowly. *No.*

He pulled out another glass and closed the cabinet. He poured some milk and brought it to the living room and set it in front of Nina. He'd never seen her have a sandwich without it.

"Where are you living, now?" Sylvia said. There was no expression on her face when she added, "With April?"

"April," Nina said. "Who's that?" She pulled a strip of meat from between her pieces of bread and dangled it over the floor. "Come here, Nyx."

Dan said, "I bought an RV."

Sylvia laughed. It was a quick, loud, chirp of a sound. *Ha!*

Dan checked his watch. Jenny would be leaving work in an hour, and he needed to get the car for his meeting with April. "I have to get going."

Nina twisted on the couch and looked at him. Her cheeks and forehead were still fresh and bright from all the wind and cold, as if it had sanded away a layer of winter gray. "Bye … Dan. Right?"

She didn't appear sad, or wounded, or even angry. The level of nothing behind her eyes could almost have convinced him that she truly didn't remember him, that he was once again every bit the stranger he'd been to her when they'd met in the elevator one fall morning eight years ago. While most of the female janitorial staff had avoided making eye contact with him—supplies on the cart would suddenly need organizing, or their smartphones would require an improbable amount of concentration—Nina had smiled at him, said, "Hi," and asked, "What floor?" before pushing the button with a gloved finger.

Right now, with no obvious pain owning her soft mouth and hooded eyes, she just looked like Nina, and he had missed her face. The compulsion to go to her was almost overpowering. "Right."

"I'll walk you," Sylvia said.

They didn't talk until they were outside and Dan remembered the money in his wallet. He gave it to Sylvia and explained what it was for.

"So, what do you think about all this?" she said.

Dan said he didn't know. "But I think maybe it's better this way." He zipped his coat. "Her forgetting."

Sylvia wrapped her arms around her t-shirt, an advertisement for a wildlife organization, its cartoon koala bear tugging at a eucalyptus branch. "What do you mean?"

"If this is what she needs to get over things."

"Jesus." She squinted at him, smiled in a way that wasn't happy. "You *are* an asshole." She walked back to the house and took the stairs slowly, opened the door and closed it—solidly—behind her.

TWENTY SEVEN

Dan drove. Jenny, done for the day, opened her purse and pointed inside and said, "Look."

A messy pile of green.

"That's a lot," he said. "They'll catch you." He'd wanted to skim, too, when he was younger. Sixteen and working at the video store. Was there a kid behind a register who hadn't? But as much as he'd enjoyed the stolen book—both the act of stealing it and the satisfaction of having stolen it—the thought of going through with anything like that again had made his teenage bowels churn.

"Not the way I'm doing it."

"What about the camera?"

"I turned it." She set her purse on the floor. "I don't work by myself enough, though. Andy comes in, and then he's always around."

He asked her how much she'd managed to take, so far.

"Total?" She looked out the window and shrugged. "I don't know. It's only been two days, but there's a conference, which is just what I needed. So, maybe two fifty? A little more? I don't know. I'm trying not to count so I don't get impatient. I'm just collecting. I'll count it after a week and see where I am. I know it's not seventy-six thousand dollars." She played with her expensive coin purse, clipped to the handle of her regular purse. "I should be glad he took it, you know? Because if he hadn't, who knows how long I might have been with someone who could do such a thing?"

It made odd sense. Dan said, "Mm."

"I know I've said some things and that I act a certain way around him, but I did love him. Or … whatever."

Andy was thoughtful, she said. Tender. Protective. Funny, "believe it or not." And responsible—or, she had thought so, until Las Vegas.

Dan joined a pack of slow-moving vehicles, speed adjusted for the sudden heavy snow. At thirty-five miles per hour, they were keeping up with traffic. It was twenty-five after four.

He would be late.

A yellow Renault that looked like April's passed on his right in a faster moving lane. He tried to get a look inside, but it was dark and the window was spotted with melted snowflakes. He pressed the gas, said, "Sit back," and used his arm against Jenny's upper chest to push her against her seat. "Get out of the way." He strained to look past her.

"What? What is it?" Jenny said. "An accident? What happened?"

April pulled farther ahead, leaving an opening behind her car. Dan spun the wheel and pulled into it. The snow was thick and new enough to provide traction for braking before his bumper would have cracked into hers. He honked the horn—*Ho-ho-ho-hoooooonk!*— and rolled down the window. He stuck his face into the cold air and shouted, "April!"

Jenny slid down in her seat. "Oh my god, what are you *doing*?"

"April!" he yelled again. His flashing brights bounced off the hatchback's rear window.

"Will you stop it?" Jenny said. "This is so embarrassing."

Dan flashed his brights again, screamed her name into traffic, and read the bumper sticker spotlit by his headlights: SHUT UP HIPPIE.

Dan eased off the gas and looked for an opening in the center lane. He slammed his palm against the steering wheel.

"Watch out!" Jenny said, her finger pointed at a large pickup truck slowing in front of them.

He pumped the brakes, useless on the slick spot, pressed his head against the headrest, and waited for impact and pumped and pumped. "No no no no no," he said, pumping, pumping.

Traffic moved forward.

No impact.

He breathed.

His hands were wet. He wiped them on his pants and shifted into fourth gear.

"If she makes you like this, living with her should be really exciting."

Dan parked next to the RV with ten minutes to spare, giving him time to calm down. Bright headlights filled the rearview mirror and he flipped the lever to dull the glare. The vehicle parked a few spaces away with no cars between them.

"Um," Jenny bit a fingernail, "you can stay the night if you want. I know I was weird about us staying here together, but that was just about living together, the idea of it. But we can be friends who ... who ... you know."

Her face gave away more than she probably wanted it to. "Jenny," he said, "are you stupid? Do you *want* to get hurt?"

She looked at him with those eyes. Those big, brown eyes too young to be glazed with the kind of protective barrier he saw there now, the one that hadn't been there before.

Andy.

"I ..." She closed her arms tighter around her purse. "I don't—"

"Stop."

She wiped her eyes and reached for the door handle. "I didn't even do anything. You're the one who drove us h—"

"Shh." It wasn't her face, but her hair he saw—pulled back tight, the long ponytail—in the window of the car a few spaces away. He whispered, "Get down."

"No." She pulled the handle and Dan reached for her coat, but she was too fast. She slammed the door and ran for the RV. He was afraid Nina might chase her. It wasn't something he thought would be characteristic of her, but she was being anything but the Nina he thought he knew.

She didn't. Instead, she sat in her car looking at Dan. When she turned away, he saw Sylvia, leaning forward to look at him. She held up a cup of coffee in a "cheers" and then leaned back again.

He got out of the car and kicked toward them through the snow. Their faces were pale circles watching him from behind the window. He knocked on Nina's door and said, "Put it down." He mimed rolling it down with a handle.

It slid down. "I'm sorry," she said. "Syl … via … thought it would hel—"

"You followed me before," he said.

Sylvia's head tipped low so they could see each other. One of her hat strings swayed against the emergency brake handle. "She thought if she saw where you lived she might remember something." She looked around. "Is this where you live?"

"For now."

"Who's the little girl with the big boobs?"

"She's no one. I'm helping her out."

"I thought you were after April. How many of these do you have?"

Nina said, "This isn't working. I want to leave."

"It was your idea," Sylvia said.

"And now I want to leave. Okay?" The window started to slide up and Sylvia said, "She's too young, Dan, even if the world really *is* ending," before it closed. Nina backed out of the space and pulled away, driving deliberately past the Pace Arrow to the on-ramp.

The RV's curtains were open, the lights on behind them. Dan knocked on the door and wasn't told to come in. He tried the handle, found it unlocked, and went inside.

Jenny sat on the couch in sweatpants and a sweatshirt, her body in a tight ball. The window closest to where he'd been talking to Nina and Sylvia was open just enough for sound to carry in. Her nose and eyes were red and streaks of paler skin emerged where makeup had been scraped away by tears. "I don't know why people hate me," she said, the words muddled by slime clinging to her lips, distorted by a stuffed-up nose.

He tore a paper towel from the roll in the kitchen and handed it to her. "People don't hate you." He sat beside her. "I didn't think it was any of their business." He waited while she wiped her face. "Do you want me to stay?"

She shook her head, tilted down so he couldn't see her. She said she was embarrassed, and that it was less about him than it was about everything. She told him it was okay to leave, and then asked him if he would, please.

"Pick you up for work in the morning?"

Jenny blew her nose and said, "Yeah."

Deep tire tracks led away from the line of garages attached to April's building. A fresh set of footprints made a trail from the front door to April's stall. Still, he went up and knocked.

From the couch, he heard the bedsprings in the back creaking and the sheets rustling, Jenny tossing and turning. She whispered "Dan?" and he pretended not to hear.

He had been fourteen minutes late getting to April's. He remembered, now, her intolerance for tardiness. And then he wondered whether that was true or a detail about her he'd just created. He thought he should know the difference.

A hand caressed his chest and began the slide down his stomach, smooth nails tracing a wide trail. He grabbed her fingers. "I don't feel well."

"But maybe this could make you feel better."

"No," he said, and to soften it, "Not tonight."

She pulled her hand away and sat on the floor. "You're not sick," she said. "I think it has something to do with me. Would you tell me? If it did, I mean?"

He suddenly remembered the thought that had kept him awake. Here he was, just as he knew he'd be, and even after relinquishing ownership of the Pace Arrow.

He imagined the quiet of the basement, comfortable enough as long as there was plenty of padding between his body and the floor, a kitchen and living room and full refrigerator just up the stairs.

Jenny asked again what was wrong and Dan threw off his blanket.

TWENTY EIGHT

The windows were blocked with white. He heard the painful scrape of metal on pavement, Nina's grunts, and the *fwop* of the load landing somewhere near the house. She was leaving for work later this morning than she used to, but she'd left an hour earlier the day before. Her hours had typically only been this erratic when Valbon needed her to replace a no-show or help with training, but she'd never worn nice clothes to do that. On one of his daytime voyages upstairs he'd come across her cleaning clothes in the laundry basket. They were still there the next day.

He grabbed a cracker from the stack he'd been hoarding on the shelf, a collection amassed over the last six days he'd stayed in the basement while trying to get in touch with April. She'd not answered a call, not returned a message. He'd driven to her building twice, but knocks had gone unanswered.

Time passed slowly when Nina was home and he was confined to the basement. So slowly he'd almost walked up the stairs more than once to show himself to her and assert his right to the house. When he played out the scene—her screaming, frightened; her admitting to faking amnesia and crying; her admitting to faking amnesia and screaming; her looking at him one more time the way she had from the living room, as if she had no feelings for him at all—he would change his mind and find something to do, some way to keep himself busy in the basement where it was quiet and where he had space to himself, and where, now and then, Nyx would visit. To pass time, he would wet the straggling black sock in the sink and use it as a rag to clean the shelves where he kept his food. He rearranged. He wiped layers of dust and grime from the windows and told himself to remember to buy a couple of books.

Dan pulled up his jeans—loose around his waist, these days—and bent to pet the cat, who trailed him up the stairs.

He followed Nina's noises and found her out back, not dressed for work. From a distance, he watched through the window as she maneuvered the shovel on the lawn, around the wood she'd been pounding into the grass while the temperatures had been high. When she stopped, he readied himself to hide, but she just adjusted her mittens and started again. He went to the kitchen.

She'd gone grocery shopping a few days before. There were plenty of sealed containers and cartons he'd have to wait for her to open before he could take anything, but some she'd already snacked on: a bag of his favorite cheddar chips, a netting of tangerines, a box of granola bars. Dan grabbed a handful of the cheddars, two tangerines, and a granola bar and brought them downstairs to add to his growing pantry.

He drank some water from the utility sink faucet using the glass he'd never remembered to return, then sat cross-legged on the floor and closed his eyes. He made himself imagine the end of the world, whether Farling's or any other. It was an activity he'd turned into a daily meditation.

Today it was a silent end, something mysterious originating at the edges of the universe, a phenomenon even cosmologists hadn't considered. It would arrive at Eastern Standard nighttime, engulfing the planet while he slept.

Yesterday, it had been a sneak attack. Nuclear waves shattering metal and stone in a series of explosions.

He didn't know what it would be tomorrow.

And then he reminded himself, as he did every morning in his spot on the floor, that there was no tomorrow. Imagining no tomorrow, accepting it, was more difficult than fearing it. Accepting it meant dismissing hope, but his fear couldn't seem to separate itself from hope. Hope implied the possibility of an alternative, and that invited complacency.

Dan's phone vibrated and he pulled it out of his back pocket. A text from Jenny: *911.*

He dialed. Jenny picked up after the first ring. Without saying hello, she told him Margaret had called from the hotel about a guest who hadn't been registered in the computer, but who, somehow, was there to check out that morning.

"I'm busted," she said. "I was going to be the one to check him out. But there's all this stupid, *stupid* snow and the interstate's closed, so Margaret came in, instead. She lives, like, two blocks away from the hotel. I can't even get out of the rest stop."

Dan asked if she might be able to explain away the room as some kind of mistake.

Her heavy breathing—animal, bull-like—into the phone tickled his ear. "Yeah," she said. "I guess. I could just call back and say something. I'll say I don't remember him. He could have broken in, right?"

"Or," he said, "you could try something that might actually wor—"

She hung up without saying goodbye.

Dan wriggled his fingers at the cat and pet her when she came close. He'd found the litter box on one of his walks around the house, tucked inside a closet in the spare bedroom on the second floor. Nina kept the folding doors open a crack, just wide enough for the cat to squeeze through.

Dan's phone vibrated. A call, this time.

"Um ..." Jenny's voice broke and Dan thought he heard something else. "They—"

"Hold," he said, his voice low. It came again. The floorboards, creaking over his head.

Jenny whispered, "What is it?"

Dan cupped his hand over the phone and his mouth and said, "Shh ..."

Her weight shifted from the hallway to the kitchen where he heard the refrigerator open, and then close. More floorboard noise across the living room. The back door opened, closed.

"Okay," he said.

Jenny said, "Anyway. It, um … it turns out they do have more than one … more than one camera." She was crying. "How am I supposed to get more money, now? I'm never getting out of here, am I?"

Margaret had initially sounded like she might consider believing her, Jenny said—"The whole break-in thing could have worked because these doors are old. They don't close all the way when you let them go, the way regular hotel doors do."—but the guest had said he remembered Jenny from check-in.

Jenny said, "Margaret said he said I have 'a substantial chest.' Who says that? Why would someone describe someone that way? 'Oh, yes, ma'am, I remember the robber. He had blond hair, blue eyes, and a big, enormous dick.' Because that's helpful, right? I remember that room one-thirty-two guy, too. You know what he looked like? He looked like someone who was too cheap for a regular room and took a handicapped room, instead, even though we only have two and he's not handicapped. What if someone checked in who needed the bars on the bathtub and toilet? It's a ten dollar difference. That's it."

Dan asked what they got on camera.

Jenny said, "Everything."

He asked if Margaret knew where she lived, and Jenny said the last residence they have on record is her mother's house.

"And my mom doesn't know where I am, now, either. I haven't called her since I left."

He heard the cabinet doors on Jenny's end closing, closing. He said, "What about Andy? Does he know where you are?"

"He asks, but I don't tell him." The squeak of couch springs and Jenny's exhale. "Anyway. I can't go back, but I can't stay here, either.

They went over the video and matched all the guests I actually checked in with the ones who showed up at the counter. The times and dates are recorded on the computer, you know. Plus, they went into the safe and counted the money."

"How much have you taken?"

"I told you I don't count it every day. Four hundred, maybe. Five?—What? Do you think that's—I wasn't going to take that much so fast, but it just got easier and easier. Andy's been sick, so I had all that time alone. And they didn't notice when I took a little, so I took a little more. And yesterday was really busy, and it's never busy on Mondays, so I checked in, like, ten people without actually checking them in. Margaret never works on Mondays, either. That's her day off. So there was no way I was going to get caught. There was *no way*."

She'd been thinking again about California, she said, because Andy said he thought she would do well on reality TV. "As soon as this stupid snow stops, I'm just doing it. I'll tell you where I'm not going—Canada."

The last time he'd come home after checking April's, Jenny had dropped him off. She had the car with her at the rest stop.

He said, "I'd like to see you before you go."

"You liar. You want the car."

"I'm not lying."

She was quiet.

He said, "I'll see you when the snow stops and the roads are clear." He didn't hear anything outside and wondered what Nina was doing.

"I wish you could come over now," Jenny said. "It's so quiet out here. Spooky. And I want some pretzels, but there's no way I'm going into the rest stop by myself."

"Why not?"

"Are you kidding? A girl alone in a deserted rest stop?"

"If it's deserted …"

"You never know with crazy people. They could be anywhere." Dan heard a dull click over the phone. Another. Nail-biting. She said, "What am I going to do out here all day?"

Dan said he was sure the plows would be by soon. Jenny said she hoped so, because the more she thought about how alone she was, the scarier the trees and the silence and the emptiness behind the rest-stop windows.

"It's morning. It's light. You have nothing to be afraid of."

"You're not a girl," she said. "There's always something to be afraid of."

TWENTY NINE

Dan lay on the floor with the cat on his chest. He followed Nina through the house by listening to her movements upstairs. Back and forth, back and forth. Kitchen, living room, brown room, hallway, kitchen, garage, kitchen. Up the stairs and down the stairs. No phone calls, no words. It occurred to him how little speaking people did when they were alone. She had woken that morning and had spent the six hours since living her life without saying anything. If not for the call from Jenny that morning, he, too, would have been silent all day. He wondered how long it would take to forget how to make sounds or use the tongue and lips to form words. "Ahhh-ooo-waaah," he said, just loud enough for his voice to be a voice. He grimaced, puckered, and exercised his tongue by rolling it around inside his mouth.

At three o'clock, he called April. As it had all week, his call went to voicemail. He waited for the beep. He said, "It was just fourteen minutes."

He hung up.

The day before, he'd called at two o'clock. Standing at the living room window while Nina was at work, Carl's car gone and the old couple gripping the railing on the way down the porch stairs, he'd said, "I'm convinced my life isn't my life without you in it."

Sunday, he'd called at one-thirty. Without naming Jenny, he'd explained that "someone had needed help" and that he'd had no choice but to be late.

Saturday's call had been placed after too little sleep, his bones sore from rolling around: "What happened on the train doesn't happen to everyone. It would be irresponsible not to … We have to give it another chance."

Friday, he'd called Howie. The first time Howie called his cell phone—early that same morning—Dan hadn't previously thought to turn the phone to VIBRATE and was midway through urinating in the utility sink when it rang. Nina had been home, the house quiet.

It had not been the tidiest run a man had made across a room.

Instead of answering, Dan had pushed at all the buttons until the phone silenced. Only one full ring had released into the basement, but he'd been sure Nina had heard it and he'd listened for five minutes from a dark corner near the water heater before believing it was safe to come out. He'd used one of his t-shirts to clean up the rug as well as he could.

Later, after Nina left for work, he'd returned Howie's call.

"You coming back?" Howie said.

"Is that why you keep calling my house?"

"Your wife says she doesn't know who you are."

"How did you get this number?"

"She gave it to me." He coughed. "Don't ask me to make sense of it."

Dan said he wouldn't be back.

"You're the best we had," Howie said. "Head cases aren't responding to these threats from the new kids who don't even know what 'can't squeeze blood from a rock' means. We're losing money. Speaking of money, you get a new job?"

Dan said he did, and that it was called living.

Howie snorted. "How's the pay?"

"I'm not coming back," Dan said.

"We need you to train the new class. These kids, they keep getting their feelings hurt, give up every time. And, as it is, you still owe two weeks. You didn't tell anyone you were leaving."

"It's not a good job. People leave all the time without notice."

"That's true for most. You got me, there. But it's been a good job for you. And besides, you're not that kind of person."

Dan said, "No."

Howie said, "Damn it." He said, "It was me that got the bonuses raised when you made a thing of it, remember. And you remember how much you made in bonus that year and every year since. Come on, now, Dan. What else have you got to do?"

The call had ended with Dan trying to explain exactly what it was he had to do and why, with Howie laughing and saying, "You're one of the crazies, you know that," and, "I'll see you when you run out of money. I can hold your job for a while, yet. Good luck to you, you damn nutbird."

The basement window was still buried, and Dan couldn't tell whether the snow was still falling. He didn't need to know for any particular reason, and still the desire to know was overwhelming. But Nina was home, and he was stuck.

He tapped his chest and the cat walked over from a dark space under the shelves and climbed on.

It was dark, ten o'clock according to his phone, when he opened his eyes. He heard TV noises upstairs. The cat was gone. He felt around for his gloves and put them on, then made his way to the wall and climbed his hands up the cinderblocks to find and open the window. The snow was so hard-packed against it that not even a chill came in. It would have to be pulled inside if he wanted to get out.

He made a pile on the floor that, for the most part, could be scooped in his arms and brought to the sink. The rest melted into a dark circle on the rug.

THIRTY

The streets were smooth and white. Light flakes, remains from the day's dumping, floated in circles. It was the same time of night, the same kind of untouched winter, that years ago he and April had watched the snow falling outside the narrow bedroom window of his rented attic apartment. He remembered her fingers playing with the waist of his briefs, tracing the sensitive skin beneath, and her breath on his cheek when she said, "Oooh, beautiful," before climbing out of the blankets. He reached for her thigh, but she was already at the window, close to the cold glass and very much exposed to anyone on the street who might think to look up.

"Take the blanket," he said, but it was chilly, so he picked up his t-shirt from the floor, instead. "Take this. Here." He tossed it at her. It hit her arm and fell, and she looked at him and smiled.

"I'm going to brush the snow off your car windows," she said. Goosebumps dotted her stomach and chest. "Want to come?"

Dan pulled the covers to his neck and said, "Out there?"

"Yes, 'out there.'" She picked up his shirt and he watched her body stretch as she raised it over, and then pulled it around, her head. It covered her to mid-thigh, and sleeves that were short on his arms reached past her elbows.

"Maybe later," he said.

He stayed in bed while she slipped into jeans and boots. She left with his t-shirt hanging below the elastic waist of her coat and thudded down the stairs. He hoped it wouldn't be long before she'd be back in bed.

He waited five minutes, then raised himself on an elbow to look out the window. In a cone of light under a street lamp, April pushed at the snow on the roof of his car with her arms and the snow brush. Some, she pulled down toward her and then jumped away to keep it out of her boots. He could hear her laughter and squeals through the glass.

He lay back down and waited another few minutes, then sighed, pulled himself out of his underwear, and masturbated to the image of her standing shirtless by the window. By the time she returned he'd already cleaned himself off with another t-shirt he found on the floor and was on his way to sleep when she took off her clothes and climbed in with him. "Are you sleeping?"

"Mm," he said.

"Did you see me?"

"Of course."

She kissed his cheek. "I loved knowing you were watching. Did you see what I wrote?"

Had he not looked out the window at all, he knew, she'd be offended. Not quite as offended as she would be to know he'd started watching and then stopped. He said, "M-hm."

The bed bounced and her knee pressed against his thigh. He opened his eyes. She was studying him, her head propped on her palm. "Did you even look outside at all, Dan?"

"Yes. I already—Yes."

"What did you see?"

"I love you," he said, hoping to distract her.

A lucky guess.

She pressed her body to his.

It didn't take much to wake him up again.

Dan looked back at the house to make sure Nina hadn't turned on any lights after a noise he might have made, then felt his back pocket again for his phone—still there—and pushed through the snow to the end of the road, where he hoped to find plows had been through.

They hadn't, but there were tire tracks to follow to Main Street, and he could see that it, at least, had been cleared.

He called Jenny and asked if she'd been able to get out, yet.

"The plows came through almost right after we got off the phone," she said. "I would have left, but you said you wanted to see me first, so I—I guess you want my car, now."

The gas station down the street was open. He told her where it was and said he'd be watching for her.

"You're so thin," Jenny said. They sat in their usual spots, her on the couch, him on the chair. An old, loose-knit cardigan had replaced her usual snug sweater. A large green pendant lay bright against her black tank top. Her jeans were faded and torn. When she looked away from him, when all he saw were her clothes and her hair, she could have been April.

He said, "You look pretty."

She touched her sweater with one hand, her necklace with the other. "Do you like it? I see people who dress this way, and I always think they look so comfortable. Not just because the clothes are ratty and old and soft, but in their hearts. Like they don't care what anyone else thinks about them, and like they think and say things that mean something. They're the kind of people other people remember."

"I think you're the kind of person people remember."

"Yeah, for these." She cupped and bounced her breasts, then pulled her sweater closed. "Do you think when you wear someone else's things, you can sense them, in a way?" She reached for her pendant and rubbed it with her thumb. "Like the woman who owned this necklace. Maybe she was the kind of woman who … she liked to give hugs, and she was accepting. And warm. And … and maybe I would feel that. The psychics on TV get information from people's stuff."

"I don't know."

She laughed without smiling and went into the kitchen. "Well, a lot of different people probably owned all the things I'm wearing, so

I guess that could be pretty scary." She opened a cabinet and said she was making a late dinner and asked if he was hungry. He pulled a sandwich from his pocket and set it on the counter before taking off his coat.

"Oh my god, is that peanut butter and jelly?"

She used her finger to wipe jelly or peanut butter off the bread's crust. She smeared it on the top layer of bread and took another bite. "Hey, Dan?"

"Yes." He got up when the microwave timed out and brought a cup of hot noodles back to the living room and sat across from her. A chunk of a peanut butter nut clung to the corner of her mouth.

"Do you think we could," she looked at the ceiling, "… um … I guess—This is so embarrassing, and I feel like you're going to think—Well, it's not like it's going to kill me, and nothing matters, anyway, right?"

He had forgotten a fork.

"It feels so free to know that, you know?" She had one small bite left of her sandwich, but she set it on the paper towel on the arm of the couch and rubbed crumbs off her hands. She closed her eyes tight and said, "Could we maybe just be together one more time before I go?"

At the same time, he said, "I have to ask to borrow a little bit of money."

Jenny opened her eyes.

Noodles still in hand, Dan got up and went to the kitchen. He opened the silverware drawer. The tray, sitting higher than it had before, wobbled on her earnings. He grabbed a fork, closed the drawer, and stirred the noodles on the way back to his chair. "Not a good idea," he said.

"Being together or giving you money?"

The honest answer was both, but he needed the money. "Sleeping together."

"Did you think it was a bad idea before, or just now?"

"Legally, always," he said, but it had been Nina's reaction to her, Nina's knowledge of her, that had changed things. When he'd left Nina, it wasn't so he could be with some young girl, as Nina might now think. He was spending his time, in bed and otherwise, with the wrong person.

Dan burned his tongue on the noodles. He spit them back into the cup and stirred, then blew on the next forkful before putting it in his mouth. He watched Jenny over the cup. She ate half of the remaining sandwich bite and looked at the floor.

She said, "I'll pay you."

In a string of seconds Dan couldn't begin to count, all of which passed in silence, he didn't even taken a breath to say no. He didn't tried to say anything. No one had ever offered to pay him for sex, before. She had struck him dumb.

"I feel like I should say, 'Oh, I'm just kidding.' But I don't feel that way at all," she said. "It's like I don't even care. If I give you fifty dollars and you feel like you have to at least kiss me out of guilt, or something, the rest will just happen naturally and it won't be like I had to pay you for it at all."

He found himself thinking that he would need a lot more than fifty dollars. For gas and food alone.

He tried to catch one of three floating peas on his fork. Nina didn't buy much microwaveable food, anymore. Nothing frozen, nothing ready-to-heat like the soup and noodles in a cup. In the refrigerator he would see snow peas and green beans in twisted cellophane bags, real garlic cloves in white nets. Chicken breasts defrosting under plastic wrap. All for last meals he'd never get to eat. With Jenny's money he could put something besides stolen crackers and sandwiches on the basement shelves, just enough to last until he got April.

Jenny went to the kitchen and pulled a bottle of water from the refrigerator. "I bought three cases a few days ago, just in case. What if this is the start of an ice age? Tucker Farling said the asteroid will be a mile long, and the one that caused the Ice Age—or might have, anyway, because they don't know for sure—was just half a mile bigger. I looked it up. It was called Altesian or Elatin, or something like that." She twisted off the top and brought it to the living room, stopping midway to stare out the window. "But if I thought it might really happen, for real, I mean, wouldn't I be hoarding gas and propane?" She flopped on the couch and folded her feet under her thighs. "What if *nothing* happens?" Her phone chimed. Dan poked at his soup while she pulled it out of her pocket and looked it, then set it beside her on the couch. "Margaret. She wants to 'discuss the situation.' She said before that she wouldn't fire me, but she wants the money back." She looked at him with her mouth in the small circle Dan was learning communicated anything from fear to defiance. "I could just go be a truck stop whore."

One of the peas stuck in his throat and he coughed.

"Why not?" she said. "It's just sex. And it's my body. If I need money, what's the big deal? If they're dirty or sweaty or drugged-up, or whatever, all I have to do is take of my clothes, close my eyes, and fake it."

Jenny was too inexperienced for this game, too young to understand he had no reason to truly care, though he did. He said, "That's right."

"I'm serious," she said.

"I believe you."

She put the final bit of sandwich in her mouth and talked around it. "How many truckers do you think I could do in a day?"

He knew she wanted him to be protective, a concerned father figure, but it wasn't something he could offer long-term, and he didn't want to give her anything he would have to take away. So he told her he estimated she would spend fifteen minutes on oral sex and about the same on traditional. Assuming she took a lunch break, he said, and in the unlikely event that she was the only whore at the truck stop and that the trucks rolled in steadily, she could count on about thirty-two jobs every day. At twenty to sixty dollars for oral sex and two hundred for intercourse, figures he remembered from a special he and Nina had watched with some horror, her earnings could be as low as six hundred a day or as high as sixty-four hundred. The top figure, he told her, wasn't realistic, but if she worked hard and managed to evade the police and the sex traffickers undoubtedly trolling the parking lot, she would have enough to get to California in no time.

Jenny took a sip of water and twisted the cap back onto the bottle. "Anyway, I'm not going to meet with her."

"Don't do it."

"I just said I'm not."

"That's not what I mean. Don't.—Jenny."

Jenny looked at him, and then she looked down at the bottle. She scraped a fingernail against the cap's narrow ridges. When she looked up at him again it was with a thick tear glaze in her eyes. She set the bottle beside her on the couch and got up, walked over to Dan, and sat side-saddle on his lap. She hugged him for a long time.

They were back in their seats, she folded up on the couch and he on the chair with one of her bottles of water. He asked what time she was leaving, and she said she hadn't made a plan, that she would start the trip when she woke up. The gas tank was still full from a post-Las Vegas filling, she had food and, of course, water, and warmer weather waited just a few hours away. She yawned and stretched and said she was going to bed.

Dan was tired, too, but he didn't want to leave. He was warm and comfortable, and the basement floor was harder than he'd remembered the last time he chose it over the RV, no matter how many folded sweaters he put down. It was a risk to ask her, but he thought he might have felt a shift in their dynamic. One that had eliminated him as a romantic possibility.

He asked to stay, quickly following up with an assurance that he wanted nothing from her, just a night off the floor.

She took longer to answer than he'd expected she would. He waited.

Her knee bounced. She rubbed her pendant. "Did you know it's my birthday?"

He said he didn't.

She got her purse and fished out her ID and showed it to him. "Why didn't you say anything before?"

"I don't know. I guess I haven't felt very 'birthday.'"

"Happy birthday."

"Thanks."

He really did want a night of sleep on something that didn't numb his limbs and bruise his bones.

And it was her birthday.

Jenny's bra, dropped to the bed when she'd taken if off, wrapped around Dan's foot. Her noises, like afterthoughts of moans, distracted him, too. Her awkward and stilted efforts, which he hadn't noticed before, made him impatient. She nipped rather than nibbled. Her balance was off. She arched her back too intentionally, almost grotesquely, and she parted her lips in a way he'd seen performed in most pornographic movies. Her toenails, too long, scratched his ankle bone. He forced pressure into his ears to block out the sound of her, and when she leaned forward to kiss him on the mouth, he dodged, ducked, pulled her up and over and gave her nipple a lick. She said, "Ooh, yeah."

Jenny kept on, dragging her hair across his chest, sliding around on top of him, and he enjoyed it—as much as having sex with a facsimile of a woman could be enjoyed—until his orgasm washed through, a pleasant involuntary reflex.

She lay beside him breathing heavy in the dark, her ankle tossed over his, her open palm on his chest. She pressed down and said "Mm" and kissed his arm.

He ran his fingertips up and down her back to help put her to sleep.

"That feels so good," she said. "I wish you could do it forever."

"Go to sleep," he said.

She lifted her chin to look at him. "What's the matter?"

"Nothing," he said.

"You sound mad, or something."

He cupped the back of her head and pushed it down, against his chest. "Shh," he said. "Nothing's the matter. You're reading into things. Go to sleep."

She struggled under his hand. "Stop—*stop* it. Let go!" She slipped her head out and crab-crawled backward to the end of the bed. "What's the matter with you? What are you doing?"

"Rubbing your head. You don't like it?"

She smoothed the back of her hair. "I like rubbing, yeah, but you just—"

"Then come back here," he said. He patted his chest.

"You held my head down," she said.

"I did?" he said. "No."

"Yes."

"Well, that's not what I meant. Come on. Come here."

Dan opened his arm to her, and he touched her head lightly when she rested it on his chest.

He lifted the silverware tray to pull out the bulk of the cash and brought it to the window to count some off in the diluted light from the parking lot. She'd taken, in all, just over seven hundred dollars. Dan pocketed two hundred and returned the rest to the drawer.

Jenny couldn't have lived on what she originally had much longer than she would live on what Dan left her. He wrote a note on a torn receipt, an IOU, that he intended to honor later (if later came, he reminded himself). He tucked it under some bills before sliding back into the big, warm, soft bed.

THIRTY ONE

Nina paced upstairs. She called, "Nyx!" She turned on the television with the volume high and vacuumed, dragging the wheels from room to room, the floor rumbling over Dan's head. He'd been so comfortable in the Pace Arrow the night before that he considered a night—just one—in a hotel, but he couldn't waste the money. His phone vibrated. He didn't have to look at the number to know it was Jenny. Since six that morning, it had been Jenny. She'd left only one message in over three hours of phone calls: "You didn't say goodbye."

Sunlight speared a bright, dust-flecked ray from the window to the floor. He hadn't repacked the snow outside. A sloppy decision, but one he wasn't concerned about. Getting to the window meant walking far around the unpopular side of the house, and Nina had no reason to do that.

He rearranged the things on the shelves. He kicked the rug closer to the utility sink. He turned on the lamp.

He was thirsty.

Nina would hear the water running through the pipes, coursing through the house. He opened the window and scooped a handful of snow into his mouth.

He was restless.

He wondered if he was waiting too long, giving April too much time, not being assertive enough.

When the cat came down the stairs, Dan found a piece of paper to crumple into a ball. Nina called "Nyx!"—tapping a cat food can and whistling until she came—and Dan was once again alone. He sat on the floor and closed his eyes. He envisioned a plague. Sickness and open sores.

Life was many things, he told himself. One of those things was this, this sitting in a basement in good health, and sitting in a basement in good health should not be taken for granted even if it wasn't what he wanted to be doing.

He would go to her apartment, and this time he would sit outside her door until she had to walk through it. If he could live this long in a cold basement, he could certainly spend a few hours on a warm landing.

He gathered his folded and stacked clothes and stuffed them in his duffel bag. He slung the bag over his shoulder and took the stairs like someone who lived there. When he opened the door to the main floor, Nina was standing in the kitchen, coffee mug in her hand.

He said, "I'm going."

The coffee that splashed his face wasn't hot. Not so hot it burned. He wiped it away with his coat sleeve and walked to the door while Nina screamed that she would call the police.

PART III

THIRTY TWO

Dan parked Jenny's—his, now—car in front of April's open garage. The handlebars of her red mountain bike, dulled by dust and hanging from hooks twisted into wood rafters, dangled inches from the roof of her Renault.

He took the stairs to her floor and knocked without listening for voices inside. Shadows appeared in the light under the door.

"It's me," he said. "Are you alone?"

"Yes."

"Can I come in?"

He heard her fingers sliding down the wood and imagined her leaning against it.

"I bought you something," he said.

Without opening the door she asked what it was.

"Something you'll like."

She cracked the door just enough for him to see her face, so naturally beautiful that he'd always suspected the makeup she'd been forced to wear when she was little could only have detracted from what was already there. She said, "I don't want things."

"I know."

She looked at him and waited. The foot blocking the door from opening any wider was encased in a slipper-sock.

He said again, "Can I come in?"

She shook her head, said, "No."

Dan slipped a leather portfolio through the opening. He'd stopped at an art supply store on the way, saw the purchase as an investment.

She took it from him, lightly touched the embossed cover, and then opened it and ran her finger along the raw suede interior. "It's magnificent," she said. "What do I do with it?"

"It's for your stories," he said.

"Oh. Oh! I see how they'll fit in the—I see. Thank you. Really, it's … I'm sure I'll be able to use it for something."

She rolled it into a tube and looked at him through the hole.

"Please," he said. "Let me in."

She shook her head. Her eyes glinted.

Dan inched his foot forward until it almost touched hers. If she tried to close the door, she wouldn't be able to. He said, "I'm sorry."

She leaned her head against the door. He sensed it was a calculated gesture meant to be irresistible. It was.

"You mentioned on the phone that you might say that," she said. "But sorry for what, Dan?"

"For …" His hands turned cold, dry. He put them in his pockets. His stomach felt like it was folding in on itself. "For … for being late the last time we were going to do this."

"And?"

And for calling her when he was drunk, he said, and for saying whatever it was he'd said. He apologized, too, for not remembering what that was.

"You wanted to tell me about the hooker."

"I'm particularly sorry about that."

"You wanted to talk about how beautiful she was."

"Ah. Sorry."

"You said she wasn't as beautiful as me, which was cheap."

"Nice, though."

"Nice enough."

She smiled. "You can't do it, can you? You're still insisting it was—"

He said, "April. I'm sorry for—I'm—for …"

The word she wanted to hear wasn't an honest word, wasn't what had happened. But she needed it to be what had happened, so he would say it once. For her.

He repressed the urge to vomit as he did.

April stopped smiling. She pulled him into her arms and whispered, "Thank you."

April made green tea. Dan watched her glide through the kitchen, slipper socks floating, her arms swaying rather than swinging, each turn like a body moving through water.

Even though he had taken off his coat, a line of sweat slid down his side. "Is there no way to fix this?"

She rolled up her sleeves. "Wait in the living room."

He remembered he was wearing a t-shirt underneath his sweater and took off the sweater. He folded it and set it on the kitchen table next to the portfolio and waited until the tea was done, then followed her into the living room. She sat on a pillow on the floor. He sat on the rug, facing her, and set the cup on the rug near his feet. April picked it up and put it on the table "just in case, because this rug cost—well—too much, and jute, dyed or not, doesn't clean easily."

The jute was red, dark red, to match the rest of the room. Dan didn't say a spill would probably go unnoticed. Something like that would get them both excited about principles and control, all the things people used to inflate small arguments about things that didn't matter. For example, the way a tea spill on a rug shouldn't matter now that they were finally together. Dan watched April handle her cup, one hand wrapped full around it and her long thumb tucked through the handle, her breath blowing it cool. She smiled at him while taking a sip, then set it beside his on the table and leaned back on both arms with her legs extended and crossed at the ankles. A distracting song played from her stereo, a version of Joe Cocker's

"Leave Your Hat On" performed by a woman whose voice gouged an obsessive urgency, a predatory aggression, into the air.

"So," April said, "what now?"

There were things he wanted to say, things about a quickie wedding at the Point, April holding a tangled bunch of wildflowers that would match the buds in her hair. A cloud-smeared sky and wind on the water throwing waves against the rocks. Two fat-stuffed suitcases in the back seat of the car on a long and straight nowhere road with the windows rolled down. April's hair, loose and long, blowing in the wind and her hand on Dan's thigh while he drove. The two of them hiking through forests with walking sticks, finding the edge of the world together before it was gone. This was it, he wanted to tell her. This was all they had and they'd taken it too lightly, and if they didn't make it matter now, it could be lost. They'd already lost time, a decade, that could have done without waiting. He could only be grateful neither of them had died before now, because they still had the chance to do something, to make it count, and he wanted to tell her these things but the blankness in her eyes locked his words somewhere behind his teeth. He'd seen her this way once before, just before it had ended, when—after hours of a closed bathroom door between them and her doctor's appointment behind her—she'd come out and stepped over him, her old, bell-bottom jeans stained at the center seam. He'd scrambled after her into the bedroom and watched her pull her suitcase from under the bed and slide open the zippers. Her eyes had been red—but a dissipating red, a disturbing red because there was a serenity there that hadn't made sense to him—when she'd said, "You're no different from them, after all. You're not the person I thought you were." Pants: packed. Shoes tossed one by one on top as she'd said, "I loved who I thought you were. I don't love who you are." Shirts being pulled from their hangers as she'd said, "I hate who you are."

Dan reached for his cup and drank from it. He studied her face for a hint of something. Raised eyebrows would mean she was testing him, and as madding as it could be, it would give him hope.

Tight lips meant she wouldn't hear anything he said. A smile would mean she'd given in. A smile would ruin him, would inflate him, would arm him and conquer him. He wanted a smile from her—that smile, the kind that began in her hairline and worked its way into her eyes and her cheeks before reaching her mouth—and he would do anything it took to get it.

He said, "I want to read that story."

April rubbed her throat, curved hand closing around and releasing her own neck. "I don't know if I'm ready to show it to you," she said. "I have others."

"No," he said. "I want to read that one."

"Because it's about you."

"And you."

"What if I said another one is about you, too? Would you want to read that one, then?"

"You made me curious about this one."

She sighed and leaned forward and held her feet. She thumbed the arches absently. "Everything hasn't magically gone back to normal. Or whatever we could call what it would be."

"But it's a step," he said. Her feet were close to his. He moved his left foot until it touched her right, bracing himself for an attack.

She didn't react.

He rubbed his hands together to warm them.

"It's a step, yes," she said.

He got up for his sweater. In the kitchen he noticed that a cheap wood frame glued to the wall held a picture of April and the waiter wearing white helmets and harnesses on a crude platform in the woods. It hadn't been there before.

"When was this taken?" he said.

"Summer."

April faced a clearing through the trees with her hands wrapped around a thick, twisted rope. She looked ready to leap, her life entrusted to a clip and a cable. The waiter, behind her, had a hand on her shoulder and smiled like a boy nailing the kind of woman he could never hope to nail again for the rest of his life.

Dan put on his sweater and went back to the living room. "The story?" He reached for his tea and took a sip. Cool, thinly flavored water. He had never liked tea. He put it down.

She massaged her feet again, pressing her thumbs hard into her flesh. Her shirt was a loose, knit tunic with a low collar, and hair that had fallen forward dipped inside the open neck and curled at the ends against her skin. He reached for it, using a finger to hook it and lay it over her shoulder—but without touching her. He had taken her lack of interest in his foot as a no to touching, and he would do no more of it until she told him he could, or until she touched him first, and he hoped she would touch him again soon, very soon, anywhere, with any part of her, before the day ended or better yet right now, kissing him with her arms wrapped around his back and her thighs weighing on his and her hair a scented curtain around his face.

"Did you hear me?"

He said he hadn't.

"I said thank you. The way you did that with my hair—it was nice. It felt nice. Sincere. I don't—" She smiled, but not the way he wanted, and said, "I didn't even see you check out my tits."

He laughed. "You missed it."

April got up and he thought he felt her touch his head.

She came back with her folder and plopped on the floor to look through it. It was gray at the edges from use and the corners had worn to rounding.

He got the portfolio from the kitchen table and laid it on the floor by her knee. She looked at it, then went back to searching. Dan sat on his floor pillow and blew warm air into his hands. It was so cold in the living room that crystals frosted the corners of the windows.

"Here." She held a single sheet of paper to her chest with both hands. It crinkled under her palms. "This means something to me," she said.

Dan held out his hand.

"I don't know if you're going to get it."

"I guess we'll see."

"I'm—I'm a little afraid you *will* get it."

"Let's assume I'm not stupid."

"I can't help thinking you're going to do something that'll make me regret this."

"How many times do I have to say I'm sorry?"

"I'm just—"

"You have to trust me."

"Don't make me regret this," she said.

He disregarded the no-touching rule he'd given himself and took her hands. They were warmer than his. "Do you want to know what means something to me?" He squeezed. "This, right here—holding your hands in this ice palace—is the most intimate thing I've ever done."

"Oh, well." She shrugged and giggled and blushed, and Dan felt frozen in that simple storm of charm. "Who can resist that?" she said. She gave him the story.

He took it to the couch, where the just slightly higher air was just slightly warmer.

"It's untitled," she said.

"I can see that. Sh."

> Lunelle had spent her life a buttercup, slender and bright and cheerful and light, her happiness smudging the men who held her. They reveled in her gaiety, smiled "I've-found-her!" sighs at her movie-girl mood that never changed and ever pleased, at her baby lotion soft (and deceptively youthful) skin. They, the men, licked her buttercup dust from their fingers until even their nails were clean.

She, Lunelle, was the kind of girl (before *him*) who—in the meat-freezer cold of New England winters—refused to ride in a car or a bus from the college where she taught compassion for Oates's broken *Beasts* and *Solstice* women. She walked, thighs flaming fire-cold, without complaining or grumbling or cursing the "goddamn" New England winters the way the others did. She, Lunelle, ran ahead, *skipped* even, and giggled, swinging her hair around to smile and rub-rub-rub her silly-cold thighs and say, "Brrr!" She, Lunelle, picked up snow and tossed it high, raised her face, closed her eyes, and collected soft powder on her lashes. She laughed, then, and skipped back to him (more specifically, to *him*) and took his hands and led him forward and onward, saying, "Oh, grumpy-grump!" when he complained he couldn't feel his toes. Once inside her cozy and well-lit apartment (sunlight hit her hair just so in the afternoons), she offered hot chocolate and peeled off their clothes and sat naked atop him while water heated on the stove.

He was the dashing dapper-doll she'd spotted one fall crossing the street with a parrot on his shoulder, its feathers boasting vibrant rainbow shades. He— *he*—wore a sleeveless t-shirt and handed sunflower seeds to the beak hovering cheekside. Lunelle had waved from her side of the street and said, "Hi, there!" Giggling, she'd asked the parrot's name, and from then and on they were together. For their one-year, her first long-term, he'd planted a patch of sunflowers in the soil under her kitchen window and she'd clapped her hands and kissed the air.

Today, *now*, the sunflowers peak, now in full autumn, *Gillian's* season since three years before when, parrot shouldered and one uprooted sunflower dragging, he—*he*—left under a ghost sheet. "Getting candy corn," he lied.

He left, he later sighed, because she was too perfect. (She didn't argue the impossibility of being "too" perfect.) He flipped her hair, said, "Thick and bouncy!" He spat in her eyes. "They sparkle, for Christ's sake!" But also, she was too optimistic, too chipper about "goddamn everything." To prove him wrong she, Lunelle, had said, "No, it's not true, baby blue. Listen to this, to what I was thinking, and you'll see I, too, am some days sinking into the depths of sadness and gloom, and that I am hardly(!) like a flower in ... in ... bloom! Listen," she said. "Sometimes? Sometimes I think my heart could just break from autumnal beauty that's too much to take, the rusts on brown trees ... I could fall to my knees!" But she knew. That was too beautiful, too. "You make me fucking crazy," he said.

So she, once Lunelle, became an Oates woman, because they, damaged and *im*perfect, are loveable, sickly adored the translated world over.

She, *Gillian,* breasts shaved to *Beasts* nubs and hair permed curly, buys lipsticks called *Tangerine Tango* and *Mazetlan.* Her students snicker at the bold smears coloring her teeth and at her pronunciation of "Rastafarian" (Rah-stih-*fay*-rien), roll their eyes when she uses words like "stichomythia" and "brackish" for their ugliness.

She is Lunelle only on Halloween nights when, gold-lit under the porchlight, she drops dried buttercup buds in children's cheap plastic pumpkin buckets.

He handed the story back to her.

"Why are you looking at me like that?" she said. "It's fiction, obviously. I was never a teacher, never mind a professor, and I don't know one single person with a parrot."

"I'm sorry," he said again, but this time, though he didn't tell her, it was for never having considered that a woman like her could be vulnerable.

THIRTY FOUR

Dan woke up several times throughout his first night at April's to pull his feet into warm spots on the couch. In the deepest hour, when darkness was absolute and the thinnest noise could yank a person from sleep, he heard the walking sounds of feet sticking to the floor and felt her drape more blankets over the two light covers she'd left folded on top of the extra pillows. She didn't touch him before walking away, didn't whisper something she might want him to hear but not hear. He hoped for hesitation, listened for a pause in her step before she closed herself in her bedroom—a pause that didn't come—and then kept himself awake for as long as he could in case she changed her mind.

When morning came, and every morning of that first week together, he made her breakfast before she left for work. There were only a few places things could be in her small kitchen, so he didn't make much noise looking for frying pans and spatulas not glued to the wall. Sweating even in his underwear and socks, he cooked her eggs the way she liked them and made the coffee the way he liked it. She didn't drink coffee, but she tried one morning to brew a pot for him. When he said it tasted a little bit like a gas station puddle, she laughed and punched him hard on the arm.

Before she left each morning, he asked her to quit her job, go away with him, "drink the ocean or lie in tree sap, or whatever it was you said you wanted to do." She didn't need the money, he reminded her.

"Aren't we happy now, like this?" she said one morning, standing in the open doorway. On a different morning, organic orange juice and ice in a travel mug and an art magazine tucked under her arm, she said it wasn't about money but her responsibility as a job coach to Nick, Tracy, and Monique.

"I'm not ready to be trapped out in the middle of the country with you, yet," she winked on a more recent morning, the wink not entirely convincing.

Evenings, before bed, they sat together on the couch in almost the same way they had when they were younger. Missing were her fingernails scraping his scalp through his hair, the perfect roundness of her shoulder under his arm, the way her body tucked and fitted into his under a blanket. Her hand, the few times he reached for it, would be pulled away to scratch an itch, cover a cough, or change the channel. But it was always followed by a quick touch on his arm, or a casual lean that pressed her body against his.

They watched sitcoms and the nightly news—Dan had time for that, now, could relax a little and be in the world now that he was with her—and drank their wine and listened to a young, bright-faced policeman speaking at press conferences about crime rates, whose numbers, he said, were unchanged. Some isolated "incidences" were, however, baffling law enforcement, he said, citing cases that included suburban vandalism—patches of siding stripped from the facades of mcmansions, tops sawed off of decorative sapling pines—and prank attacks. The most recent involved three college boys who'd tackled a businessman outside of a breakfast restaurant, inked his overcoat with a "priority mail" stamp stolen from the post office down the street, and taken his briefcase and phone. The victim recalled one of the boys screaming "Farling!" into his ear.

"You really get a sense of who people are when they react to something like this Farling nonsen—business," she said one night. "Give them the right opportunity, and they ooze the slime that must have always been there, bubbling just under their skin."

Dan thought she was probably right about some of them. The pressure to be civil had to be overwhelming for people who weren't. But he thought there might be something else to it, for some of them. Some kind of hope or security they gained through bad behavior. People believed in justice, and the fear of punishment had to be easier to tolerate than the fear of death.

That first week, Dan looked forward to mornings the most, to stretching the pain from the couch out of his back and knowing he would see her step out of her bedroom and into the hallway with her hair lumped-up and tangled and her morning eyes squinted.

He spent the days when she was at work listening to her music, going through her drawers and closets, and wondering how many calls she was getting throughout the day from the waiter, who'd left behind a pair of black-and-blue striped briefs rolled up in a ball in April's sock drawer. Dan received four or five text messages from Jenny, who'd made it *all the way to some fucking place called Aquia Harbor* before realizing he'd stolen from her. Her final text was Andy's address, where Dan was to send the money he owed her. But it wasn't time, yet, to talk about it with April.

Dan found little outside of the picture on the kitchen wall and some scattered books in the living room to give him the details of her life since their breakup. Reading material included *Photographs that Get Noticed, Secrets to Growing Award-Winning Plants, 10 Steps to Getting Your Story Published, Small Paintings that Sell, May-December: Stoke the Embers*, and Goldie Hawn's *A Lotus Grows in the Mud*. Pressure point oils smelling of smoke and wood and flowers crowded the shelves of her bathroom medicine cabinet, and the sink faucet held various sizes and colors of bands for her hair. In the bedroom he found that her socks were all white, her underwear cotton pastels, and she still kept suitcases under the bed.

When on Friday afternoon there was nothing left to look through, Dan opened her folder of stories, shelved and lying on top of the portfolio he'd given her. Within an hour he was surrounded by loose pages scattered on the couch, where he sat on the twisted and wrinkled sheets and blankets he usually folded minutes before he expected her home.

He was in the middle of "Beauty's Offspring," a short story told from the point of view of an unattractive girl whose celebrity parents were widely known for their good looks—"Fucking genetics, man," said one of the fictional paparazzi who'd snapped a picture of the girl—, when April opened the door. When he looked up from the pages and saw her, he wished he'd known earlier, and thought he really should have known earlier, that this was all it would take to get her to smile her someday-April smile, to put her arms around him for more than a hug.

Her kisses were light and teasing, more playful than he remembered, and then hard like the ones he'd known. She groped at his hair and neck, the fingers pulling at his skin either urgent or frustrated and with a need that both excited him and made him wonder if he was enough, if there was something she was trying to get at that he didn't have.

She traced lines on the side of his ribs with her fingernails, then scratched. "Feel good?"

"How'd you know I had an itch?"

"I always knew."

He grabbed her hand and brought it to his mouth and kissed it.

"What do you think is worse," she said, "pain or fear?"

"Fear of pain. Why?"

She outlined his mouth with her fingertip and said, "No reason."

The tracing tickled. He nudged her hand away and scratched his lips. "Jesus," he said, using his bottom teeth, ridged and sharp. "What did you do?"

"Nothing." She laughed and tapped his nose with her fingertip. "Maybe Nina gave you a disease. Itchy mouth disease."

The sun had fallen and shadows shaped the room. Lights from passing cars swiped the walls. They lay together naked on the couch with the pages of her stories torn and crumpled on the cushions and scraping Dan's side and thighs. April's elbow and knee poked into him. He inched a gap between his body and hers and tried to remember the position they'd fit into when they used to mold together like soul mates, their bends and curves sealing neatly into place. He'd assumed it had been natural, there from the beginning, but now he wondered if it had taken some time to find.

"That wasn't nice," she said. "The Nina thing. I didn't mean it."

"Not nice."

"I said I didn't mean it."

"Don't worry," he said. "They heard you."

"Who's they?"

"Whoever it is you're afraid will get you for it. The spirits in the ceiling."

April propped herself on Dan's chest. "You know, I never thought you really knew me."

"What about now?"

"Now I think maybe you did."

"I did."

"I always had the feeling you found me amusing."

"You are amusing."

"Did you love me?"

"Yes."

"What I mean is, did you *really* love me? The way you say you love me now."

"I did."

"Did I ever tell you the day we got married was the happiest day of my life? I know the day you get married is supposed to be the happiest day of your life. At the very least, you're supposed to pretend it is. But it really was."

"You never told me."

"I cried that morning before you woke up. It was four o'clock, exactly, when I looked at the clock, and I remember thinking, 'We're getting married.' Something came over me, and I—I didn't know it was possible to be happy like that."

He stroked his thumb under her eye until it was dry. "I loved you, too."

She pulled her hand away, tucked it against herself. "Your apology didn't blow amnesia dust up my nose. You know what I mean?"

He nodded.

"It's going to come up again. I just want you to know."

"Noted."

"But we don't have to talk about it now. Do you want to talk about it right now?"

"No."

"Then I'll talk about something else." Her chin still rested so close he could feel her breath on his neck, but all he saw of her face in the darkness was a speck of light in her eyes. She said, "Tonight, you didn't initiate—You weren't very ..."—tapping his skin with the hand she'd wedged between them—"I kissed you. I took off your clothes. I put you inside."

"You did do all those things. Wonderfully."

"Did you want to have sex with me? Were you at all interested before I came onto you? I don't remember you ever being very subtle about wanting sex, so when you didn't come after me, I thought ..."

"If you thought I didn't want it, how did tonight happen?"

She smiled. "I took a chance. But you did genuinely want to have sex with me, didn't you?"

"Yes."

"More than I did?"

"Is that important?"

"Yes."

"Much more."

She rested her cheek on his chest. "Make it more obvious next time."

He closed his eyes and touched her back. The slightest of bumps, blemishes—not rounded like pimples or moles, from the feel of them, but sharp, pointed—roughed her skin.

"You know," she said sometime in the night when both of them were awake for no reason, "I didn't expect you to read those stories."

"You wrote them. I wanted to read them."

"It's funny. I don't really care about any of them. Just the one about you."

"Then, it wasn't seeing me buried under a pile of your writing that made me so irresistible to you?"

"Oh, I don't know." She stroked his hair. His scalp tingled and his eyelids fell. "Daniel Nathaniel Palace, you could have been surrounded by anything of mine and I would have torn off your clothes. What girl can resist a man so interested in her that he goes through her things?"

"Some people would call it creepy."

"Did you sniff my underwear?"

"Not yet."

"Not creepy yet." She kissed him, her mouth hard on his. She reached for his hand and pulled it to her waist, slid it lower for him. She put his other hand on her breast. She stroked his chest and slid a hand into his hair and pulled until it hurt. "Do *something* on your own."

Her alarm buzzed in her bedroom and she left him on the couch. He pulled the blankets close and listened to her movements through the bedroom, the shuffling in her closet, the closing of the bathroom door for her shower before a short working Saturday. Water hit the bottom of the bathtub with varying intensity, changing as she stepped into and out of the spray. She would be going to work, the same way she did every day. And then she would come home, and he would be there, the way he was every day. He would buy wine because they were out, and they would drink it in the living room later in front of the TV.

They were on day twenty-eight, he realized. Twenty-seven days down.

He tried to remember when he'd stopped paying attention.

He began one of his basement meditations on the end of the world, rolling through a list of possibilities before giving up.

He didn't know how it would come. It didn't matter.

She didn't startle when he opened the shower curtain, but smiled and stroked a razor along her exposed armpit. "Yes?"

"Don't go to work today. Have someone cover it for you. When you get out, we'll pack suitcases and go somewhere."

"Where?" She bent to rinse the hair from the blade in a weak stream of water dripping from the faucet.

"Anywhere you want to go."

"Where do you want to go?"

"I don't know. We can talk about it while we pack."

She raised her other arm and soaped the stubble, dragged the blade across the skin.

"Say yes. If you have to have a destination before you can say yes, okay. We'll go to Montana."

"I bet it's gorgeous in the winter."

"I bet it is."

She set the razor in the shower caddy and twisted her body under the water to wash the soap from her armpits one at a time. He watched the water fall over her like veins, tracing lines around her neck and between her breasts and straight to the shallow hole of her bellybutton, where it paused, collected, and overflowed, spilling over the small bump of her abdomen and drawing a line to her pubic hair.

"Alaska," she said with what he thought was a glance at his crotch.

"From Connecticut?"

"It can't take more than four or five days." She poured shampoo and rubbed it into her hair with both hands.

He put his hands in his pockets and imagined yanking her out of the water and onto the floor. "Alaska. Okay. You'll go? I'll start packing for both of us if you say yes."

"I can't today. I have to give some kind of notice so they can find someone to take over. Maybe we can go next week."

"We could be dead before next week."

"We could," she said. "I forgot. It is the year for that kind of thing." She winked at him and soaped her arm. "But we could also be alive and on our way to witness the splendor of Alaska. And because it's impolite for you to keep living on my income, you'll get to find an exciting Alaska job. We both will." She tilted her head back to rinse away the shampoo. "Alaska. How exciting is that?" When her hair was slick and clean she wiped her eyes and stood facing him, then sighed and pulled the curtain closed.

Dan went to the kitchen to start coffee.

"I guess I get to buy really big snow boots," she yelled. He thought it seemed a little loud. Something banged, and he called out from the kitchen to ask if she was okay.

"Oh, I'm *perfect*."

His mouth and teeth stretched and rounded in the coffee pot. He, *he*, was the man planting sunflowers under her window.

Dan didn't believe in a god, but he liked to think, at times, there was a benign energy or force. He thanked it for giving him April. He asked it to keep the world intact for at least another two weeks.

THIRTY FIVE

Dan watered the plant in the pot on the kitchen wall and wiped down the counters and sink before leaving. He pretended to lock up in case someone was watching from behind the other doors. April had taken her key and there was no spare.

He stopped for gas on his way to clean out his desk and pick up his final check, pay plus unused vacation time and sick days. He'd thought Nina would receive it and pass it on to him, but since she hadn't, he knew it must not have been mailed. He watched the cars go by and wondered whether the tired-looking faces behind the windows were on their way to make the most of things.

When a car with Utah plates pulled up to the pump behind his, he remembered he had forgotten to tell April he'd been there. And then he remembered that while winding through the mountains under that vast, moonlit sky, he had forgotten to think about her.

It hadn't snowed in days and the roads were clear, but the temperature had stayed below thirty and the trees along the interstate were frosted white, the sloped clearings on the hills bright squares in the sun that made him squint. His phone vibrated in a construction zone just outside of the city. He pulled it from his pocket and read a text from Jenny saying she had no choice but to come home. She'd used too much money before counting what she had and could afford only to hide out with her mother unless Dan gave her what he'd taken, which would at least cover propane and keep her warm and independent for a while. Another text followed: *Andy said you never sent anything. Will txt u when I get there to meet up & get my cash.*

Another came as he was pulling into a parking space in the crowded lot of the office park: *Is this still your number?*

He plucked out the keys and shook the ball on the keychain Jenny had forgotten to take with her. He asked it if he and April would go to Alaska.

BETTER NOT TELL YOU NOW.

When his phone rang in the lobby and he saw Jenny's number, he didn't answer. He would text her when he had the check in hand. He stepped into the elevator and pressed the button for the sixth floor. The distorted, gold-tinted reflection of himself, contrasted with the figure he'd last seen in those doors, was one he liked. He'd lost weight, intentionally or not, and the bags under his eyes had smoothed, disappeared.

A loud and happy chime announced the passing of the floors until the elevator stopped at six and his reflection split in the middle. He stepped out onto the hard, gray carpet and looked out over a cubicle grid until he spotted the one closest to the floor-to-ceiling windows teasing freedom, his books still propped against the monitor, the small spider plant Nina had given him spindly and brown in death. Supervisors walking the floor bent to answer questions, take over headsets to speak with confused, doubtful, or disputing debtors, or chide collectors for not asking before getting up to use the bathroom.

Dan wandered in and watched for the thick blond hair he would always see coming toward him over his cubicle wall before he ever saw Howie himself.

"Palace," Howie said behind him.

They shook hands.

Howie guided Dan into the break room. "See your desk? No one touched a thing. No one but the night cleaners, I mean. I think they dust it now and then."

The teams, Nina had told him, were divided: one team for the top three floors, one team for the bottom. Once they'd started seeing each other, Nina had asked Valbon for the bottom three. "We would have to break up if I had to dust your desk and empty your trash," she'd said.

"You should have given my cube to someone else," Dan said.

"I knew you'd be back. And here you are. You miss it. You miss us. Face it. You miss me. And Kathy misses you."

"No, she doesn't."

"'I sure do miss that meaty Daniel Palace,' she said."

Kathy had had the second highest collections, when Dan still worked there, and made double her base pay in bonuses. He knew this because they had regular award ceremonies—collector of the month, employee of the month—and, behind Dan, she was the most frequent recipient of collector of the month. Her picture, unflattering and bright, looked out at the sea of cubicles from its spot on the wall between the men's and women's restrooms.

Dan's picture was no better. Now and then he would try to collect just short of her to keep his face off the wall, but he invariably failed. He wasn't good at not being good at something he was good at.

Howie slapped Dan's back. "We've missed having you around."

"Thanks."

"You won't have to retrain. I have to tell you, though, I can't hold it much longer. Doug's looking at applications soon."

"What are you doing after this?" Dan said.

"Tonight? Want to grab a beer?"

"After all of it. The job."

Howie shrugged. A single, lustrous wave of yellow hair framed his forehead, and his face was smooth and rosy. He looked like a porcelain shelf angel. "Stay here, I guess. Get Doug's job someday. It's good money."

"Be better at it than Doug."

"Look," he said. "He made the right call with that guy. If you believed them all, you'd spend all your time filing disputes instead of collecting money. Doug saved you time, and your paycheck was better off for it."

"It was a legitimate complaint."

"Maybe."

"Not maybe, Howe."

He shrugged a shoulder. "It's not our job to help them, unless it's to help them get off their asses to pay their bills." Howie smiled and stuck his hand in his pocket, pulled out change and dropped it in a vending machine. He pressed the button for a bag of plain potato chips.

The window between the break room and the work floor was lined with streaks from a squeegee. Nina said her boss didn't do windows. There was a separate company for that. Dan thought window washing might not be such a bad job with squeegees. He'd asked Nina if she would prefer window washing to cleaning, and she'd said it was all the same to her: not enough. "It's not a worthless job. 'Cleanliness and order are important in a productive, civilized environment,'" she'd said, quoting a Valbon-ism, "but I can do more for the business than that. I want to do more."

In the checkerboard of cubes a hand shot up from Molly's desk, a short-fingered hand attached to a slight wrist that ended at the cuff of a loose purple blouse, and it stayed raised until Doug walked over and tapped her arm. She stood up and weaved through the cubes to the restroom.

"You can start back Monday," Howie said. Chewed, liquefied potato chip clung to his teeth and the corners of his mouth.

"I should have a final check waiting," Dan said. "Unused vacation and sick days."

"If you leave today without a commitment to come back, Doug won't hold your spot."

Dan said he needed a box for his things.

Howie chewed another handful of chips and asked Dan if he was sure.

Molly came out of the restroom and returned to her cubicle. She slid the headset over her hair and adjusted the mic to her mouth and pressed the key that would bring up a new screen and auto-dial a new number. He could almost hear her conversational, sympathetic appeal.

As collectors went, she was average. She rarely hit bonus.

Dan told Howie he was sure, and Howie crumpled the empty chip bag, tossed it in a trash basket in the corner, and said he'd find Dan a box. "But I'm not giving up on you yet. I'll talk to Doug and call you in two weeks. But that might be your last chance."

Dan went to his cube and waited. Howie brought him a white box with a picture of a headset on the side. Dan packed his books and threw away the dried plant. Howie watched with his hands in his pockets and said he didn't know how Dan could have done the good job he did while getting all those books read. "Imagine what you might have done for us if you weren't reading all that DeMille."

"If I weren't reading now and then I would have jumped through that window, Howie."

Howie walked Dan to the elevator. "I couldn't get you the check," he said in front of the doors. "They said they mailed one out, but it came back 'return to sender.' They'll cut a new one and mail it in a few days. It won't include vacation and sick days, though. Give me two weeks on that, 'kay?"

Dan gave him April's address for the check and asked if he could get an advance of some kind.

"For a job you're trying to leave? You *are* a nutbird. What's the burning need for cash?"

"Going to Alaska," Dan said.

Howie laughed. His bottom jaw bounced as if to underline his amusement. *Haw. Haw. Haw.* "What the hell is there to do in Alaska?"

Dan saw, reflected in the elevator doors, the cubes and cubes behind him, heard the din of murmurs from collectors trying to lead debtors into bonus territory. April would be home in two hours and he would have both of their bags packed and lunch waiting, a flower in the vase on the wall. He would convince her to leave with him in the morning, and if she didn't want to leave, yet, it wouldn't matter, because he would spend every morning and every evening with her until the day they finally did leave, doing something memorable in the days between to make each possible last day one whose violent end would be a shame.

Kathy stood up inside her cube and arched her back in a stretch that pulled her shirt tight across her chest. She brought her hand to her face and Dan could see her long, white nails even in the distorted metal doors. She scratched the tip of her nose and then her nail slipped briefly inside a nostril to scratch some more before she lowered her hand. When she saw his reflection in the door she smiled and waved. He waved back.

THIRTY SIX

The noodles on top of the heap were cold from the wintery air passing through the open window, but it was the only way they could eat at the kitchen table without sweating. April held her fork over her plate while she chewed. After she swallowed she said, "This is the best spaghetti I've ever had. I don't think I've ever had it for lunch, but it's definitely worth any midday sleepiness."

Over her head, the flower he'd bought for the vase drooped at the bud, but was otherwise fresh-looking and bright. Blue petals faded into a yellow center, and narrow, pointed leaves spread out of the mouth like open arms. April had noticed it as soon as she came in—"Oh, it looks just like the paper daisy!"—and had rushed into the kitchen where he was preparing their plates and hugged him tight.

"Did you do something different with it?" She tapped her fork on the plate.

"Cloves," Dan said. "Not whole. Ground."

She hadn't been to the bedroom, yet, hadn't seen their packed bags. After lunch, he would ask her to marry him as he opened a bottle of wine, a Cabernet Sauvignon Larry had talked about that wasn't nearly as expensive as his Eagle. He hadn't bought a ring, hadn't known he would propose until he walked in the door, but April wasn't the kind of woman who needed a ring. Nor had Nina been, for that matter. His proposal to her had been a spontaneous word burst at Bob's Batting Cages after their fourth turn on the go-kart track.

April swept her linguini-wrapped fork through a red puddle and put it in her mouth. Sauce stained her lips, and her cheeks expanded to accommodate the bite.

"I used to wish I'd met you at ten," Dan said.

She covered her mouth to laugh and fell into a coughing fit. A segment of a noodle shot out of her mouth and onto the table. She took small sips of water and breathed through her mouth until the choking passed. Her eyes wet and her face still red from coughing, she picked up her fork again. "Oh, yes, I'm finishing it."

Two candles flickered on the kitchen table and air promising more snow replaced the smell of pasta and sauce. April drank the Cabernet with her attention on the window. She fingered the base of a candlestick, turning it a little bit at a time. "If we're going to do a better job this time, we have to ... well, we have to do a better job."

"What does that mean?"

"I wasn't finished."

"I'm sorry. Please finish."

"Well, to begin with, you don't get to be mad at me for saying no to something I've had no time to think about, and that you laid on me after just one week of us seeing each other." She kicked him hard under the table. The pain was so sharp and sudden that, without thinking, he got up from his chair. She didn't move, but looked at him, fingers circled loosely around her glass. He sat back down and she said, "Can I finish, now?"

"Please."

"For example, I really—*really*—want to be able to tell you to stop waiting for me to initiate sex."

"I see."

"You don't do anything unless I start it, Dan. Even Jeremy, who can be a little shy, would have put a hand under the water."

"Jeremy."

She reached across the table and took his hand. "I apologize for how this sounds, but truth can be ... well ... unattractive. I can't help it. What frustrates me—what makes me the most insanely mad about all of this, Dan—is that you weren't the one damaged by what happened. I should be the one afraid of you, not the other way around. That you won't touch me until I do something first makes me feel … it makes me feel like you've decided to play the victim in all this. But there can only be one, and it's not you, Dan." She took a long, deep breath. She let it out. "It's just this, too: If we're afraid of honesty, which our past says we are, then this thing with us will never work. If I'd been more upfront early in our relationship … What if I'd told you right away that I didn't want kids?"

"Excuse me?"

"Excuse you?"

He tried again: What did she mean? he said. What would her not wanting kids, or his having known about it sooner rather than later, have to do with anything?

"Isn't that what made you so angry? Isn't that why it happened?"

"I wasn't angry."

"You must have been, Dan. I had marks on my wrists."

A sharp, icy breeze blew the candles sideways, but didn't extinguish them. Dan rubbed his hands together, cupped them one over the other. "You had marks on your thighs this morning. And your back."

April opened her mouth and looked at him, her head tilted, but said nothing until Dan reached for the window.

"I want it open," she said.

"It's cold."

"And if we close it, it's hot."

"Why don't we move to the living room?"

"Because I want to sit here. Leave it, Dan. It's my goddamn window and I want it open."

He had to stand to push it shut. Over the years the wood had expanded and contracted in the heat and the cold until it warped. "I live here, too, and I want it closed."

After he sat, April stood up to open it—"You stay here with my permission, in my apartment"—and sat again. "But let's not get distracted," she said. "We could do this all night."

"Is there something else you'd rather be doing?"

"I'd rather talk this out."

"It was a joke."

"I'm ignoring it."

Dan refilled his glass.

"I want to know why it happened," she said. "If it wasn't because you were angry, then I have to know why." She leaned back in her chair.

She'd warned him, but he hadn't really believed it would come up again. He realized, then, that it would never stop being an issue. Whether she held onto her version because she needed to reassure herself that she'd done the right thing by reacting so severely, or whether it was to punish him for her reaction, she would only acknowledge the truth she'd created, one he knew she didn't believe.

He would have let her have it, had she been able to let things go with his apology. He couldn't, now. It was more than a desire for her to acknowledge that he wasn't what she said he was, though he did desire that. It was that he couldn't go on living that particular lie. He couldn't have her believing that he believed it.

He said, "In the RV, you said—"

"I didn't say anything in the RV." The tightness of her face revealed the magnitude of her struggle to convey, in her tone and in her features, a combination of light amusement and confusion. Anything but anger or fear or guilt.

Dan tried to keep his own voice calm, his own features relaxed and nonthreatening. "You s—"

"Drunk on two bottles of wine and passed out on the couch I supposedly said something? How do I know you're telling the truth? Even if you are, it wouldn't matter, because—"

"Because why?"

"Because. Words don't alter facts, Dan.—Okay, what's that look?"

"April, I can't …"

"What?"

He considered his wine, but he couldn't drink. Couldn't eat the last of the food on his plate. He laid down his fork and said softly, "It didn't happen. Not like that."

She half-groaned, half-screamed and clutched the table with both hands. "Jesus," she said, her teeth clenched. "This must have been how you felt when you raped me. Enraged, right, Dan? Because I think I could actually kill you. I think I might enjoy killing you. Did you enjoy raping me, Dan?" She exhaled a short burst of air through her nose, a little scoff. "I have to say, though, even that was probably better than the sex we're having now. When we have it, that is. Dan, you made me embarrassed for myself this morning. It humiliated me to think I'd ever wanted you—that I'd actually slept with you. So weak. So sad, standing there, like some peeping teenage virgin, with your hands in your pockets to hide your erection instead of actually *doing* something with it."

She kicked him again, hard, the force of it piercing like a split in his bone. He picked up the wine bottle and flung it past her against the wall. When she turned to avoid spraying glass, he reached across the table and grabbed her shirt at the collar. He had been afraid to start, to give her any reason to misconstrue, but if she wanted him to start, he would. Without letting go of her, he slid out of his chair and yanked her out of hers and pulled her to standing, backed her against the fresh stain on the wall and pressed his lips to her throat. Her shirt came off. Her hands pulled and groped at his back and he heard her breathing, heavy and excited, when he carried her to the couch. He threw her down and lay on top of her. "You want me to do something?" he said. "I'm doing something." He hovered over her. Her chest rose and fell and her skin was pink and hot. He pushed down his pants and yanked her jeans over her hips and down her thighs. He kissed her mouth and thrust himself inside her until he came.

She said, "God damn."

She moved under him, hips rocking, rocking, the last one a powerful jerk, abrupt and strong and throwing his balance. He fell off the couch. The jute was rough on his skin.

"What's the matter?" he said.

She looked at him. "Are you actually smiling?"

He walked to her on his knees, each step a small agony, the bumps of hard fiber pressing into the soft spots of his joints. "I thought—"

"I'm not playing," she said.

"I'm not either. April. What are you—Why are you so upset? I thought you—"

"I wanted it. Again."

She kicked out fast with both legs, her heels catching him between the ribs. He toppled back, lost his breath. He grasped at the rug and tried to breathe and something hard and cold struck his cheek and sent a stinging, throbbing shot through his face and head. The next blow was flesh on flesh, her feet slamming into his side. His breath was slowly coming back, and he could move. He grabbed an ankle to secure it, but she twisted her foot in his hand and slipped away. She didn't pull up her jeans and run. Instead, she sat on the couch with her feet tucked out of reach, jeans down around her knees, hands in her lap, her eyes on him.

Something warm trickled over his ear. "What did you hit me with?"

She stood to pull up her pants, zipped and buttoned them, and then sat back down. Her shirt was still somewhere on the kitchen floor.

Dan put his fingers to his face and the salt of his skin burned the open cut. He pulled it away. "What did you hit me with?" he said again.

"Did I hurt you?"

"It felt like a rock."

"Rose quartz." She walked to the kitchen to pick up her shirt and put it on while standing over him in the living room. "You bought it for me, remember? You have five minutes. Then I want you to get up and pack your things and leave." She lifted something—the rock, he saw, with just a spot of red on it—from the couch and carried it out of the room. He heard her bedroom door close. It opened again, and his clothes, which she'd been allowing him to mix with hers in dirty laundry, fell in a pile on the floor. The door closed again.

Dan pulled himself up and eased onto the couch. He saw his underwear on the floor. He stretched out a leg and dragged them close with his toe, hooked his foot in a hole and lifted it high enough to grab. Moving his head as little as possible, he slid them over his feet and up his thighs and around his waist. He sat back, the velvet cushion soft against his back.

The candles on the table in the kitchen burned low, flames jerking on stumpy wax sticks. Broken green glass bits lay scattered on the wine spill near the baseboard. April's chair had been knocked to its side—Dan saw only the legs and metal feet through the doorway.

Cold air from the open kitchen window spread into the living room and raised goose bumps on his arms and legs, on his stomach and chest heaving and bouncing with the breaths he took through his mouth so she wouldn't hear.

THIRTY SEVEN

Nina pounded with a hammer in the back yard under a blue sky. The crack of metal on wood and nails echoed through the quiet. A wide circle of yellow-brown grass surrounded her, cleared the day before with steaming water carried out in buckets. Dan watched from the basement, as he had for the last week since leaving April's, Nyx sitting nearby on a high shelf and licking her paws beside the lamp. Nina, in her old jeans and what she called her "yard work" baseball cap, had been going in and out with buckets, off and on for hours. When Dan got hungry, he'd waited for her to go back outside and had taken the stairs two at a time to the kitchen, where he'd discovered an uncorked bottle of wine while snatching a handful of chips. He'd had time to pour half a glass before running back down to the basement.

Nina concentrated her hammering and pounding on one spot, a triangle base supporting a long board that stood what Dan judged to be, based on its height relative to Nina, about seven feet high. She tossed the hammer in the grass and rubbed her shoulder and wrist, then checked the high board for sturdiness. She smiled at it and wiped her hands on her jeans.

There was much to love about her. He wondered why he'd not properly loved her before.

When she picked up the second long board and dragged it through the grass to the other side of the wood base, Dan went upstairs, checked her from the dining room window, and pulled two pieces of bread from the cabinet. The loaf was only a third gone, which meant she wasn't likely to notice a missing piece or two. He would have to find a food substitute soon, but few sandwiches were as quick or as satisfying as peanut butter and jelly.

A noise sounded at the back door and Dan saw her figure behind the slats of the angled blinds. He ducked behind the counter with bread pieces in hand, the bag left in the open. The blinds rattled against the window with the opening and closing of the door and Nina coughed. The radio turned on and the volume went up. Windows slid open. He wedged himself into the corner. And then she was there, at counter's edge beside the bathroom door, dirty hand dangling at her side. Dan didn't breathe and didn't blink. Nina stepped into the bathroom, flipped on the light, and disappeared behind the wall without closing the door.

He couldn't get to the basement without her seeing him in the bathroom mirror, so he edged around the counter and hid behind the recliner, his legs folded tight to his chest, bread in both hands. Deep bass sent a rhythmic, thudding pulse through his sore cheek. When the toilet flushed, he watched for her, but she didn't come. He felt the shifting floorboards beneath him and then heard, on the counter not far above his head, cellophane crinkling with the twisting of the bread bag's neck. "I think I'm going crazy, Nyxy-Nyx," she said. "Oh, Nyxy-Nyx. Come here, Nyx." When Nina next walked by, Nyx's full, brown tail dangled from her arms and went outside with her to the back yard.

When he heard the pounding again, Dan came out from behind the chair and got a knife and the peanut butter and jelly. He finished making his sandwich.

She worked out there until the house's shadow covered the lawn and she had to work by patio light. Dan watched the final stages from a safe spot in the dining room.

It was a door. Raw wood secured on a triangle base in the middle of the yard.

Nina stood back to look at it and then curled her hand around the knob. She pulled the door open an inch, maybe two, and then closed it without stepping through. She walked across the lawn to pick up the cat from where she sat in the dry birdbath. Dan went downstairs.

He got his bed ready under the vent. He lay with the back of his head on laced fingers. Thanks to his work box he had books to read, but he didn't feel like a mystery.

Nothing happened outside the window. No snow fell, no wind pushed at the glass. He was angled wrong to see the stars.

He moved to a better spot, where he could see just one.

He tried to imagine the end of the world, but couldn't.

Outside a car door slammed and a young boy shouted something. Dan heard Carl's muffled, "Hey. Cut it out. Get inside."

Nina stayed up later than she used to. He'd seen her old work clothes come out once, but for most of the week she'd worn something professional, pressed, fitted. Clothes that made him think of his own job and Howie, who he would have to call soon. Tomorrow. He would also have to pick up his check from April.

He had a hard time sleeping on his back, but the wound on his face, healing slowly, made sleeping any other way uncomfortable. Gravity pulled least painful if he lay with his face aimed up. He closed his eyes and listened to the sitcom sounds falling through the vent. He faded during a car commercial, but snapped awake when the doorbell rang. He looked at his phone. He'd been asleep half an hour. Stairs creaked and Dan went to the window, where he could see only a section of the porch and the Pace Arrow parked in front of the house.

He heard the front door open and Nina's "Can I help you?"

"Is Dan here?"

"I'm sorry. Who?"

"Dan. Dan ... um ... I can't believe I don't remember his last name. He was—Remember? I came here with him? We dropped off the cat.—It was raining ...?"

He heard her boots shuffling on the porch. The back of Jenny's coat appeared and then disappeared. Appeared and disappeared.

"I was asleep," Nina said.

"I'm sorry. I'm—This is really awkward, but I don't know what else to do. I just—We came here, right to this porch. I know I have the right place.—There! That cat. That's the one we dropped off. I wouldn't have come here if I knew where else to go. I already tried the other place, and … I just thought you'd know where he is. I need—He owes me some money. Can you please, plea—"

The front door closed and Jenny stepped back, but didn't leave. Instead she looked at the front door and nodded. Jenny spoke, but he couldn't hear her. She gestured at the RV and then put her hands in her pockets, taking them out once to wipe her eyes. She laughed. She nodded. The front door opened and closed with Jenny still on the porch. He heard Nina walking overhead, down the hallway and into the kitchen. A pause, and then her footsteps carried her back to the foyer. The front door opened and closed. Jenny placed her palms together like a prayer. Her lips said "Thank you." She moved closer to the house and out of sight, and then she was going, bouncing down the stairs, an envelope in her hand. The front door opened, closed, and Nina's light, slow footfalls didn't go down the hallway and up the stairs, but instead into the brown room. The floor croaked and groaned over his head near the window looking out to the street. The Pace Arrow pulled away from the curb.

Nina was up early the next morning, her high heels tapping down the stairs and into the kitchen where they clacked loud on the tile. Back and forth across the room, making breakfast, making coffee Dan could smell from the basement. He heard the back door open and went to the window. It had snowed a dusting in the night, frosting Nina's door. She folded her arms to her chest and walked toward it and then stood in front of it. For a time, she didn't move, and then she reached for the knob, turned it, pulled the door open and stepped through to the other side. She stood there for a long time before closing it behind her, walking around the side, and returning to the house.

She clipped and clopped some more, back and forth from counter to counter, before opening and closing the front door with a sing-song goodbye to Nyx. Dan watched her car pull out of the driveway and waited a minute before going upstairs.

On the counter, he found hot coffee in the pot, a clean mug, and a peanut butter and jelly sandwich beside a note: *Go through the door. Start over. This is your one time. See you tonight.*

ABOUT THE AUTHOR

Kristen Tsetsi lives in Connecticut and, outside of the observation that there are indeed a lot of old White people living there, does not share Jenny's opinion of the state.

Her other novels are the auto-fictional *Pretty Much True* and the post-post-Roe *The Age of the Child*, available wherever books are sold. Her award-winning and Pushcart Prize-nominated short fiction, along with some previously unpublished short stories, appear in her collection *Carol's Aquarium*, available on Amazon.

The short story April has Dan read in Chapter 33 is titled "Becoming an Oats Girl" and was previously published in, and selected as the winner of a short fiction competition hosted by, the (late) literary journal *Edifice Wrecked.*

For more information, visit kristenjtsetsi.com.